Praise for the Carol

BEYOND A

"A high-speed chase of a mystery, filled with very likable characters, a timely plot, and writing so compelling that readers will be unable to turn away from the page."

— *Kings River Life Magazine*

"Will keep you turning pages late into the night and make you think twice about the dark side of the Hollywood Dream."

— Paul D. Marks,
Shamus Award-Winning Author of *Vortex*

"Radio host Carol Childs meets her match in this page-turner. Her opponent is everyone's good guy but she knows the truth about the man behind the mask. Now Carol must reveal a supremely clever enemy before he gets the chance to silence her for good. Great read!"

— Laurie Stevens,
Award-Winning Author of the Gabriel McRay Series

"A story of suspense, raw emotion, and peril which builds up to a satisfying climax...Silverman has given us another book where we can sit down and get our teeth into, and I look forward to the next in the series. Highly recommended."

— *Any Good Book*

"Fast paced and cleverly plotted, an edgy cozy with undertones of noir."

— Sue McGinty,
Author of the Bella Kowalski Central Coast Mysteries

SHADOW OF DOUBT (#1)

"Silverman provides us with inside look into the world of talk radio as Carol Childs, an investigative reporter, finds herself in the middle of a Hollywood murder mystery, uncovering evidence that may point to her best friend. A hunky FBI Agent and a wacky psychic will keep readers guessing from beginning to end."

– Annette Dashofy,
USA Today Bestselling Author of *Lost Legacy*

"Silverman creates a trip through Hollywood filled with aging hippies, greedy agents, and a deadly case of product tampering. Forget the shower scene in *Psycho*; *Shadow of Doubt* will make you scared to take a bath!"

– Diane Vallere,
Author of the Material Witness, Style & Error,
and Madison Night Mystery Series

"A thoroughly satisfying crime novel with fascinating, authentic glimpses into the world of talk radio and some of its nastier stars... The writing is compelling and the settings ring true thanks to the author's background as a newscaster herself."

– Jill Amadio,
Author of *Digging Too Deep*

"Carol is a smart, savvy heroine that will appeal to readers. This is a cozy with a bite."

– *Books for Avid Readers*

"Absolutely engaging, I could barely put it down. The characters in the book were well-developed and the plot was chillingly genius."

– Lyn Faulkner,
Netgalley Reviewer

BEYOND A DOUBT

BEYOND A DOUBT
A Carol Childs Mystery
Part of the Henery Press Mystery Collection

First Edition
Trade paperback edition | July 2015

Henery Press
www.henerypress.com

ISBN-13: 978-1-941962-73-2

Printed in the United States of America

BEYOND A DOUBT

A CAROL CHILDS MYSTERY

NANCY COLE SILVERMAN

To Nadine,
Enjoy,
Nancy Cole Silverman

Dec. 10, 2015

HENERY PRESS

The Carol Childs Mystery Series
by Nancy Cole Silverman

SHADOW OF DOUBT (#1)
BEYOND A DOUBT (#2)
WITHOUT A DOUBT (#3)
(May 2016)

To Bruce

ACKNOWLEDGMENTS

One of my favorite paintings is *The Water Lily Pond* by Claude Monet. When I look at it I feel the breeze against my skin and hear the wind rustle through the tree leaves, as it forms small ripples across the water. It wasn't until I actually visited Monet's home in Giverny, in northern France, that it occurred to me that while Monet was a great painter, and a pretty good gardener, too, that those who worked for him, had to have been a fantastic support. There was no way he could have done it all alone. That's how I feel about writing. I may have the ideas and the vision, but without the aid of good editors, beta readers, family and friends, I'd be lost in the woods. I'd like to thank a few of them.

My agent and publisher, Kendel Lynn, who found me and thought I had something to say. My editors at Henery Press, Erin George and Anna Davis, both brilliant young women who see beyond the printed page and are master craftsmen themselves when it comes to story writing. Stephanie Chontos, whose uncanny ability to design a cover that captures the tone and theme of my books, continues to amaze me each time, and Art Molinares, who pulls the team at Henery Press together.

My beta readers, first editors and friends: Rhona Robbie, my hiking partner and person with whom I test plots while we visit parts of the city I might not otherwise go, at least not alone. Marjorie Palmer, my sister, a retired Methodist minister, whose prayers for me I know have saved me more than once. Sue McGinty, a fellow member of Sisters in Crime, who stepped up, read and offered wonderful advice and support as I came through with my final draft for *Beyond a Doubt*. My mother and father, and children, Christin and Larry, whose love makes my world a safe place. And of course, my husband, Bruce Silverman, without whose love and support, I would find it difficult to do all I do.

Thank you all.

Nancy Cole Silverman

CHAPTER 1

"Tyler, can you hear me?" The sound from the heavy buffeting of the helicopter's rotor blades above me and the cool wind whipping through my hair made it impossible for me to speak in a normal voice. Pushing the hair from my face, I sheltered the mic into my shoulder and screamed, "I'm up on Mulholland. I can see the body!"

From the roadside, the canyon, with its rolling hills and sage green chaparral surrounding upscale Southern California mansions, loomed beneath me. A body, barely visible through the early morning fog, appeared tucked beneath a sprawling oak tree. It looked as though it had fallen from the sky and somersaulted down the hill. A red high heel was several hundred feet away, and bits and pieces of clothing, like scrap ribbon tied to a tree, hung from the branches above the body. Like a ragdoll that had come to a stop, its bare back was exposed to the roadside, the head and shoulders slumped forward at an awkward angle only partially covered by the victim's long, curly blonde hair, hanging limply to one side.

I heard Tyler. "Hold for two." Then, "We're live with KCHC's reporter Carol Childs. Carol."

"Residents along this section of Mulholland Drive woke up this morning to the sound of helicopters above their homes. Police were alerted by commuters who called to report what looked like the body of a partially clad young woman lying several hundred feet from the roadway. But I can tell you, Tyler, among those standing here with me and watching this recovery, there's speculation as to how this girl got here. I'm getting conflicting reports from people who believe they heard the sound of a low flying chopper maybe an hour *before* LAPD's helicopters arrived to investigate."

I returned to the station, my hair stringy and matted against my head, my lips chapped. Tyler, my boss, had called before sunup alerting me there'd been a possible body dump less than fifteen minutes from my home. He wanted me on the scene, and I'd been there since before six a.m. Right now, I was a mess. I hadn't brushed my teeth, I had a headache from the sounds of the helicopter, and already I was feeling mentally exhausted. I couldn't shake the vision of the young woman's naked body, covered with a thin Mylar blanket, as it was lifted onto the helicopter's gurney, or stop thinking about how horrendous her last moments must have been. From the looks of the shrubbery, undisturbed around the body, and from what some of the residents were telling me regarding the sound of a low flying helicopter, earlier that morning, before the police arrived, this young woman just might have been pushed to her death. I couldn't imagine a worse scenario. My own daughter Cate was only a couple years younger than the body they pulled from canyon. My stomach turned. This was every parent's worst nightmare, and what I wanted now was a shower and a cup of hot coffee, but before I could do any of that, Tyler had insisted on a meeting. He wanted to see me ASAP.

With Tyler everything is ASAP. KCHC's boy wonder, our news and programming director, has ants-in-his-pants when it comes to being the first to know. For Tyler everything's a race. Second best is never good enough. Already there was speculation that the body might be that of Monica Channing, a twenty-four year old kindergarten teacher and daughter of a prominent federal judge. She'd been missing for the last week, the subject of a massive manhunt, and today was our first break in the case. Tyler would want information. If it was Monica, he'd want KCHC to be the first to report it.

The trouble was, I couldn't be certain the body I'd seen up on Mulholland was Monica. Over the last eighteen months three other young women had disappeared off the streets of Hollywood. LAPD Missing Persons Unit has listed them as possible runaways, or probable kidnappings, but nothing had been confirmed. The only facts the media had concerning their disappearance was that they were all young and attractive and were believed to have been into the Hollywood club scene. If Monica had met the same fate, she'd be the fourth victim and the first to show up dead. The only difference was that Monica, while young and attractive, was hardly a party girl.

Throughout the last week, news about Monica's sudden disappearance had been everywhere. Newspapers, billboards, and the evening news all carried stories with photos of her singing in her church choir, feeding the homeless and reading to her kindergarten class. The woman was a saint. Her parents described her as a naïve young woman, an innocent, who would have been vulnerable to someone who wanted to hurt her.

I stopped in the doorway to Tyler's office. He looked like he hadn't slept. His skin was blotchy and his short red hair stuck straight up from his head like he'd finger-combed it. He was focused on the computer monitor. His eyes never left the screen.

"So give me your take. Is this our girl?"

"Maybe," I said. I sat down in the chair in front of his desk. "Stat-wise it all fits. Young, pale blonde, probably about the right height, although I couldn't tell for sure. Could just as easily have been any of the other missing girls, except for the hair. Other two were brunettes. One was a redhead. As for cause of death? We'll have to wait on the medical examiner's report, but my guess is a broken neck. From what I could see the body looked pretty banged up."

Tyler looked up at me.

"You okay on this? You look a bit pale yourself."

"I haven't showered yet, and I'd like get a cup of coffee before I start my shift." Tyler was oblivious to the fact he'd called me before five a.m. and that I wasn't scheduled to clock in until almost ten. "Other than that," I said, "I'm good."

I stood up and moved toward the doorway. I was desperate for coffee. If there was any chance of my making a connection between Monica Channing's murder and that of the other missing girls, I needed caffeine and lots of it, quickly.

"Great, 'cause before you go, I have another story for you." Tyler pointed to the chair and indicated he wanted me to sit down. We weren't done. "We've got another missing blonde."

Another young girl? I sat down. The shock on my face must have registered my surprise.

"Relax, Carol. This is different, a little story to make up for this morning. I think you might actually like it."

I knew I was in for it. Tyler was up to something. The look on his boyish face had suddenly changed from weary to smug. He smiled impishly at me.

"Really," I said. There was a heavy touch of sarcasm to my voice. "And just what might that be?"

He paused, looked back at his computer, printed out an assignment sheet and handed me the paper. "This just came in."

I glanced at the paper and sighed. My window of opportunity for running home and taking a shower before my shift began was growing ever smaller. Now I'd be cutting it tight.

"Kari Rhodes," he said, "is doing an on-air tribute to the Hollywood Walk of Fame. She's got the boulevard's honorary mayor Tommy Banks in studio with her. All that would have been fine, except it turns out someone's removed, or stolen, Marilyn's star."

"Marilyn?" I interrupted. "Like in Monroe?"

"Who else?" He leaned back in his chair, crossed his skinny arms across his chest and smiled confidently. "We're going to need a reporter over there for an interview. You interested?"

"Do I have a choice?"

He shook his head. "No. But on the brighter side, it appears a group of street impersonators have launched a protest. Seems they don't think the city's paying enough attention to security. They're upset about Marilyn's star. I'm certain there's a little human-interest story there somewhere. See what you can do."

I groaned. The Hollywood Walk of Fame was a tourist trap, a nightmare of ghoulish looking impersonators that roamed the boulevard. Most of them were out-of-work actors, hoping to be discovered while making a few bucks on the side posing with tourists in front of what was formerly Grauman's Chinese Theater.

CHAPTER 2

I left Tyler's office clutching my cellphone like a compass and hurried down the hall towards the station's lobby. Staring up at me was a returned text from my best friend, Sheri. I had texted her as I left the house before dawn. I explained Tyler had called and asked if she'd put in a wakeup call for my son Charlie. Her reply read: "Not a problem. Boys and I did pancakes at Dupar's. Don't forget, big game tonight. Call when you get a minute."

I laughed. Pancakes. That was so Sheri.

Sheri's a single mom like me, but the similarity ends there. She refers to herself as a member of the lucky sperm club, a trust fund baby, who doesn't need to work and dabbles in special projects. I suspect I'm one. She admits to living vicariously through me. Physically we're exact opposites in everything from our height to our hair color—I'm blonde and scraping five-nine and Sheri's brunette and barely five-two—but our sons, Clint and Charlie, are best buds. They're both freshmen at Princeton High around the corner from my condo.

I stopped in the lobby to catch my breath and leaned up against the wall. It was still early, but there was a chance that if the body up on Mulholland had been Monica Channing, the LA Coroner might already have an answer. The identification of a judge's daughter would have top priority. Every reporter in town would be making the same call right about now. I listened as the phone rang, my foot tapping against the floor nervously as the call went through to voicemail.

Dammit! I hung up and stared down at my two left feet. In my rush to get dressed this morning I'd grabbed a wrinkled t-shirt off the hamper, torn blue jeans, and a mismatched set of pink tennis shoes. Thank goodness this was radio. I glanced up at the big clock in the lobby. It was nine-fifteen. I had an hour and half before I had to be in Hollywood.

I drove home with my cellphone to my ear. Like an addict, I continued to call the coroner's office nonstop. Fortunately, I had Dr. Gabor's inside number, something only a few reporters in town had. Plus, I knew right about now he'd be taking his mid-morning coffee break.

"Hello?" Dr. Gabor answered. His heavy Hungarian accent echoed through the line. He had me on speaker. "May I help you?"

"Let me guess," I said. "You've been in the office since before five, you've completed two autopsies, checked your emails and you're just about to sit down and crunch into a pickle from Jerry's Deli. Am I right?"

"Carol. You know me too well." I pictured Dr. Gabor in his office, his lab coat on the coatrack by the door. He'd be dressed in a three-piece suit with his trademark red bowtie, and right about now he probably had a pastrami on rye neatly laid out on a cloth napkin in front of him. For him it was already lunchtime. "What can I do for you?"

"I was hoping you might be able to tell me something about the body of the young woman the police recovered this morning. I know it's early, but by any chance have you been able to get a look, maybe make an ID?"

I heard what sounded like crumpling paper and envisioned him tossing the sandwich wrapper across the room and into the basket.

"Right now all I can tell you is if it's the missing teacher you're concerned about, we'll know soon enough. Judge Channing and his wife are coming in to view the body. I'd say there's a good chance they'll make a positive ID."

"So then, you must think it's her."

"I didn't say that." I knew with the sensitivity of the case, Gabor had to be very careful.

"May I ask a favor then?"

He paused.

"Always with the favors, Miss Childs. Just what is it you'd like me to do for you this time? Call you first with the ID, perhaps?"

"Wouldn't hurt. Or you could text if you're busy." I waited for him to consider his options then added, "I've got tickets to Disney Hall. Dudamel's doing a concert this weekend." In the past I'd thanked the doctor for his help with station tickets to the LA Philharmonic. It's not exactly how things are supposed to be done between reporters and city officials, but I knew he was a big fan, and it seemed like an innocent enough gesture.

"I'll text you once I have an ID. But you need to understand, if this *is* Monica Channing, her father's going to want answers quickly. I'm already getting pressure from LAPD to get the autopsy done this morning, and once I get a cause of death your people will be all over this like locusts." He paused, I heard a series of clicks and realized I was no longer on speaker. "However, there is one piece of information I can share with you, off the record."

"What's that, Doctor?"

"The girl was recently tattooed on her wrist." Dr. Gabor explained that the police believed the markings might have something to do with the kidnapping.

CHAPTER 3

As I drove home from the radio station I kept thinking about Monica Channing and the other three missing girls we'd reported on. Over the last year and a half, each girl had had her fifteen minutes of distressed fame and when they didn't turn up, the news moved on. That's how the news works. There just isn't enough time and space to carry every story beyond the initial report. But as a parent, I couldn't imagine not knowing what had happened to my daughter. What I did know was that the clock was ticking, that the police had yet to officially tie the crimes together, and that in the absence of any new information, in a week or two, this story, like the stories before it, would die. Other stories would come and fill the headlines and in time people would forget. I wasn't going to let that happen. Both as a parent and as a reporter I was determined to find out if there was some connection.

I entered my condo, threw my keys on the kitchen counter and was about to run upstairs when I noticed a yellow Post-it note on top of a stack of mail on the counter.

Happy Birthday, Mom. Don't forget the game tonight. Four p.m. @ Notre Dame. Sheri said she'll meet you there. See you then, Charlie.

I couldn't believe I'd forgotten my own birthday. I glanced down at a stack of mail Charlie had brought in. Directly beneath his note was a postcard. At first I thought it might be from a travel agency, some piece of junk mail. I picked it up and was about to throw it in the trash when I turned it over and noticed it was postmarked from Mexico. I knew instantly it had to be from Eric.

FBI Special Agent Eric Langdon is my tall-dark-and-handsome. The man in my life I want to kiss hello and whose arms I wanted to fall asleep in at night. The man who, up until he sailed off with his *Sea Mistress*, his sixty-foot seafaring yacht, was, and is, my steady.

On the front of the card was a photo of Cabo San Lucas with clear blue waters and palm frond structures. On the back was simply written 10/07/2014 with a hand drawn heart, followed by a happy face and a birthday cake, candles blazing. The coded message on the back of the card made my heart smile. Eric and I have our own special codes, shorthand for when we can get together. The numbers meant Eric was headed home. If weather permitted and the sea gods allowed, I expected him to be in port sometime around October tenth. Next week. The thought of his homecoming tickled me and refreshed my wearied spirits. I grabbed the card, hugged it to my chest, wished myself a happy birthday and headed upstairs like a giddy teenager.

I showered and finished blow-drying my hair, pulled it back into a ponytail, patted a little moisturizer on face and looked into the mirror. I looked tired, but a little concealer and blush worked wonders. I slipped on a bra and panties, walked into the closet and grabbed a short black tailored dress off the hanger. Most of what I own is casual Friday wear, but today being my birthday, I wanted something a little snazzier. Plus, if anything came up concerning Monica's disappearance, and I suddenly needed to be anywhere downtown, i.e. a courthouse, I wanted to look professional. I wiggled into the dress, struggling with the back zipper as I simultaneously slipped on a pair of black heels, then smoothed the body of the dress over my legs. I glanced back in the mirror. Not bad for a forty-five minute makeover. *Happy Birthday, Carol.* I smiled at myself one last time in the mirror, threw my leather jacket over my shoulder and headed out the door.

CHAPTER 4

Nearly ten million people a year visit the Hollywood Walk of Fame. The three and half mile stretch along Hollywood Boulevard and Vine Street is a magnet for tourists who want to check out the location of their favorite star's monument. Marilyn Monroe's star is on the south side of the boulevard at Highland and Hollywood, in front of Ripley's Believe It or Not. There's a huge dinosaur on top of the building. I parked my car about a block away, and as I approached I was greeted by a sea of pale skinned, platinum wigged, high-heeled Marilyn impersonators. They were all running in my direction.

"There she is. The reporter. Over there."

I glanced over my shoulder. I was thinking a TV crew must have pulled up behind me. Perhaps Mario Lopez from *Extra*? What else could explain this gaggle of Marilyns running in my direction? How could they possibly know who I was? Radio people aren't exactly recognizable. I wasn't carrying, or wearing, any identifying logos on my person. My microphone was in my bag and far as I knew, dressed in black, I looked like any other businessperson about to dash into Musso & Frank's or maybe the Roosevelt Hotel for lunch.

"Are you Carol Childs from KCHC?" The first of the Marilyns to reach me grabbed my hand and, turning me around so that my back was to the others, made a quick introduction. "I'm Norma Jean Baker. I called the station this morning to report the theft. I organized this protest."

I was surprised the young woman in front of me was using

Marilyn Monroe's real name. Certainly it was an alias. I asked, "Your name's Norma Jean Baker? For real?"

"It helps in this town when you work as an impersonator to be as authentic as possible. So for today, yes, I'm Norma Jean Baker, a.k.a. Marilyn Monroe." She smiled and feigned one of Marilyn's famous poses, one hand on her hip, the other in the air. Beneath her platinum blonde wig, strands of dark hair had worked their way loose and were threatening to escape. She was as much Norma Jean Baker as she was a natural blonde.

"How did you know who I was?"

"I'm a big fan of the Kari Rhodes show. I listen every day. Love all the gossip. She described you to me, but..." She stood back, held my hands out to the side of my body and studied me, her eyes giving me the big once over. "She didn't mention that you were so..."

"What?" I asked.

"Well, pretty. I actually thought since you were in radio that you'd be more...you know..."

My cellphone started to vibrate. I was happy for the intrusion. I could only imagine how Kari might have described me. Our relationship was at best professionally strained. Kari viewed any female with whom she shared a broadcast booth to be competition. From her perch as the mid-day entertainment host, I was the enemy. I held up my index finger. "Excuse me, I need to take this."

A text message from Dr. Gabor filled the screen. *Positive ID on Miss Channing. Cause of death TBD.*

I sighed and glanced back at Norma Jean. I didn't have a lot of time. Behind her the Marilyns were approaching like a group of platinum wigged bobbleheads.

"I need to make a call. Can you ward off your blonde impersonator friends for a moment?" From the look on her face I could see she thought I was being rude. I felt bad. I didn't mean to come off as dismissive. I softened my voice and with as much constraint as I could muster, I said, "Look, I'm sorry. I need to call the newsroom. It's important."

"Is this about that body you reported on this morning? I heard your report. Awful news. Do the police think it's the schoolteacher?"

I held the phone to my chest. I'd already hit the speed dial to Tyler's office and could feel the ringing vibrate against my heart.

"I really can't say. But if you'll wait with your friends, I'll be right with you. I know Kari wants me to get an interview."

I turned my back and waited for Tyler to answer then whispered into the phone. "It's the schoolteacher. Her parents identified the body a few minutes ago."

"Hold on a minute, Carol." In the background I could hear Tyler, his quick fingers flying across the keyboard. "Cause of death?"

"Don't know yet. We're still waiting. I'm thinking maybe I should blow this boulevard thing off, go over to the morgue, talk to the coroner, see if I could get an interview with her parents."

"No. Absolutely not." Tyler's voice was firm, there was no room for negotiation. "You stay where you are. I'll take it from here." Tyler hung up. A dial tone droned coldly in my ear. I felt as though I'd just been told to stand down. I turned around and looked back at Norma Jean. She was standing in the middle of the Marilyns. All eight of them, identically dressed in Marilyn's iconic white dress, like she'd worn in *The Seven Year Itch*, stared back at me like they were awaiting stage directions.

"Alright then." I tried to sound optimistic. "Let's do this." I reached into my reporter's bag for my earphone and mic and with eight Marilyn impersonators trailing behind me like baby quail, I walked across the street to the location where Marilyn's star appeared to have been jackhammered from the sidewalk in front of Ripley's.

A bare-chested young man stood in front of the museum and was preparing to swallow a sword while tourists walked past him. Some stopped to watch, most appeared oblivious. With coffee cups and cameras in hand, the majority simply walked past or stopped briefly to take a selfie. Others sidestepped the area where Miss

Monroe's missing star was blocked off with yellow crime scene tape and orange traffic cones.

I gathered my group of Marilyns and glanced at my watch. It was almost the top of the hour, and I dialed Kari's inside line. By now she should be in the middle of a station break and able to talk freely, off the air.

"Kar—" I hadn't even gotten her name out of my mouth.

"Well finally, Carol, you're there. I thought I was going to have to do this show all by myself."

I resisted the urge to remind her that while she was sitting in the studio, I had been out since five o'clock that morning. I had already viewed a dead body and I was now standing in the middle of a crowd of crazed tourists with a bare-chested sword swallower behind me and a gaggle of Marilyn impersonators in front of me. Instead I said, "The natives are growing restless, Kari."

"Ha-ha-ha." She laughed, a very affected stage laugh. "I take that as a good sign the celebration's underway. It certainly is here."

In the background I could hear the muffled clatter of plates and utensils. I knew Kari would have had a cake brought in for today's Walk of Fame Celebration. Part of me wanted to tell her to save me a piece, but I knew there was no point.

"Things in la-la land are getting busy," I said. I explained the streets were packed with shoppers and tourists and I could see what looked to be a marching band down the street preparing to do a number.

"Fantastic. I'll cut to you after the station break." She paused. I heard her chatting in the background, then she came back on the line. "By the way, Tyler just told me, that body this morning? It was the teacher. Thought you might like to know."

I bit my tongue and waited for Kari to come back on the air. She opened with Mayor Tommy, the two of them reminiscing about old Hollywood. The area had once been lemon groves and then became a kind of silver screen Camelot with its midcentury architecture, views of the Hollywood Sign and movie stars like Clark Gable and Carol Lombard, who secretly rendezvoused at the pool at the old Hollywood Roosevelt Hotel. Today it was in the midst of an exciting building boom. New apartments, eateries, theaters, museums and scores of nightclubs were attracting LA's young hip professionals like free tickets to a rock concert. They came in droves.

Turning her attention back to the anniversary celebration, Kari said someone had called into the station to report Marilyn Monroe's star had been stolen from the boulevard. "Carol, what can you tell us?"

"I'm sure you can hear from all the noise in the background we have a lot of excitement out here today and a bit of mystery, as well." I reached into my bag and took out a mic sponge to shelter my microphone from the background noise. I explained I was standing with a group of Marilyn impersonators and fans staring at a hole in the ground where Marilyn's star had been.

"Of course, we really have no idea if the star was stolen or perhaps removed as they sometimes are for cleaning." During the station break I'd quickly Googled a history of star thefts. I was about to include a list of those stars that had been stolen, Kirk Douglas, James Stewart, Gene Autry and Gregory Peck, when Norma Jean surprised me and grabbed the mic from my hand.

"It was stolen." She yelled and then turning her back to me and facing her fellow Marilyn followers she screamed, "We know it, don't we? It was stolen, right?"

As though on cue, the Marilyns, all of them, began chanting. "Bring back our star. Bring back our star..."

"Goodness, it does sound like you have your hands full, Carol." I could barely hear Kari through my headphone. "Perhaps you might ask them if there's something we might do?"

I was helpless. I didn't have the mic. Norma Jean did. Like a cheerleader she hollered at the Marilyns. "What do you say? How about a song, ladies?"

Suddenly the speaker from behind me, atop the Ripley building, started blasting music.

"A kiss on the hand..."

Then leggy dancers with long white gloves and rhinestone jewelry appeared from out of nowhere while in front of me the eight Marilyns started to sing. The marching band down the street began to advance and tourists everywhere started snapping photos. It was chaos.

Only it wasn't.

It was a flash mob. A public relations promotion, perfectly timed for my arrival, and I was right in the middle of it. Up and down the boulevard traffic had been cleared and people were dancing and singing in the street. I took the mic back from Norma Jean. I began broadcasting a play-by-play; the dancing Marilyns, the bare chested sword swallower, the impersonators, the marching band. Behind me, from inside Ripley's, and along the street on both sides, shopkeepers began rolling out carts with sheet cakes decorated for the event and offering slices to passersby. It was like a scene out of a 1940's musical.

I was about to sign off when Kari interrupted me.

"Before you go, Carol, I understand you're also celebrating a little something today. Your birthday, right? What is it? Thirty—"

I stepped into the street. To my right the band approached, their drum major leading a corps of drums and big brass instruments, the sunlight gleaming off their shiny horns to the beat of *Hoorah for Hollywood.*

"What? I can't hear you, Kari. Sorry, the USC Marching Band is coming our way. Listen." I held out the mic, their sound totally drowning out Kari's last words. "Thirty-nine again" was lost to crescendo of the beating drums and the brassy sound of the big horns. I signed off.

"This is Carol Childs, live from the Hollywood Walk of Fame."

I turned back to Norma Jean. "You knew about this?"

She nodded. "It was part of a promotional stunt. I'm a hired hand. An actor. Impersonator. I do parties, standup, wait tables, and on weekends I drive a tour bus." She handed me her business card. "You ever want to see the boulevard at night, give me a call."

I looked back down at the card. On one side was a classic

swimsuit shot of Norma Jean as Marilyn Monroe. On the other side was a picture of a customized tour van with the words *Holly Wood Tours* painted on the side beneath a pair of red hot lips. A phone number was printed on the bottom.

"Holly Wood?" I asked. "That's your name?"

She smiled. "Like I said, this isn't my only job. Call me sometime."

Then with a wink she turned and sauntered away, swaying her hips from side to side in a very Marilynesque way. I looked back down at the card in my hand and shook my head. This morning I'd been at the scene of a body dump and this afternoon the middle of a flash mob dance. The day couldn't get any stranger.

CHAPTER 5

By the time I got back to the car, every radio station in the city was broadcasting that the body found up on Mulholland Drive this morning was that of Monica Channing. KNX, the all-news station, said her parents had made a positive ID. Down the dial KFI was reporting LAPD would be doing a press conference with Miss Channing's father, Judge Byron Channing III, at two p.m. on the steps of the Federal Courthouse. I was about to pick up the phone and call Tyler and tell him I'd cover the conference when a second news report caught my attention.

"In what may be a related incident, police are also reporting the disappearance of another young woman from North Hollywood. Gabi Garrison, former news anchor for KCBS-TV, was reported missing by friends and family who became alarmed when she failed to come home Tuesday evening."

Oh my God, not Gabi. I knew Gabi. She and I had lunched together. For a brief period of time, Gabi Garrison had been a TV reporter, a fresh face that quickly faded when the ratings hadn't worked out in her favor. Rather than fire her, CBS had given her a shot as an account executive. She and I had crossed paths back when I was selling time for the radio station. We'd met outside the office of a mutual client in Westwood, quite accidentally. Our client had kept us waiting in the lobby and told us he'd be about an hour. Gabi and I went down into the village and grabbed a light lunch, and we talked. I liked her right away. She was attractive and vivacious and despite our age difference, we had a lot in common. Gabi was single, like me, and had made a recent career move from the talent side of the business into sales. Something I was hoping to do, only the other way around. She also mentioned she was dating a resident at UCLA Medical named Dr. Ericson. I didn't recall his first name, but she said she was going to catch coffee with him right after our meeting. I remembered the name because I'd just started dating Eric and had plans to see him later that afternoon as well.

News of Gabi's disappearance had a very uncomfortable feel about it. Not only did she look a lot like Monica Channing, with her high cheekbones and all-American Pepsodent smile, but I knew she lived in the same section of town. I also knew, like the other missing girls I'd reported on—other than Monica—Gabi liked Hollywood's nightlife. She had mentioned several times while we were lunching how much she and her doctor friend loved to go clubbing.

I glanced at my watch. It was just now twelve o'clock. I was about to pick up my phone and call Tyler and share my concerns about Gabi's disappearance when it started to ring. It was Tyler.

"The coroner sent over a copy of his report for the Channing girl. Hope you don't mind, I saw it in your inbox and snagged it right away. We've got a cause of death."

I let the fact that Tyler had obviously rifled through my emails go. I knew better than to think if I were working on a breaking news story that he'd consider my inbox my personal sanctuary. In his mind, anything that flowed through a newsroom had his name on it. No questions asked.

"Broken neck, right?"

"Along with a cracked skull, shattered collarbone and fractured humerus. Report says death was probably instantaneous. Most likely a fall. Good news is there are no ligature marks on her wrists and ankles, no mention of rape or signs of sexual abuse." He paused. I could hear him typing, the keyboard clicking in the background. I imagined he was searching his computer files for something. "Odd though—"

"What's that?" I asked.

"Her body was dumped in Stone Canyon. Judge Channing and

his wife live in the canyon. Monica grew up there, graduated Emerson Middle School. Almost like somebody was trying to send a message."

It was hard enough to imagine anyone wanting to kill a kindergarten teacher, but then to dump her body behind her parents' home? The whole scenario bordered on macabre.

"But why?" I asked.

"Might be easier if we start with the how. I'm looking at a map of the area. It's relatively remote and I don't see any hiking trails."

"She wasn't out hiking, Tyler. Not in stilettos. There was a red high heel not far from the body. She didn't lose it hiking."

"And you didn't see any evidence that she might have been pushed out of a car? Maybe slid down the hill? Bushes trampled, that kind of thing?"

"Nothing. In fact, other than a few broken tree branches *above* where her body landed, the bushes around it appeared untouched. It's like she fell from the sky."

"So, could be the neighbors are right. Maybe they did hear a helicopter early this morning and she was pushed from it. The injuries would be consistent with what the coroner listed in his report. The body was pretty beat up."

I noticed as Tyler read through the report we'd both stopped using Monica's name. It made it impersonal, easier to deal with a body than to think that twenty-four hours ago Monica had been alive and breathing. That she was someone's daughter, a teacher, a young woman, just starting out.

I grabbed my notebook, made a note of the helicopter theory, and told Tyler I wanted to take the press conference this afternoon.

"Meanwhile," I said, "I heard Gabi Garrison is missing."

"Yeah, CBS broke the story this morning."

I could tell Tyler was unhappy not to have been first with the news. I wondered if for the sake of the story he'd wished it'd been me. At least then he would have had a jump on the competition.

"I was thinking between now and the press conference, I'd head over to LAPD's missing persons unit. Seems to me with Gabi's disappearance and Monica's death, they might be rethinking the disappearance of those other three missing girls. Could be a connection. Maybe they weren't so random after all."

"Don't expect to be greeted with open arms, Carol. Not with a federal judge breathing down their necks and another girl missing this morning. They're not about to spend their day idly talking with news people. If you want any information that isn't an official LAPD stamped press release, you're going to have to give them a reason to talk to you."

I knew Tyler was right, but I also knew a few things about Gabi and her boyfriend and her interest in Hollywood's nightclub scene that detectives might not know. It was worth a shot, and if that didn't work, I planned to track down Gabi's boyfriend and talk to him. Perhaps he'd tell me something he hadn't already told the police. At least I hoped so.

I told Tyler I'd call him after the press conference and hung up the phone.

I could feel a sense of excitement about the case. I had reported on the disappearance of the other three missing girls and they all had inconclusive ends. But this, I felt, was going to be different. This was somehow connected. I knew it. I could feel it in my bones. I texted Sheri and told her I'd be late for the kids' game. *Save me a seat.*

CHAPTER 6

There are lots of reasons why people disappear in a city like Los Angeles, everything from teenage runaways to people simply walking away from a bad situation. The fact is, it's not a crime to go missing, and there is no forty-eight hour waiting period before a report can be filed with the missing persons unit. Not in LA anyway. Fortunately, despite the fact that the unit handles more than three thousand cases a year, and with just six officers, most people show up within three days. They don't all end up as a homicide.

But when one does, detectives know the press is going to be looking for mistakes, particularly like today, when the coroner's report was about to reveal that up until twenty-four hours ago Monica Channing was very much alive. A worried public was going to want answers. Something to explain how a kindergarten teacher had disappeared and then shown up as a body dump, just feet from her parent's expensive west side home. Had the cops missed a clue, an opportunity? Or maybe failed to identify a location where she might have been held or to arrest a suspect?

After this morning's grim discovery, standard procedure would be for the cops to gather their troops like an old-fashioned wagon train, their defenses up while they doubled down on the investigation. Today they'd all be tightlipped, facts and dates only. Any reporter walking into LAPD's missing persons unit knew their reception was going to pretty icy, if they got one at all. Fortunately, as a radio reporter, anonymity has its advantages. I wasn't exactly identifiable.

"May I help you?" An elderly gentleman from behind the desk glanced up at me as I approached the counter. He looked like a volunteer, dressed in civilian clothes, tan khakis and a white shirt with a black and white nametag above his pocket. Mr. Martin Porter. He had a friendly face.

I smiled. From time to time, LAPD allows volunteers to staff the reception desk at some of the divisions inside their downtown headquarters. Most of what they do is assist the officer in charge, answering the phone and greeting the public. I was in luck. It was obvious the volunteer was alone, but only temporarily. The outline of the desk sergeant's body was still warm in the chair next to him. Mr. Porter appeared eager to help. If I worked fast, I just might make it by the gatekeeper and speak with the detective investigating Gabi's disappearance.

"Yes, I was hoping I could talk with someone concerning Gabi Garrison. Her disappearance." I looked away and focused on the walls, the pictures of officers and their awards. I was hoping I looked like a nervous first time visitor, perhaps a distraught friend of the family hoping to help.

"You're a friend, right? Not a reporter?" He looked up at me.

I could tell this was a trick question. I laughed like it was an absurd assumption. If he knew I was a reporter I was sure he'd tell me to come back, that they were busy, and refer me to LAPD's press relations department. I figured a little white lie wouldn't hurt.

"Actually, Gabi and I are friends. We had lunch not long ago. I thought maybe if I talked to the detective in charge I might be able to help."

He looked over his shoulder. The desk sergeant would be returning any moment. I didn't dare wait. I knew when the sergeant returned I'd be busted. Cops have a sixth sense about reporters.

I leaned a bit closer and whispered, "I'm sorry to be in such a rush, but I'm worried about Gabi. Traffic was awful getting down here, and my son has a game this afternoon."

He looked up at me and his eyes softened.

"Game, huh? Why didn't you say so? Got a grandson myself,

he's playing this afternoon as well. Can't afford to miss that stuff. Important. Why don't you wait here, and I'll see what I can do."

Moments later he reappeared. Behind him, a tall heavyset black man, who looked like he could have been a former NFL linebacker, approached the desk. He was dressed in a blue blazer that fit tightly across his muscled chest, and I noticed his LAPD shield on his belt.

"How can I help you, miss?" He extended his hand, held mine a moment longer than necessary, and stared directly into my eyes. "Name's Detective Harry Browne. I'm the detective investigating the disappearance of Gabi Garrison. And you are?"

"Carol Childs." I sensed before he released my hand he knew exactly why I'd come.

"Mr. Porter here tells me you're a friend of Miss Garrison, that the two of you had lunch recently. But something tells me maybe friendship's not really why you're here. Am I right?"

I folded my hands in front of my face, prayer-like, and bowed my head, looking up at him. There was no point in carrying on my charade. "How'd you know?"

"Your knapsack there gave you away." He pointed to my scruffy looking reporter's bag with my recorder and notepad inside. I'd set it on the floor, next to my feet, thinking nobody would notice. "Looks pretty beat up, more like a feed bag than a purse. And judging by the way you're dressed—little black dress and all— I'd bet your taste runs a little more Neiman Marcus than Goodwill."

"You got me there." I threw my hands up and shook my head.

"So what do you want to know about your friend, Ms. Childs? 'Cause what I'm going to tell you right now is we're doing everything we can." Browne folded his arms across his chest and what followed felt canned, like he was reading from a script.

"One, we've got Miss Garrison's picture out to the media. Two, we have officers in the field who've talked with her employer. And three, we spoke with her boyfriend. Plus we've uploaded her photo and profile to our national database for missing persons."

I locked eyes with Detective Browne.

"That's standard procedure, Detective. What I want to know is if the police think Gabi's disappearance is related to Monica Channing."

He continued as though he hadn't heard me.

"We know Miss Garrison didn't show up for work Wednesday morning and that her boyfriend reported her missing when he came home from the hospital on Thursday evening."

"The doctor, right? Dr. Ericson."

Browne unfolded his arms and took a step closer to the counter between us. Finally, I had his attention, and I hoped I could get him off script.

"So you are a friend?"

"Business acquaintance actually. But I did know she was dating a doctor, although I don't know his first name."

"Miles Ericson, first year resident at UCLA Medical. He says he was on call at the hospital and hadn't been home in the last forty-eight hours. So we don't know exactly when Miss Garrison went missing."

"You think he's involved?"

"Too early to tell. Right now we're just chatting. Purely procedural. Nothing more. Could be she'll just show up. We see that sometimes. Usually within three or four days."

"But you don't think that's the case, do you?"

"What I think, Ms. Childs, is that when a couple of white girls go missing, like Monica Channing and Gabi Garrison, you and every other media outlet in town are all over this story like a Fourth of July fireworks show. And what I'd like to know is why I can't get two lines about what's happening in South Central LA in any major media outlet in this town. Answer me that. "

I felt like I'd just been tied to a stake, blindfolded, and asked if I wanted to make any last statements. I knew what Detective Browne was saying was right. Stations like my own catered to an audience that responded to their advertisers and South Central wasn't it.

"So what's happening in South Central, Detective?"

"I've got girls missing there too. Just not white girls. What I got are a couple of black girls, 'bout the same age, one a little younger, than those three who went missing in Hollywood this last year."

I felt like I'd just been slapped across the face. The police never had proved there was any connection to their disappearances, but after the third girl had gone missing, an alert was issued; a warning to young women about the dangers of being out alone at night in certain parts of the city.

I remembered reporting on each case and thinking their connection to Hollywood was not just curious but bothersome. The first girl, Jessie Martin, lived in North Hollywood and had an abusive home life. A picture of her, a small boyishly slim brunette with her mother, had run in the paper. The mother's face looked like a fighter's punching bag, and she was quoted as saying she hoped her daughter wouldn't come home, that she was better off somewhere else. The police had listed her as a runaway, desperate to get away from a bad situation.

The second was Marilyn Ann Billings. She was from a small town in Nebraska, a Midwestern girl with a real milk and honey complexion. She had told her sister, after being discovered online by a talent agent, she was headed to Hollywood for a role in the movies. Her "agent" had sent her a ticket, and her sister said she had driven her to the airport and then never heard from her again. The airline had no record of a Marilyn Ann Billings, nor did the police find any evidence that she'd ever arrived in LA. That in itself, the police said, wasn't unusual.

A lot of young wannabes changed their name, going for something that sounded more Hollywood. The police thought it was possible Marilyn Ann had a ticket in another name, perhaps something her agent had sent to her. That, and the fact that a lot of young actors came to LA and worked odd jobs, in cheap productions they didn't want to write home about, wasn't unusual. Some ended up shacking up with other struggling actors, and between the odd jobs, the name changes and hopscotch residencies, some of them got lost in the shuffle. After an unsuccessful search that included Marilyn Ann's computer and various low rent hotels and youth hostels, the police had listed her as simply missing.

The third girl, April Hansen, was a dancer at a strip club on Sunset Boulevard. April had a string of DUIs and a pending court date that threatened to land her in jail. The police believed April took off to avoid serving any time. They had a warrant out for her arrest, but the Hollywood connections, as far as the police were concerned, all appeared to be random.

I pulled out my notepad and looked Detective Browne directly in the eyes. "What are the names of the two girls, Detective?"

"Leticia Johnson, seventeen. And Brandy White, fourteen. Both of them students at Garfield High and disappeared off the streets while walking home from school one afternoon."

"Kidnapped?" I asked.

He nodded.

"And these two black girls you're looking for, you think they might be connected to the three young women who've gone missing and that maybe they might all be related to Gabi Garrison's disappearance and Monica Channing's murder?"

"I'm not at liberty to tell you that, Ms. Childs. This is an open investigation. But I will tell you these two, Leticia and Brandy, they weren't runaways. You get their names in the news and we'll talk. Until then, like I said, we're doing everything we can to find your friend Gabi."

He took his business card out of his wallet and slid it across the counter. I could see he had nothing more to say. The rest was going to be up to me.

CHAPTER 7

By the time I got to the courthouse the street was lined with media vans. TV crews with their cameras and oversized news trucks were parked everywhere. A small dust devil had grabbed a plastic trash bag and was whirling leaves and papers amid arriving reporters, creating havoc on the courtyard where LAPD's Chief of Police Bradley Walker and Judge Channing were expected to address a nervous public. Officers on bicycles with bullhorns began sweeping the sidewalk, advising vagrants and those loitering to move on. Anyone within earshot knew something big was about to go down.

I weaved my way through the crowd. Usually for things like this it's mostly media people, print and broadcast journalists, but today's group was much larger than I expected. Interspersed throughout the crowd were dozens of plainclothes officers wearing dark glasses with earpieces and mobile walkie-talkies disguised as wristwatches. I nodded casually to some reporters as I made my way towards the makeshift podium at the top of the stairs, then stopped. Standing directly in front of me was a pair of broad shoulders I recognized.

"Mark?"

"Carol. I thought you might be here." He turned and looked at me through mirrored sunglasses.

Special Agent Mark Delfino and Eric had been through the academy together. The two of them were sailing buddies and Mark was Sheri's plus one at her frequent dinner parties. They were an odd pairing—a little like Rachael Ray and Jack Sprat, with no chemistry between them—but together the four of us enjoyed a lot

of good wine and laughs, despite Mark's finicky eating.
"I didn't know you were working the case." I knew the FBI had
been called in to investigate Monica's disappearance; when a
federal judge's life is threatened, or any member of his family for
that matter, the big guns are always called in. But with Eric away, I
had no idea exactly who was involved in the investigation, nor was I
privy to anything they might know.

"Just lucky, I guess. So what do you hear from our old man
and the sea?"

Mark never passed up a chance to remind me Eric was his
senior. At forty-eight, Eric was as fit as a man half his age. And with
his hair greying about the temples, he looked a little more like a
college professor than a federal agent. Something I was really into.

"Got a card in the mail this morning. At least I think it was
today." By now so much of the day was starting to blend together, I
wasn't certain if the mail I had seen on the table this morning had
been from the day before or two days ago. It was all a blur.
"Weather willing, he's due back by the tenth. But you know how
that goes."

Moments later, LAPD's Chief Walker appeared from inside the
courthouse. He looked strained, with dark circles beneath his eyes,
his salt and pepper hair slicked back from his leathered face.
Following him was Judge Channing. Without his black robe or
seated behind his courtroom bench, he looked smaller than I
imagined him to be. He appeared almost frail, his grey hair
thinning. Next to him, coming barely to his shoulder, was his wife,
Melissa. She was dressed in a fitted black dress, and with her dark
hair pulled back in a bun, looked equally as gaunt. They walked
hand-in-hand towards the podium, as though they'd never let go of
one another. As they centered themselves, three more plainclothes
officers came and stood behind them. We all stood quiet while the
police chief adjusted the microphone and prepared to address the
crowd.

"This morning, at five a.m., LAPD received a call from a
commuter traveling west on Mulholland Drive above Stone Canyon.

They reported what they believed to be a body beneath a tree several hundred yards from the roadway. We immediately dispatched a car and discovered the body to be that of Monica Channing, the daughter of Judge Byron Channing and his wife Melissa. Miss Channing, as you all know, has been the center of a massive manhunt headed up by both LAPD's missing persons unit and the FBI. And in light of this news, Judge Channing has asked for this press conference. But before I turn this over to him, I'd like to say this morning's discovery has now moved this case from that of a missing person to a homicide. This is an active investigation. Both LAPD and the FBI will be pursuing all possible leads, and we are asking anyone for any information concerning this case to please come forward." Chief Walker exhaled a heavy sigh then turned and nodded to Judge Channing.

The judge and his wife stepped forward to the podium like stiff soldiers, grim-faced, their jaws locked.

"My wife and I would like to make a brief statement." The judge paused, cleared his throat and for a moment pinched his eyes shut, the creases around them deepening. He looked as though he was fighting tears. My own throat tightened as I watched the scene. Chief Walker stepped up behind him, put a hand on the judge's shoulder and another gently on his wife's back.

"After that," the judge said, "I've asked Chief Walker to answer any questions you may have. I hope you'll understand this is a very difficult time for my wife and me and respect our need for privacy and to be left alone."

The judge bowed his head, put his fist to mouth and choked back what was clearly a sob. Cameras clicked, catching what was a palpable moment as his wife leaned closer to him, her arm about his waist. We all knew this was the money shot, the judge fighting back tears, the wife pressed close to her husband with her head bowed. Tomorrow morning it would be on the front page of every paper in the southland.

"This last week has been a horrendous rollercoaster. A ride no parent should ever have to take. Our Monica was a wonderful young girl. She was a devoted daughter, excited about life, and she loved being a teacher. Her young students were everything to her. Just the other day she said, 'Dad, I really know I'm doing the right thing with my life. I just hope I can give back as much as the kids give me.'"

Clenching his jaw, the judge turned his head away from the crowd momentarily and appeared to be searching his wife's eyes for strength, and then finding it, looked back at the crowd.

"One week ago today Monica disappeared and suddenly became the subject of a massive manhunt. I'd like to thank LAPD and the FBI for their concern and their help."

He paused again and a silence that could have deafened a football stadium at halftime followed. Nobody moved. We all knew the next words out the judge's mouth would be the lead line in tomorrow's paper, immediately below the photo of him holding back tears with his wife at his side.

"Early this morning, that search came to an end when we learned that Monica may have been the latest victim in what the police now believe has been a string of kidnappings targeting young women in Hollywood. This is a devastating loss for us, and I would ask that you allow my wife and me our time of mourning, and that if anyone has any information at all concerning Monica and her disappearance that they contact the authorities. Thank you."

The judge looked back at his wife, took her hand and then stared back out at the sea of reporters in front of him. There was an immediate clicking of cameras and a volleying of questions. Chief Walker held his hand up, demanding we all remain silent. No questions. We all watched as the judge and his wife disappeared, like shadows of their former selves, behind the courthouse door. It was so quiet we could all hear the door close behind them.

The Chief stepped back in front of the microphone and reminded us all this was an open investigation and that he had time for only a few questions.

From within the crowd of reporters I thrust my mic forward, while those around me all did the same. Shouting questions, vying for his attention. Chief Walker pointed to me.

"Chief, do you have any idea how many women may have been kidnapped?"

Before he had a chance to answer, someone else in the crowd yelled, "Are we going to wake up tomorrow and find their bodies in Mulholland as well?"

"What about Gabi Garrison?" A reporter from CBS pushed me aside. "Do the police think she's also a victim?"

The chief stepped closer to the mic, his face red.

"Folks, we don't have answers to all your questions. I'm sorry. This is a very fluid situation, and we've got officers, not just here but all around the country, combing through records of missing girls who either lived here or were believed to have come to Hollywood for work or to visit. Let me remind you all that this is a big city, and people go missing in big cities. As for how many of those missing may be connected to this case, we don't know. Could be as many as a dozen, but most missing people don't show up dead. But to whoever kidnapped Monica Channing and any other young women in our city, let me say this: We will find you. Hollywood is not your hunting ground."

Without further statement, Chief Walker, his shoulders squared, backed away from the mic and disappeared behind the same doors Judge Channing and his wife had gone through moments before.

I filed my report from the steps of the courthouse.

"In an emotional and shocking statement to the press just moments ago, Judge Channing announced that his daughter, who has been the center of a massive manhunt this last week, may have been the victim of a series of kidnappings targeting young women in Hollywood. Speaking before a crowd of reporters, the judge asked for anyone with any knowledge of his daughter's activities, or information that may lead to the arrest of those responsible for her disappearance, to contact the authorities. Police Chief Walker said detectives working with LAPD missing persons unit have been combing their files and believe there may be as many as a dozen missing girls, including two young black girls, seventeen year-old Leticia Johnson and fourteen year-old Brandy White, previously suspected of being runaways. Meanwhile, there is no news concerning the disappearance of former CBS reporter, Gabi Garrison, who disappeared four days ago. Investigators close to the investigation would not say if they believe Ms. Garrison may have also been kidnapped by the same person or persons responsible for Monica Channing's death, only that she bares a remarkable resemblance to the judge's daughter..."

I was about to wrap up my report when Tyler interrupted me. "Carol, hold on. I'd like you to stay where you are. We have a few questions."

CHAPTER 8

What was supposed to be a brief wrap-up following Judge Channing's press conference ended up running longer than I expected. Tyler kept me on the air pressing for more information about what the station was now reporting as Hollywood's Missing Girls. For the next hour I reported on LAPD's missing persons unit, and what I'd learned about the national database for missing persons. The good news was that because I was on the air for longer than expected, I was able to include more information about the two other missing girls Detective Browne had asked me to make public. The bad news was that I was now running late to my son's game and wouldn't have time to go home and change.

It was the middle of fourth quarter by the time I managed to get from the courthouse downtown to the high school in Sherman Oaks. Tonight's game was an away game and I was unfamiliar with Notre Dame's campus. I found a parking space on the street off Woodman in front of the school, and slipping off my heels, grabbed a pair of tennis shoes I kept in the car and hurried towards the field. The sun had set and temperatures dropped. It was perfect football weather, cool with a slight breeze in the air that kicked up a few of the fall leaves on the ground. I arrived at the edge of the field to the sound of cheering fans and the band dressed in blue and gold with their big brass horns swaying side to side. They were playing the Notre Dame Fight Song. I stared at the scoreboard. Home: forty-four, Visitors: thirty-eight.

"Carol. Over here."

From midway up the bleachers, near the end zone, Sheri stood waving enthusiastically, her dark curly hair poking out from beneath her knit cap, her cheeks red from the cool night air. I hurried in her direction. Then stopped. Next to her, with a big smile on her face, dressed in an SDSU hoodie, was my daughter, Cate.

Surprise, she mouthed, standing up, a big smile on her face.

I hadn't expected Cate to come up from San Diego State for my birthday. She had called yesterday to say she was sorry she wouldn't be home this weekend. Homework. With a second wind of energy I hurried up the stand. Then ducking my head, trying to make as little interruption as possible, I crawled over the laps of cheering fans to the empty seat Sheri had saved next to my daughter and hugged them both. I thought I'd been successful until somebody tapped me on the shoulder. Expecting to be told to sit down, I turned around to see a young woman sitting behind me, wearing a dark hoodie, with a set of pink earphones stuffed in her ears.

"Are you Carol Childs?" she asked.

I leaned down, still holding my daughter's hand, and over the roar of the crowd shouted, "Yes. Do I know you?"

"You're the reporter with KCHC, right?"

I nodded, anxious to get back to Cate and Sheri.

"My brother's the coach on Charlie's team. He told me who you were and that the parents would all be sitting together in the visitors section. I took a chance and hoped you'd be here. I need to talk to somebody. My name's Bethany Richards. Monica and I were friends. We taught school together."

I didn't know what to say. I was at a loss for words. She looked crushed, her eyes strained and worried. I stumbled for something more than "I'm sorry for your loss," but I could think of nothing. Suddenly the crowd all around me was on their feet. The Notre Dame Knights had dropped the ball and the crowd was going crazy. Cate let go of my hand and started jumping around. I sat down while the cheers from the crowd faded to mere background noise, providing Bethany and me with our own private huddle. She pointed to her pink earphones and told me she'd been listening to

Judge Channing's press conference.

"This is crazy," she whispered. "Judge Channing's got it all wrong."

"What do you mean, wrong?" I had no idea what she was talking about.

"What he said about Monica. It was all wrong. Everything. To start with, she wasn't a kindergarten teacher. Maybe he was just upset, but she was my assistant, a teacher's aide, not a teacher. Not that it mattered. Not that part anyway. She was great with the kids and they loved her. So did I. But I think the judge just preferred that people think she was a teacher. But she was...well, you know..."

I shrugged my shoulders. I wasn't sure what Bethany meant. "She was what?"

"You know, slow. Not like mentally slow, but naïve and sweet slow. Overprotected, maybe? I guess that goes with being an only child. Her parents didn't do her any favors. I don't think she ever did so much as go to the mall by herself. So when she got her first job and started living alone, I think she just went a little crazy. She just wanted to have fun, fit in."

I grabbed her wrist gently and looked at her. "What do you mean by fun? Did you know where Monica was or what she was doing?"

"Not really. Not at first anyway. She told me she had been going online and she had all these relationships. I think she thought they were real. And then she met this one guy—or this man—and she started to talk about him all the time. I didn't think much about it, until he invited her down to some of the clubs in Hollywood, the really cool ones, where a lot of the stars go. She was so excited about it. Like a groupie. She'd never done anything like that before—you know being a judge's kid, an only daughter—she was pretty sheltered, particularly for growing up in LA. She kept telling me I should come with her, but I'm just not into that scene."

"Have you spoken to the police?"

She nodded, her head shaking nervously. "Right after she went missing, but not since...you know, this morning...when the police found the body. They asked me all about her. I told them she'd been dating some man she met online. But I didn't want to say anything that would get her in trouble with her father. He's something else. I think he thinks I might have been a bad influence, but there was no way I was. Besides, the police had her computer and with that they'd know as much as me. I really thought maybe she'd gone a little crazy with this guy and run off. That she'd come back. Like you said in your report this afternoon, sometimes missing people just show up, right?" She paused, her eyes searching mine, almost pleading.

I took a deep breath. Ironically, what she was telling me about Monica made me hopeful about Gabi. The Gabi I knew would never be involved with someone online. She was too smart.

"So why are you telling *me* this? Don't you think you should go back and talk to the police?"

"I listened to the station, and I liked the way you covered those other missing girls. You talked about them like they were real people. Like you really cared, and I thought maybe if I talked to you—you'd understand, maybe help."

It wasn't unusual for a listener to connect with an on-air host or a reporter, and clearly something I had said connected with her. I asked her how long this affair had been going on.

"Not long. Maybe a month, month and a half."

"Did she describe the man she was meeting? Give you a name?"

"No. All she'd tell me was that he was really nice. Someone important, and that they needed to keep it a secret. I think he might have been like her father's age or something. Monica, she has—she had—you know, daddy issues. She was always into older men. It wasn't the first time. In college she'd had this crush on a professor." She stopped and looked down at her hands. She was wrenching her fingers like she was struggling to tell me something.

I put my hand on top of hers. "Go on."

"It's just, she kept saying how much he respected her. Her working with kids and all. And that he really liked clean cut girls. It sounded odd. You know, kinda off somehow. And then he started pushing her to do things."

"What kind of things?"

She paused, bit her lip, and looked down at her hands again. I could feel her discomfort.

"Like sex?" I asked.

"Oh, no. Not like that. Monica wouldn't. She was a..."

"Virgin?"

Bethany nodded her head nervously up and down.

"I think that's why she liked him. He wasn't pushing her. Not like that. I couldn't tell the police all this. You understand, right?"

I nodded.

"You see, Monica and I, we made these virginity promises in high school. We weren't going to have sex until we were married. She told him she couldn't do it, and he said that was okay with him."

"Did she say what they did do?"

"Just go to the clubs, meet people. Mostly she said it was men. He got her all kinds of really sexy clothes to wear. You know, short glittery outfits and really tall spiked heels. The type of clothes girls wear to the clubs, only hotter. That was it. She said he had business people he needed to meet in the clubs and wanted her to look good. Nothing more, not really, 'cept she said he was always asking her to go get him a drink at the bar, and when she would, they'd all look at her. She thought it was fun. You know, because he liked it when men looked at her. I think he got off on it, and Monica, she just didn't get it. Like I said, she wasn't real smart about men. She may have thought they were in a relationship, but if you ask me it was strange, like he was using her."

"And you think she was really falling for him."

"Oh, I know she was. Only, then all of a sudden, he just drops her, and she's really devastated. She thought it was 'cause she'd told him who her dad was, that he didn't want get involved with a judge's kid, but she just wouldn't let go."

"So, she pursued him?"

"Not only that. She went and got this tattoo, on her wrist. She said one of the girls that hung around the club—a friend of his—had one and that he thought it was cool."

"Did you know what it symbolized?"

"She said it made her his girl. You know, like how some girls tattoo their boyfriend's name on their arm or maybe a butterfly on their ankle. I think she hoped if he saw it he'd realize how much she cared."

Suddenly the pictures and the stories the paper had been running since Monica's abduction were taking on a whole new meaning for me. The girl in the photos with her parents, singing in her church choir, feeding the homeless, reading to her kindergarten class, they weren't just of the saint her father described her to be. She may have been a naïve young woman, an innocent, but if Bethany were correct, she was very definitely into the Hollywood club scene.

"She begged me to come with her. She wanted to see him again, but I wouldn't go." Bethany put her head in her hands and started to cry. "I can't believe she's dead. Maybe if I'd gone with her, she wouldn't be."

I wanted to put my arms around her, but she wiped her eyes with the back of her hand, then reaching into her pocket, handed me a crumpled piece of paper. It was a flyer, some type of Hollywood advertisement promoting an event.

The headline read: *Pub Crawl. Free Entrance into Hollywood's Hottest Clubs. No cover. No wait.* Beneath the headline, in fine print, was a description of the various bars, clubs and hot spots promising anyone looking to party an "Awesome Night." A telephone number was printed in bold for reservations.

"She wanted me to come with her. She said it'd be fun."

I folded the flyer and asked her if I could keep it. Tears began welling up in her eyes as she nodded her head. I pressed my business card into her hand.

"If you think of anything else, or if you need to talk, call me anytime. Alright?"

I wanted to tell her it'd be okay, but I knew better. I could see in her eyes she was blaming herself for Monica's murder. Around us people started jumping to their feet, cheering. Cate was going crazy. Charlie had scored a touchdown. She grabbed my hand. I jumped to my feet and turned to look at the scoreboard. It was flashing a winning score for the Vikings. Home: forty-four. Visitors: forty-seven. By the time I turned back Bethany was gone.

CHAPTER 9

Despite the lilt of my daughter's laughter and the smell of roasted garlic and tomatoes coming from Sheri's kitchen, I was having trouble feeling festive. Standing in front of the living room's large plate glass window I stared out at the city lights below, my mind wandering back over the events of the day. How many other missing girls might still be out there? Alone and afraid, they might end up like Monica.

"Champagne?" Sheri entered the living room with Cate. She was carrying a silver tray of hors d'oeuvres and three perfectly frosted champagne flutes, chilled and bubbly. She handed a glass to me, then one to Cate, and suggested we toast.

"To your birthday."

"And to a little girl time," Cate added.

The boys had gone off with Charlie's dad for a weekend of football and Boston baked beans. My ex had tickets to the USC/Boston College game—which obviously trumped my birthday—and Charlie asked Clint to go with them. They'd been packed and ready to go for days and left right after their game.

The three of us clinked glasses. Dinner would be another few minutes. Cate wandered over to a bookcase filled with old LP's; an antique Victrola was on the shelf in front of her. I looked back out the black window at the lights. Traces of my conversation with Bethany continued to run through my mind nonstop.

"What are you thinking about?" Sheri leaned closer to me and whispered. "I can tell from the look on your face you're off somewhere else. What is it? "

"I'm sorry. I'm having trouble switching gears. I keep thinking about the young woman sitting behind us at the game. She was a friend of Monica Channing's."

"I knew it. You're thinking about those missing girls, aren't you?"

"What do you know about the pub crawls?" I asked.

"Is that what that woman behind us at the game was talking about?" Cate approached with an album in her hand and sat down on the couch next to us.

"She said Monica had met a man online and had gotten herself into the club scene pretty heavily before she disappeared."

"It'd be easy enough to do," Cate said. "Men are always fishing for girls online."

I looked at Cate. "You know anything about this?"

"Not this exactly. But online hookups? Everybody knows. There're girls at school who have online sugar daddies. Older guys who like young girls. We call them Sugar Babies. The men pay for their education in exchange for what they call friendship."

"That's legal?" Sheri asked.

"It's just like any other matchmaking site, only the girls aren't looking for a relationship. At least not in the traditional sense. Besides, what consenting adults do is up to them." Cate sounded very self-assured.

"But these Sugar Babies, as you call them, they're not disappearing," I said.

"On the contrary, they're graduating debt free and bragging about it."

I rolled my eyes, and took the flyer Bethany had given me out of my pocket and placed it on the table.

"Difference is, these girls aren't free at all. In fact, I think whoever kidnapped them is using them as slaves."

Sheri looked at Cate then back at me.

"It's called human trafficking," I said. "And if I'm right, it's going on right here in Hollywood, and for whatever reason the police aren't talking about it."

BEYOND A DOUBT **43**

"But why would the police want to keep it quiet?" Sheri asked.

"I don't know. Maybe because they're in the middle of an active investigation and don't want to blow it. But someone's targeting young women on the internet. Marilyn Ann Billings had an online relationship with a talent agent. Her sister said it's why she came to Hollywood. Jessica Martin was in a bad situation at home and needed to get away. April Hansen was about to go back to court for DUI. There are sites online offering financial aid. Maybe, just like those Sugar Babies, they found somebody who offered them a way out. As for Leticia Johnson and Brandy White, the girls Detective Browne told me about, I'll bet if I did a little digging I'd find they had access to a computer and also met someone online."

"But what about Gabi Garrison?" Sheri asked. "I don't see an ex-news reporter falling for an online dating scam or anything close to it."

"She's the only one that doesn't fit...Unless—" I stopped. The thought was chilling.

"Unless what?" Sheri asked.

"Unless Gabi Garrison was a replacement for Monica Channing. And whoever killed Monica, saw Gabi—she liked to frequent the Hollywood clubs—and maybe they figured she'd work perfectly. I mean look at the two of them; they could be sisters, both blonde, about the same size, same age."

Sheri put her glass down on the table and picked up the flyer.

"And you think that if you just get yourself downtown and sign up for some pub crawl, you're going to find whoever kidnapped Monica, and maybe Gabi and these other girls? That it's going to be that easy?"

"Maybe."

"No, no way." Cate grabbed the flyer out Sheri's hand. "You're not doing some pub crawl down on Hollywood Boulevard."

"Why not?"

"Well, to start with, you're my mother and you're too old."

I stood up and reached for her champagne glass. "Really?

Brave words for someone not yet twenty-one."

Cate turned away from me, shielding her glass then looked back at Sheri as though she expected some sort of support.

"Tell her she's ridiculous. She's *not* going on some pub crawl. It could be dangerous."

"Oh, stop it. This is research. Nothing more. Nobody's going to know what I'm doing, and the station will love it. They're always looking for ways to promote themselves in different areas of the city. And if along the way I uncover something about Monica and the missing girls, well, so much the better." I crossed my fingers. I'd barely mentioned the idea to Tyler. In truth, I'd left a harried voicemail as I left the game, telling him about my encounter with Bethany and my suspicion about the pub crawls. "Plus, I ran into a woman this morning that could help. So it might not be as tough as you think."

I explained the Marilyns, the dancing flash mob in front of Ripley's Believe It or Not, and how one of the impersonators had introduced herself.

"She gave me her card, said if I ever wanted to really see Hollywood Boulevard to give her a call, and I think right now that might be a good idea."

Cate looked at Sheri. The two exchanged a look, then Cate said, "Well, then you're not going alone."

CHAPTER 10

Saturday morning the front page of the *LA Times* ran a picture of Monica Channing's body as it was being airlifted out of the canyon. The headline above the photo said it all: "Judge's Daughter Found Dead." I stared at the picture for the longest time, my coffee growing cold as I read and reread the article. Even though I'd watched as the paramedics hiked down the hill and secured her lifeless body to the gurney, I couldn't believe it. The only similarity to the once happy young woman, whose smiling face had been blasted across the city on billboards and posters for the last two weeks, was a strand of curly blonde hair that had escaped the thin Mylar blanket thrown over her body. It danced with the wind as she was airlifted from the scene like some final goodbye.

The story contained a few brief details about her disappearance, including the discovery of her body by a passing motorist and that she had died as a result of a broken neck, the cause of which was yet to be determined. There was no mention as to how her crumpled body had come to be found nearly doubled over beneath the big oak tree. In fact, the entire story concerning her murder was as barebones as it gets. Chief Walker was quoted as saying the police believed Miss Channing may have been the latest victim in a string of kidnappings targeting young women in Hollywood and that an investigation was underway.

The story then conveniently jumped to an inside page and included photos of Monica's early life: Monica surrounded by her kindergarten class, Monica in college, Monica playing soccer, and Monica as a small child on a tricycle in front of the family home, a large stone mansion with a circular drive in Stone Canyon. The judge was quoted saying how proud he was of his daughter. Both he and his wife were thankful to have had her in their lives for as long as they did. At the age of five Monica had been severely injured when her mother accidentally backed the family car out of the garage and hit her while Monica was riding her trike.

She had been hospitalized and lapsed in and out of a coma for weeks. But looking at later photos of her active lifestyle, it appeared she had suffered no long-term effects. The judge said they felt blessed that Monica had survived, and admitted both he and his wife had been overprotective.

A related story, "LAPD Believes Missing Women Were Kidnapped," ran as a sidebar to the report about Monica's disappearance. The article included more quotes from Detective Browne. LAPD and FBI were now revisiting cold cases of other missing persons, including Jessie Martin, Marilyn Ann Billings and April Hansen. Their photos, along with those of Leticia Johnston and Brandy White, were included in the article, and looked like they might have come from their high school yearbooks. Leticia's picture leaped out at me. The girl was a knockout.

Even in a grainy black and white photo, it was possible to see she had a future in front of the camera. Leticia had a broad confident grin, straight white teeth, and with her hair pulled away from her face in tight cornrows, her features were model-esque.

Brandy White, the younger of the two, had freckles, wore a beanie on her head and round black-framed glasses. She looked a little like Urkle from the TV comedy series *Family Matters*. But beneath her very nerdy expression, I could see classic pretty-girl features: big eyes, high cheekbones, straight teeth and an award-winning smile. I wondered if she were trying to hide her looks behind some alter ego.

The newspaper devoted two column inches to their background. Leticia was living with her grandmother; her mother was in prison for drug possession with intent to sell. She'd served seven of her of nine-year sentence. Brandy had grown up in foster homes, the whereabouts of her family unknown. Both girls had simply disappeared off the street and were, until Monica's disappearance, assumed to have been runaways. Their names had now been added to a list of missing girls suspected to have been kidnapped.

At the bottom of the page was another photo, this one of Gabi Garrison. There was a brief description reporting that she was also missing but, despite her physical similarity to Monica Channing, the police were not convinced her disappearance was related to that of Monica or the other missing girls. Detective Browne was quoted saying that with regard to Miss Garrison, they were talking with a person of interest.

I put my coffee down, picked up the phone, and called Detective Browne's cell. He answered on the first ring, his voice amazingly upbeat for nine-thirty on Saturday morning.

"Detective Browne, Carol Childs."

"Ms. Childs, I believe I owe you."

"Really?" I liked the idea that a LAPD detective thought he owed me. "May I ask why?"

"You see this morning's paper?"

"I'm looking at it right now."

"Then you've seen the pictures of the two girls I asked you include in your report yesterday?"

"It's one of the reasons I'm calling." I explained I wanted to talk to him about the girls, but first I had some information concerning Monica I thought I should share. "I ran into a friend of Monica's, a teacher, at my son's game last night."

"Bethany Richards." He seemed to know without my saying exactly who I was talking about. "We interviewed her right after Monica went missing." I could hear him flipping through the pages of his notepad. "I'm afraid she wasn't very forthcoming about what her friend was into."

"But you know she was meeting with a man she'd met online in Hollywood."

"I'm afraid, Carol, I can't comment on that. That's part of an open investigation. You heard the chief."

I decided I'd push a little harder despite his resistance.

"Bethany says the judge was clueless about who his daughter was. She was afraid he'd come unglued if he knew what she was up to, and had run off with some man. She kept thinking Monica would come home."

"Like I said, I can't comment."

"Look, I get that Judge Channing's trying to protect his daughter. That this is an open investigation and LAPD and the FBI aren't talking about it with the press until they know something. But there's at least five other girls out there missing. The public deserves to know what's going on."

"And just what do you think that is, Miss Childs?"

"I think there's a sex trafficking ring operating inside of Hollywood and that Monica, and the other missing girls, maybe even Leticia and Brandy, were targeted via the internet, kidnapped and they're being held somewhere."

"You plan to do something with that story?"

"I plan on filing a report this afternoon that suggests Monica's murder may be linked to the disappearance of at least six other missing girls in Hollywood."

He paused and I proceeded cautiously, hoping I wasn't about to undo the good will between us.

"Detective, you started this conversation saying you owed me. Talk to me about Leticia and Brandy. Do you know if they had been going online, maybe answered an ad or—"

"Like I said, Carol, I can't, and I won't, talk about anything that might be related to the case." His voice sounded firm, like he was barking an order, but then it softened. "But, since you helped me, I can put you in touch with Leticia's grandmother, Bessie Bixby. She plays the church organ at the AME Church downtown. Nice lady. Been to church there a couple times myself and I know she'd like to speak to you."

"Good, I'd like to speak to her too." I paused. "One more question, Detective?"

"Nothing to do with the case," he said.

"Gabi Garrison. The police chief didn't think her disappearance was connected to Monica's so—anything new?"

"I talked with her boyfriend again this morning. He was at the hospital. Said Gabi was given to bouts of depression, that things at work weren't going well. She was upset with his hours. Have to admit, a resident's got worse hours than some detectives I know. He said she'd been threatening to leave. He thinks she might have gone off to some weekend resort in the desert."

I didn't see someone like Gabi just up and leaving, no matter how depressed she might be. The girl was probably pulling down a six-figure salary working for the television station. You don't just walk away from a job like that. It seemed odd.

"You think he's telling the truth?"

"What I think is that the trail is getting cold. Girl's been gone for seventy-two hours. If she were going to show up, now's about the time. Until she does, I suggested he not leave town."

I glanced at the clock. It was almost ten-thirty. Cate was still upstairs asleep. I needed to call Norma Jean Baker, a.k.a. Holly Wood, or whatever pseudonym she was using, and arrange three tickets for tonight's pub crawl. Plus, I wanted to talk to Dr. Ericson. I needed to settle the question in my own mind about Gabi's boyfriend: if he was involved with her disappearance, or if it was related in some way to that of Monica Channing and the other missing girls. Thank goodness college kids sleep late.

CHAPTER 11

There's a grab-and-go on the second level of the UCLA Medical Center. It's located directly above the staircase near the lobby, and it's where I planned to meet with Dr. Ericson. He was running late, so I got a cup of coffee from one of the vending machines, settled myself at a small table in the corner directly across from the entry, and prepared to wait. I had called the hospital after I got off the phone with Detective Browne and told him Gabi and I were friends and that I had information, something he might find helpful. I didn't elaborate. It was a white lie for sure, but enough of a connection that he agreed to meet right away.

I was halfway through my coffee when Dr. Ericson appeared in the doorway. I could have picked him out of a lineup. Not that he looked guilty, but exhausted. He was dressed in a white lab coat, a stethoscope around his neck, and badly in need of a shave. I figured between Gabi's disappearance and his nonstop schedule at the hospital, he hadn't slept in days.

"Dr. Ericson?" I started to stand. He shook his head, indicating I should remain seated, and grabbed the chair opposite me.

"Call me Miles." He took a deep breath and ran his long surgeon's fingers through his short, stylishly cut hair. "Just how well did you know Gabi? She never mentioned you."

"Actually, we were really more like business associates." I explained how we'd met at a mutual client's office when I was still working in sales. "Ironic, isn't it, how Gabi was once on-air, and now she's in sales and I'm here."

"So you're a reporter then?"

I nodded.

"This is crazy. The police think I had something to do with Gabi's disappearance. But that's insane. I love Gabi. I wouldn't do anything to hurt her. She's everything to me. Smart. Sexy. Funny. This whole thing's just a mix-up. They'll see. This'll all blow over, and she'll come home."

"Has she ever disappeared before?" I was fishing for some nervous twitch to tell me he was lying. I didn't see anything. His eyes held steady on mine.

"Sometimes. I told the police she'd left before. Gabi could get frustrated. She was worried about her job—not making her sales quota. She didn't think her boss liked her—you know how it goes. And with me working all the time, sometimes she'd just take off. She'd go clubbing or to a spa for the weekend. Palm Springs was her favorite. Sometimes she'd visit with her family, but she'd always come home."

"Had you been arguing?"

His eyes flashed to the window. He looked like he might have been recalling a previous experience.

"We had our problems. First year residency can be tough on relationships. Money's tight and time even more so. But Gabi was onboard with everything. So we decided to move in together. Gabi's parents were the problem. They're old-fashioned and weren't happy about my moving in. I think her dad was afraid he would be subsidizing my living expenses and that I'd leave when I finished my residency. But that's not going to happen. Her dad could be a real jerk."

"That couldn't have been easy. Particularly if Gabi was close to her folks."

"It was ridiculous. I love Gabi, but if I wasn't home every night, her folks were filling her head with all kinds of nonsense. And with the pressures of her job, she wasn't feeling secure about a lot of things, so we argued. Part of it was my fault. I was feeling the pressure, and I'm not in a position to offer her anything. So, lately, I started spending more and more time at the hospital, sleeping there when I really could have come home. I needed to get things straight in my own head."

"It got that bad?"

"Worse. Look, I'm telling you this because if Gabi doesn't show up soon, I know the police are going to find a reason to arrest me. Right now we're just talking. I'm their 'person of interest.'" He finger quoted the words. "I told them I don't know where she is, that I didn't have anything to do with her disappearance, but you know how the police are. They're talking to everybody. Her parents. Her boss. The neighbors. And I can just imagine what they're saying."

"So, the last time you saw her, you argued?"

"Yes. It was a Sunday. I had the day off. We were finally going to have some time to ourselves, but we got into this stupid argument, and I left. I'm sure the neighbors heard. The apartment walls are pretty thin."

"And when you came home, she was gone?"

"I didn't come home Sunday night. I went back to the hospital and didn't come home until Wednesday morning, early. I was planning on taking a nap and making dinner. I wanted it ready and waiting for her when she came in. I had been doing a lot of thinking and decided I needed to make more of a commitment to Gabi. I felt it would help her with her parents and make her feel more secure if I did."

He paused and looked like he was considering what to say next.

"So what did you do?"

"This." He reached inside the pocket of his pants, took out a thin yellow receipt, and slid it across the table. "I had been carrying around my mother's wedding ring for better than a month. She left it to me when she died five years ago. It's all I have left from her. Finally, I decided to have it remounted to fit Gabi. I wanted her to have it as an engagement ring. I was going to give it to her next week."

He stared down at the receipt, his eyes distant.

"And when you came home Wednesday morning, that's when you realized she was gone?"

"By the time I got back to the apartment, Gabi's car was still parked in the drive. She should have been at work, so I checked to see if there was a problem, but the tank was full, and it started up okay. I figured she couldn't have gone far, maybe walked around the corner to the store. Her purse was gone and the newspaper was still on the front porch. It didn't make sense. So I called her work, and they said she hadn't come in. Hey, I was the one who reported her missing. That ought to say something, shouldn't it?"

I took a sip of my coffee and considered what Miles had said. He looked tired, the lines around his eyes strained, and not just from lack of sleep, but worry. He didn't look like a guilty boyfriend. At least not to me.

"You said Gabi liked to go clubbing...that sometimes she'd go out by herself."

"Yeah. She'd go to the clubs on Hollywood Boulevard. It's close to the apartment, and one of the clients she had on the air is the old Roosevelt Hotel. They'd comp her dinner on occasion. Last week, before all this happened, we went together and afterwards walked down the boulevard to Hemingway's." He looked down at the table again, his shoulders slumped, his eyes closed as he recounted the memory.

"Did you meet anyone there?"

"No, it was just the two of us."

I paused. I needed to know exactly how much he knew about Monica Channing's disappearance. If he also thought they might be related.

"I'm sorry to ask, but you were gone a lot, working long hours. Did Gabi maybe fill her time surfing the internet? Maybe have online relationships? Someone she might have met from time to time, or gone clubbing with?"

He looked at me like I'd just slapped him across the face.

"Did she say that?"

"No. No, not at all. It's just, Monica Channing, the judge's daughter who disappeared last week, she looked a lot like Gabi. They lived in the same area of town, and the police believe she was carrying on with someone—"

"No way." He shook his head. "Absolutely not. Gabi wasn't playing around online or meeting up with strange men. We loved—love—each other."

He stumbled and paused. His hands clasped together before his face, his knuckles white.

"But you're not a hundred percent certain, are you? And the police aren't listening to you?"

He shook his head. "No. They're not. All I know is that Gabi's smart, and that whatever happened, I want her to come home. I love her."

He sounded convinced. He had probably replayed every conversation and analyzed every nuanced move she had made before her disappearance a thousand times in his mind. He was clearly searching for answers. I felt for him. I believed him. Dammit, if he had told me red velvet crumb cake was calorie free, I'd trust the man. As far as I was concerned, both Dr. Miles Ericson and my favorite dessert were guilt-free.

CHAPTER 12

Eric called when I was in the car. I was surprised to see his number come up on the Jeep's hands-free screen. The *Sea Mistress* is loaded with high frequency radio transmitters and the fact that he was calling via his cellphone and not on one of the free channels assigned for ship-to-shore communications made me wonder if he might actually be home. Unfortunately, I wasn't alone. Cate and Sheri were with me. It was almost nine o'clock, and we were dressed for a girls' night out, headed to the pub crawl on Hollywood Boulevard.

"Hey, babe, it's me." Just the sound of his voice, like velvet, triggered a warm visceral reaction. My heart started to beat a little faster, my palms sweating. He sounded like he was almost purring. "What are you wearing?"

I gripped the wheel. In the rearview mirror I saw my daughter, eyes wide, her hand over her mouth, laughing. Sheri, riding shotgun next to me, turned with her fingers to her lips and indicated for Cate to zip it.

"Actually..." I cleared my throat. "I'm dressed in a short black cocktail dress with heels, and...Sheri's got on a little sequined number and Cate, she's here with us, too, and she's wearing..." I looked back at her reflection in the mirror. "Just what is it you have on, Catie?"

Eric laughed. "So you're not alone?"

"That would be a good assumption on your part."

I could picture Eric on the deck of the *Sea Mistress*, her white sails billowing beneath a full moon with the wind in his hair, leaning against the ship's wheel, the black water slipping like moonlit glass beneath her hull.

"Sorry 'bout that. I didn't realize I was interrupting." He added that they were just north of Puerto Vallarta and wanted to call to say hello. He was thinking of me.

I explained I was doing some research. Monica Channing's disappearance had now turned into a full-fledged murder, and I was investigating a possible connection to several other missing girls and the Hollywood nightclub scene. Hence, we were headed for a pub crawl.

"And Sheri and Cate didn't think I should be out all by myself—not on a Saturday night—so they came along."

"Sorry I can't be there."

I quickly changed the subject and mentioned I'd run into Mark Delfino at the press conference. "He said to say hello; however, I think he really misses Sheri's cooking and was looking for an excuse to get together for dinner again. You know, a home cooked meal."

"Dinner, huh?" I could tell Eric had been missing more than dinner, but he covered politely and added, "Tell Sheri we've got a boatload of tuna. She can make up some of that guacamole tuna she likes, and if I get back early, maybe the four of us can set sail for Catalina before I have to go back to work."

Catalina? Sheri mouthed the word and muffled a laugh. Both she and Cate knew just the thought of sailing caused my stomach to churn.

"Sounds like a plan," I said. I hung up the phone and rolled my eyes. Eric's *Sea Mistress* was like the other woman in his life. He'd bought her at auction after she'd been confiscated from drug smugglers and took great pride restoring her to her full glory. He wanted so much for us to all get along. I couldn't wait to see Eric, but the *Sea Mistress*...I'd almost prefer if she were another woman—at least that I could handle.

*   *   *

My instructions for the pub crawl required we meet Holly at her office on Gower, just south of Hollywood Boulevard. Her note indicated it was walking distance from the famed intersection of Hollywood and Vine and that we'd find plenty of parking in back of the small white craftsman cottage. A fence post sign next to the drive read "Holly Wood Tours." Both the house and the white picket fence that surrounded it looked out of sorts for the neighborhood that was mostly office buildings and high-rise complexes. But what really surprised me was the brand new Rolls Royce parked out front. Not that a Rolls is unusual in Hollywood, but I didn't think it belonged to Holly.

Equally as surprising was the young woman who stood on the porch to the house. Holly waved as my red Jeep pulled into the lot. This wasn't the Norma Jean Baker I'd met just a little over twenty-four hours ago. Instead of the Marilyn Monroe lookalike, standing on the front porch, wearing a short, plaid, pleated skirt with red suspenders and combat boots with her dark hair spiked like a rocker, was this new persona, Miss Holly Wood.

"Holly?" As I approached I noticed a nose ring and a tattoo on the back of her neck. Something she must have covered with heavy makeup yesterday.

"At your service." She bowed. Then looking at me she raised a pierced brow. "You didn't think I was really a blonde, did you?"

"Hardly," I said, and masking my surprise, added, "I was actually thinking brunette. Probably a little more Judy Garland than—"

"Marilyn Manson?" she laughed, referring to the often controversial musician. "I get that a lot. But, hey, a girl's got to have a look and for now, this is working for me."

I introduced Cate and Sheri and knew instantly there was a problem. Holly looked at me sternly then back at Cate, the commando boots really setting the tone.

"She twenty-one? 'Cause you didn't tell me you were bringing a minor." I could hear the constraint in her voice. Already I was beginning to wish I'd come alone. "'Cause if she isn't, I gotta give her a pink wristband, and there's certain clubs she can't go into—unless you sign a waiver—and then you'll have to agree she won't order anything stronger than a Shirley Temple. You okay with that?" She glared at Cate and then back at me, her eyes like steel rods to my own, challenging me.

I looked at Cate. "Perhaps this wasn't the best idea, maybe you and Sheri ought to—"

"No." Cate stepped forward. "I'm fine with it. Just bring me the silly wristband."

Holly looked back to me for verification. I nodded, *it'd be fine*, and she suggested we take a seat on the porch. Another group was coming in from Universal City via the Fun Bus and would be joining us shortly. They were stuck in traffic.

"Like, who isn't in LA?" Sheri joked, trying to lighten the mood.

Holly shrugged, cocked her head like we were generational disconnects—totally out of it—then excused herself, saying she needed to get us wristbands for tonight's tour, and disappeared back into the cottage. I could tell we weren't getting off to the best of all possible starts.

Moments later, Holly's Fun Bus, an open-air van, pulled into the drive. The passengers, all young and good-looking, appeared as though they were already well lubricated and were dressed for a night of revelry: the men in sport coats and slacks, the women in anything short and sassy, revealing lots of skin, beautifully tanned or airbrushed, and all wearing impossibly tall heels. Like cattle, they shuttled out of the van, the men stopping to help their high-heeled-hobbled girlfriends down the steps. They joined us on the porch.

Holly reappeared from inside the cottage. She looked harried and locked the door behind her. Then, pulling a small stepstool out from beneath one of the wicker couches, she stood up on it. The effect gave her small stature the advantage of height over the crowd. Like a fitness instructor on speed, she welcomed the group and explained our itinerary for tonight's festivities.

"Are you ready for an awesome night, folks?" With her hand above her head she pumped the air, while around us, members of the crowd responded enthusiastically. "'Cause we are gonna have one hell of a time."

Rules for the crawl were easy. There'd be no lines and no cover charges. All we had to do was wear our green scrunchie wristbands and stick with the group. This was a walking tour. Holly would wave her tour-wand above her head and point out some of the highlights along the boulevard as we passed by, but most importantly, when we came to one of the clubs on tonight's tour, we'd be fast tracked to the front of the line. There were more cheers at that.

"And, if you decide you want to stay at one of the clubs, just let me know. I'll need your wristband back. But until then, keep 'em on." Holly held up a handful of the neon green bands and started to throw them into the crowd. "So, that's it, folks. If you're ready...follow me."

Holly tossed me a pink wristband for Cate to wear. "Make sure she stays with you. Last thing we need is another missing girl out here." She sounded annoyed and pushed ahead, moving the group off the porch and towards the boulevard, leaving me to bring up the rear.

I stopped next to the white fence post and told Sheri and Cate to go on ahead. I needed to adjust my heels. In an effort to appear stylish I'd grabbed a new pair of shoes, and my feet were killing me already. I leaned up next to the post, massaged my toes and was about to replace my shoes when I noticed a shadow from within the cottage pass the window. *Odd.* I'd seen Holly lock the door. I didn't think anyone was left inside. I waited. Then the porch light went out, and a man came outside, stood on the porch and lit a cigarette. For a moment I thought I must be seeing a holograph.

I'd heard about Hollywood ghosts. Every year, right before Halloween, the newspaper is full of stories about their sightings.

Legend has it that some of the greats, like Cary Grant, Clark Gable, and Carol Lombard, still haunt the boulevard. The city recently uncovered secret passageways beneath the streets of some of the old hotels that once housed speakeasies. But this wasn't a ghost. From beneath the rakishly tilted brim of his grey fedora, I could tell this was a real live gent. A silver-haired fox, with a thin mustache, probably about fifty, fifty-five years old. He was dressed in an expensive looking blue pinstripe suit with a white pocket square, and he was wearing spats. Spats. Not exactly your modern day Hollywood.

I watched as he leaned up against the craftsman's pillar and took a long drag on a cigarette, then exhaled a thin grey stream of smoke. It circled above his head. The likeness was unmistakable. Standing on the porch, illuminated by nothing more than the neon haze of Hollywood's lights, was Clark Gable.

He reached inside the breast pocket of his coat and took out a cellphone—the only thing he had on his person that appeared out of character—and stared at it. Then taking another long drag on his cigarette, he glanced out at the parking lot, and seeing me, tipped his hat. I smiled to myself. The man was an impersonator, and a good one. Then as if on cue, he replaced his phone in his breast pocket, stepped off the patio and headed towards the Rolls Royce. I watched as he got in and drove past me. The personalized plates on the car read, DRM MKR. *Dream Maker.*

I hurried to catch up with Holly and pointed back over my shoulder towards the cottage. "There was a man back there on the porch. He was smoking a cigarette and looked just like Clark Gable. You know him?"

"He's nobody, just another impersonator." Holly pushed past me, as though she couldn't be bothered to say anything else. After all, this was Hollywood—didn't I expect such things? Rushing ahead and waving her tour wand above her head like a sign girl in a fighter's ring, Holly came to the door of our first club, Cosmo, and stopped. "Hurry up, people. You don't want to miss this."

I whispered to Sheri as she passed that I'd be a minute. I

wanted to study the crowd on the street as they entered the club.

"Keep an eye on Cate, will you? I need to get a feel for this place." Sheri squeezed my hand, promising she'd do just that.

Cate passed, an enthusiastic smile on her face. She was already caught up in the scene and leaned into me as she passed and said, "And who's watching you, Mom?"

I stood at the entrance and let my eyes and ears adjust.

The noise and the lights inside were jarring. Inside the club, the interior was reminiscent of old Hollywood. It was like a step back in time, draped in a shimmering gold neon light that reflected off mirrored walls with huge chandeliers that hung from the ceiling. Secluded booths lined the dance floor, jammed with beautiful people, like something from a *Vogue* advertisement, where everybody looks terribly sophisticated and nonplussed. I joined Sheri at the bar and ordered a white wine spritzer. I was working and wanted to keep it light. Sheri had a Cosmopolitan. Across the room, Cate had already hooked up with a group of pub crawling yuppies. Sheri assured me Cate had recognized an old friend from school, an upper classman, and everything was all right. I caught Cate's eye. We waved to one another. She snapped her pink wristband, winked, then took a sip from whatever was in her glass. I assumed it was a Shirley Temple and focused back on Sheri.

"So much for my chaperone."

"You didn't really think she was going to hang with us, did you? After all, you did say you'd be doing research."

I glanced around the room and took a mental inventory. I probably had thirty to forty minutes left before Holly would be shuffling off to the next bar. "You're right, I did, didn't I?"

I nodded towards a table across the room where three young women sat with two men. They looked like they might be about ready to leave. I told Sheri I was going to talk with them and walked across the room and introduced myself. I told them I was working on a story for KCHC Radio concerning Hollywood's Missing Girls and asked if they might like to be interviewed.

"We don't have to use our real names, right?" One of the girls giggled then looked back down at her drink, taking a big sip through the straw of something neon green and bubbly. "'Cause I don't want anybody to know—"

"What goes down in Hollywood, stays in Hollywood, right?" the girl next to her interrupted. They all laughed.

"Not if you don't want to," I said, "but if you want to give me your contact information I'll be happy to let you know when this airs."

That seemed to be sufficient. The three girls all partnered up, leaning against one another and into the table so that I was close enough to interview them while the boys sat opposite me. It was difficult to tell who was coupled with whom, or if perhaps they were all just friends, out for a night of clubbing.

I began by asking if they had heard about Monica Channing.

"You mean the girl who got herself kidnapped?" One of the girls asked.

"The police believe she was picked up by a sex trafficking ring operating out of Hollywood," I said.

"Yeah, I heard that. But come on. Really?" This time it was one of the young men talking. "The cops spread those rumors to keep us from coming down here. Makes their job easier..."

"I don't believe it either. I mean, how dumb do you have to be to think some dude on the internet's gonna set you up with a movie contract? It's not like we haven't grown up around here and don't know better."

It was clear from their responses they weren't worried about being kidnapped. Two of the girls had taken karate classes. One said she'd be more afraid of what she might do to any stranger than she was for her own safety. The third girl said she didn't listen to the news, it was all bad anyway.

"You just have to be aware of your surroundings, that's all."

"Bad things can happen to anyone."

"Terrible to say, but sometimes it's just your time."

I wrapped the interview, thanked them for their time and watched as they got up and left the table.

Moments later, I saw Holly at the bar with Sheri. She was signaling to those closest to her it was time to go. One by one, our group gathered outside and some of the women, the smart ones anyway, those familiar with the rigors of pub crawling, reached into the bags for flats and changed their shoes for the walk down the street.

I sidled up next to Holly. "I suppose I should ask you, since I'm doing research. Did you ever see Monica Channing on any of these pub crawls?"

She pulled away, the look on her face like I was accusing her of something.

"No. Why would I?" She pushed ahead as though I'd insulted her. I fell in with the crowd as we approached Sayers, our next stop.

I told Cate and Sheri I'd wait outside. The live music and crowd were so loud I thought I'd lose my hearing if I went in.

I stood and watched a parade of activity. The boulevard was clearly party central with girls trotting between clubs in short tight skirts and high heels—oblivious to any sense of danger—while good-looking young men, stylishly dressed, checked their cellphones and moved on to the next bar. There was the occasional shriek of joy as groups of people met up with one another, but nowhere was there any indication that anyone was worried that girls were disappearing, or that somewhere in their midst, a predator might be hiding, waiting to strike again.

Our last stop was Hemingway's, and I couldn't wait to sit down. I was thrilled to see what looked to me to be a civilized lounge with music I could get into, books, real leather-bound books that didn't look like props, and a comfortable chair I could kick back in. I identified myself to the bouncer and told him I was a reporter and doing a story on the club scene. His name was Freddie Bleeker, and he offered me what he said was the most comfortable seat in the house: a leather lounger, facing a wall of old-fashioned typewriters and surrounded by great books. Sheri sat down next to me in an equally comfortable lounger and ordered an Asti Spumante while thumbing through a copy of Hemingway's *Old*

Man and the Sea. I glanced at my watch. It was nearly two a.m. The place was clearing out. I had some good material for the show. I didn't need anything else, not tonight. I suggested to Sheri we call it a night. Tomorrow Cate would have to head back to San Diego. I wanted her to have at least a few hours' sleep before she left. I started to get up and look around.

"Where's Cate?"

CHAPER 13

Sheri looked at me. I could tell she didn't know where Cate was. I knew she had come in behind us. I'd seen her talking to a young man and figured she had gone to the bar and ordered another Shirley Temple or something equally as innocuous.

I grabbed my shoes and purse and made my way to the bar. The barkeep was starting to clean up. With a rag in one hand and the other on the bar, he asked if there was something I wanted. "Almost closing," he said.

"No, I don't want anything. I'm looking for my daughter. Blonde. About five-foot-six. Big smile. She's wearing a black dress." I realized I was describing about half of the young women in Hollywood.

"Sorry." He shook his head and continued to wipe the bar down. "But there's still a few people towards the back of the club; you might want to check there."

I nodded to Sheri and headed off towards the back of the club. The place was nearly empty. A few stragglers got up from their chairs, leaning on one another for support, and passed me, ambling toward the door. From the look on their faces they'd all had too much to drink and were headed home to sleep it off.

"Cate," I hollered, my voice echoing back at me from the end of the darkened saloon. There was no answer. I stood in the center of the room. The loveseats and small settees around me were all empty. There was no trace of my daughter. Not anywhere. My stomach started to tighten. I retraced my steps back towards the bar. "Cate. Cate! Where are you?"

"Carol?" Holly came rushing towards me, Sheri behind her, looks of concern on their faces. "What's wrong?"

"I can't find my daughter. She's not here." I looked over their shoulders and continued to call. "Cate!"

"What's the matter?" Freddie Bleeker heard my scream and came running.

I noticed Holly's eyes clicked quickly to him and back at me.

"It's my daughter. I can't find her."

"Maybe she headed back to the office. A bunch of them gave me their wristbands as they left." She held her arm up and showed me a bunch of neon green scrunchies she'd passed out earlier. "Maybe she's with them." Holly started to reach for my hand. I had the feeling she wanted to get me out there.

"No." I pulled away. "She wouldn't do that. She wouldn't just leave. She's here. I'm not leaving until I find her."

"Did you check out back?" Freddie looked at Holly. "Maybe she went out for a smoke."

"She doesn't smoke." I could feel my heart racing. My eyes scanned the room for any sign of her. There was nothing.

"Holly," Freddie said. "Why don't you check the ladies' room? Maybe she's in there. I'll check out back."

Sheri put her arm around me and we waited like frozen statues, afraid to move.

Moments later Freddie reappeared. With him was the young man I had seen Cate with when we came in. He'd been outside smoking and looked surprised to have been summoned inside.

"Where's Cate?" I asked.

"I don't know. We were having a drink at the bar and then she started talking to someone else and I left to get a smoke. Is something wrong?" He looked genuinely surprised at my concern.

"I can't find my daughter. That's what's wrong. She's not here. Not anywhere."

"Maybe she went down the street to the Roosevelt. A bunch of us were talking about trying to get in. It's pretty exclusive. Maybe she—"

"No. She wouldn't leave. She's got to be here somewhere."

I reached into my bag and pulled out my cell. There were no messages. No text. Nothing. I pushed speed dial for Cate's number and listened as it went to voicemail.

"Cate. It's Mom. Where are you? Call me."

Sheri put her hand on my shoulder. "Stay here. Let me go find out what's keeping Holly. Maybe she's in the ladies' room."

Freddie offered me a chair. I refused and paced towards the front of bar with my phone in my hand, begging it to ring. A few more stragglers passed me on their way out and looked at me like I was mad, a crazed women standing guard at the entrance to the bar. Nobody was getting in or out without my knowledge.

"Carol." From behind me Holly called my name. "Can you come here?"

"Did you find her? Is she okay?" I ran towards her, my heart racing faster than my feet.

"She's in the ladies' room. You better go check."

I pushed through the door. In the corner of the room Sheri stood with Cate in her arms. She was leaning with her head over the sink.

"What's wrong?" I stepped forward, taking her slim body in my arms. She collapsed like a rag doll. Her head on my shoulder, her body, limp. "What's wrong, baby? Come on, talk to me."

Sheri put her arm around Cate's back and with a wet towel began to wipe her face. Cate moaned. Her eyes rolled back in her head. I began patting the side of her face.

"Come on, baby. It's Mom. Wake up. You're going to be fine."

Freddie walked in behind us. "What's going on? Is she okay?"

"No. She's not okay!" I screamed. "I think she's been drugged."

Holly turned to Freddie. "Call an ambulance. Now!"

CHAPTER 14

I barely slept after we got home from the emergency room. Instead I spent the night going back through my notes about the missing girls while Cate slept upstairs in her bedroom. Every couple of hours I'd tiptoe up the stairs and check on her, thankful she was home and that I had found her before something terrible happened. The doctors in the ER determined that someone had slipped something into her drink, but Cate couldn't remember. She said she didn't know who had ordered the drink or who put it down in front of her, only that it wasn't non-alcoholic, and when she realized, she quickly put it down. Unfortunately, she'd ingested enough of whatever was in the drink to cause her to feel lightheaded. Knowing something wasn't right, she made her way to the ladies' room where she passed out. Whoever had drugged her quickly left the bar when he realized she'd fled to the bathroom.

I glanced at the clock. It was almost eleven. My stomach was growling, and Cate would need something solid when she woke up. I wasn't going to let her drive back to the university this morning until she had something to eat and I was certain she was on solid ground. I was about to start hunting through my cabinets for something akin to a pancake mix—comfort food—when the doorbell rang.

It was Sheri. In her hands she had a basket of pastries beneath a red and white checkered cloth.

"I knew you wouldn't have anything in the house, so I made something."

Without asking, she pushed past me. The aroma of freshly

baked cinnamon rolls with melted butter wafted beneath my nose as she made her way toward kitchen.

"How's our girl? Still sleeping, I'll bet." She placed the basket on the counter. "Mind if I make myself a cup?"

I didn't have time to answer before I heard a thin voice from behind me.

"Make me one, too."

I turned to see Cate standing in the doorway. She was still dressed in her pajamas, striped long johns that hung about her slim hips like a potato sack. She toddled barefoot into the kitchen, rubbing her eyes. She kissed me on the cheek, then Sheri, and took a cup from the cabinet.

"How are you this morning, Sweetie?"

"Better." Cate sat down at the table. "I'm sorry about last night. I don't remember much of what happened, just waking up in the hospital and then—ugh." She shook her head and reached for a roll.

"I can't believe what happened last night. We were all right there, having fun, and yet, wow. It really made me see how easy this all this could happen, right in the middle of a crowd. In fact, I did a little more research while you were asleep last night about date rape drugs and some of the websites you mentioned the other night, like Sugar Babies."

While Cate slept, I went online in search of suspect websites, sites that might be targeting young women. I found several that were, in my mind anyway, very suspect. The one that stuck out the most, however, was HollywoodScholarships.com.

"If I hadn't seen it for myself, I might not believe it." I opened my computer to the webpage and read the copy aloud.

Are you young, talented and willing to travel? Top Hollywood Agent is looking for tomorrow's big names today. If you believe you have what it takes to be a star, let us help you make your dream come true.

The rest was pretty straightforward. It requested a picture—full body shot, bathing suit optional—a brief bio, and a list of close personal contacts. I assumed any young woman who had too many was immediately disqualified. An email was listed for a confidential reply.

"And things like this, they're legal? The police don't shut them down?" Sheri glanced down at my computer screen.

"From what I pulled up on the internet last night, there's probably too many to police. Lot of weirdoes out there, and when it comes down to it, I think it's really more of a buyer beware type of thing."

"Makes you wonder," Sheri said, "after what nearly happened to Cate last night, just how often this goes on."

"My thoughts exactly." I reached for a cinnamon roll and was about to sink my teeth into it when the phone rang.

It was Detective Browne.

My first thought was to share with him what had happened with Cate last night, but I didn't get a chance. He launched into conversation.

"Carol, sorry to call you on a Sunday morning, but I wanted to let you know." He sounded enthusiastic, and for a moment I thought he was calling with news about Gabi, but instead, he said, "I spoke with Bessie Bixby, Leticia Johnson's grandmother, at church this morning. I suppose I shouldn't have mentioned it, but, since I figured you'd call her anyway, I did. Long story short, I told her you're planning on doing an interview, maybe even getting her on the air."

"Miss Bixby," I said. "Not a problem." I hadn't spoken to Tyler yet, but I couldn't imagine there would any reason I couldn't get an interview on the air. I told him with any luck I'd call tomorrow with good news. "Speaking of which, anything on Gabi Garrison?"

"We're continuing to talk to the boyfriend."

"You still don't think there's a connection to Monica or the other missing girls?"

"Neighbors say they heard a lot of arguing right before Gabi disappeared."

I was disappointed, and I knew my voice reflected as much.

After Cate's close call last night, I didn't believe Dr. Ericson had anything to do with Gabi's disappearance.

"Couples argue, Detective. That doesn't necessarily mean anything."

"No, but it might interest you to know that Dr. Ericson was recently reassigned to the transplant team at UCLA, rather suddenly."

"Why's that important?"

"It's a pretty prestigious position. Applicants usually have to apply several years in advance, and it appears he was tapped."

"So? He's talented."

"Maybe. But the head of the unit just happens to be a very attractive female doctor. Supposedly they've been seen spending a lot of time together."

I wanted to laugh out loud. Why is it any time an attractive woman spends time with a man, there's talk?

"So you think because Gabi's boyfriend suddenly gets tapped to join UCLA's transplant team—by a very attractive female doctor—that he's done something to get rid of his girlfriend?"

"We are starting to run out of leads on this one."

"Well, he doesn't strike me as the type to hide her body in the desert—or maybe you're thinking he's chopped her up and is now shopping her body parts."

"Always a possibility."

"Not funny, Detective."

I hung up the phone and put my coffee down simultaneously, perhaps harder than I intended. At first I thought I'd caused the table to shake. Then I noticed the windows started to rattle. The glasses above the bar clattered like a New Year's Eve toast in Times Square and the entire house started to rock. Outside, sprinklers were going off, and car sirens and house alarms began to blare.

"Earthquake!" Sheri screamed, grabbed the basket of cinnamon rolls, and ducked under the table.

I grabbed Cate and shielded her with my arm above her head as we huddled in the doorway. We hugged each other until the rumbling stopped and the shaking, at least of the walls, certainly not my heart, ceased to move around us.

"You okay?" Sheri poked her head out from beneath the table. Her pale skin looked like a ghost beneath a mop of dark hair. In her lap she was hugging the basket of rolls like a security blanket. We laughed nervously. I offered her a hand up.

"What do you think? Three point? Maybe four?" she asked.

I looked around at the mess. I couldn't be sure. Earthquakes happen every day in Los Angeles, but this was bigger, and I suspected today's tumbler was going to have big repercussions. On the floor, dishes from inside my cabinets lay broken in bits and pieces as though they'd been hurled by some invisible monster. Other than that, I could see no major structural damage to my condo. No broken windows or water mains. But for the next few days, I knew KCHC's airwaves would be full of talk about the earthquake, and the story about Hollywood's missing girls would be bumped for news of broken glasses and the tumble of china cabinets.

CHAPTER 15

After the earthquake, I tried to call Tyler. It's standard practice for reporters to call in and report where they are and what's happened after a quake, but I was getting no answer. I tuned to the station and could hear our Sunday morning team, Jan and Dean, as they fielded calls from nervous listeners. The husband and wife duo, known for their light-hearted reviews of news and entertainment, had been on the air, sipping coffee and chatting casually when the quake hit. Amidst the clatter of coffee cups and well wishes, listeners were calling in to report their own version of shaking walls and broken dishes.

Finally, after getting no answer from the newsroom, I tried to call in via the listener line. But the screener put me on hold, and I decided my time was best spent cleaning up my own mess. I needed to help Cate pack up for her return trip to San Diego, and after last night I was feeling overly protective about letting her go. It wasn't until both Sheri and Cate left, after Cate assured me she was fine and would call when she arrived at school, that I was alone. It was then I noticed the message light blinking on my home phone.

At first when I listened I thought it was just a series of random bleeps and was about to delete it, but then I stopped and realized it was a message. It must have been there since Friday morning and I'd missed it until just now. I hit rewind and listened again. Using the keystrokes on the phone to emulate Morse code, Eric had sent a birthday message. *Happy Birthday. Miss those LSCs.* Long, slow curves. I replayed it again, several times, to make certain I had it right, then laughed out loud. After Saturday night's scare with Cate, his message provided exactly the relief I needed. I felt renewed, and grateful I knew Morse code. Several years ago when Charlie was still in Cub Scouts we'd learned it together. I never thought it'd be useful, but Eric seemed to think it was cool, and quickly it became a thing between us. It put a smile on my face, and for the first time I thought I'd actually be able to sleep through the night. I waited up for Cate's call, wished her a good night, and then fell asleep.

Monday morning I came into the station and found a Post-it note taped to my computer. *See me ASAP.*

The note was from Tyler, and I had no doubt in my mind, based upon the haste in which the note appeared to have been written, that he was dealing with his own personal upheaval and would explain why he hadn't called me back.

"What's up?" I walked into Tyler's office and plunked myself down in the chair in front of his desk.

Tyler sat facing his computer, acknowledging my presence with the mere nod of his head. Whatever was on the screen had his attention. In the background, the sound of the station's broadcast droned like white noise from the speaker overhead. Yesterday's earthquake was dominating the news.

"You're in luck." Tyler continued to stare at his computer, his voice flat like he was reading the telephone book. "Cupid's taking over the afternoon show. I'm going to need your help to fill in."

It took me a moment to grasp the meaning of Tyler's statement. Cupid was the FM jock on KCHC's sister station, KSTR, a rock-and-roll DJ who had clearly aged out from his role as the silky, romantic voice of the younger set. After twenty some odd years in the business, he no longer fit the mold.

"Cupid?" I nearly choked on his name. "You've got to be kidding. What happened to T&T, Tom and Teri, our regular afternoon drive team?"

Tyler shook his head and looked at me. He bit his tongue, then said, "Let's just say KCHC has had its own little earthquake this weekend. T&T are out. Temporarily anyway, and corporate's demanding we make a home for Cupid. 'Until further notice.' It appears someone above us all has decided the station needs to go in another direction. They'd like us to have a lighter, friendlier, more chick-lite format."

Chick-lite? I shuddered to think what that might be.

Six months ago KCHC had been bought by a midsized group of broadcasters out of the Midwest. They already owned KSTR, a fairly decent FM station in the market, and had been looking for an AM sister station to round out their holding. They liked KCHC'S format: *Chick Radio: Talk a Woman Can Really Dig Her Heels Into.* This, despite the fact we had more men on the air than we did women, or that Tyler Hunt, our news and programing director, had about as much interest in women's issues as a fish has in flying.

"You've got to be kidding. Does Cupid have any interest in anything that's *not* on a Billboard chart?" I regretted the words the minute I said them.

Tyler glared at me.

"Cupid's used to spinning records, Carol, and he's been doing it for forty years, back when the cool crowd referred to them as licorice pizzas. You want him to talk about Hollywood's Missing Girls? Then you're going to have to hand feed him everything." He turned his head back to the computer screen. I was obviously on my own. There was nothing more to say.

I stood up. I wasn't quite sure how to react. The fact Tyler wanted me to step in as co-host for this afternoon's show was a windfall. My story about Hollywood's Missing Girls was a go. I no longer needed his approval. He was clearly too busy to care. I was on my own. On the other hand, judging from Tyler's frown as he stared back at his computer screen, I could see Tyler was having one of those days, dealing with a management group from out of the market that left all of us at KCHC feeling rudderless. I knew better than to look too elated.

I'd never met Cupid. Despite the fact the FM rockers had recently moved in and occupied half of KCHC's facilities, we didn't mingle. For all practical purposes, the Walls of Jericho existed between our two stations. The FM occupied one side of the building while we, on the AM, held steadfast to the other. Fear permeated the dark hallways between our two stations. Sooner or later, we were all convinced, one staff would inherit the duties of the other, and the rest of us would be out of work. Today's reassignment of Cupid to the AM did nothing to put those feelings to rest.

I returned to my desk and quickly wrote out a synopsis of what I wanted to include in this afternoon's show with Cupid. It began with information about Monica Channing, her disappearance, the discovery of her body, and that it was believed she had been kidnapped by a group of sex traffickers operating in Hollywood.

I included the names of Jessie Martin, Marilyn Ann Billings and April Hansen along with Leticia Johnson and Brandy White as possible victims. I then listed Gabi Garrison as also missing and highlighted that at this time LAPD did not believe Gabi's disappearance was related to that of the other missing girls. However, she bore a remarkable resemblance to Monica and lived within blocks of Monica's apartment.

I then started a second section with the heading: What is Sex Trafficking? Beneath it I jotted down a series of questions: How relevant is it to the US? Who are the victims? And where do they come from? I easily had a dozen. Finally, I added a section on misconceptions and failures: why victims don't leave, why they identify with their captors, and why I believed this to be a growing problem in Hollywood.

Like a lot of people, before I realized what might be going on, I thought it was largely a problem that existed overseas—the exploitation of foreign nationals—but certainly not something that went on here in the good old US of A, and not with American women. What I learned was astounding. According to the National Center for Missing and Exploited Children, one in seven runaways in this country becomes a victim of sex trafficking, and the money to be made was astonishing. Based upon reports from eight major US cities, it ranged from $39.9 million to better than three hundred million dollars a year, per city.

I completed my notes, checked the employee roster for Cupid's personal contact info and tried his cell. There was no answer. I left a message, told him Tyler had explained to me that we'd be working together and that I would email him some thoughts I had for this afternoon's show. I suggested we meet for a brief rundown of what I knew and how we might best work together.

Then I picked up the phone and called Detective Browne and told him we had a "go" for this afternoon's show.

"Only thing is," I said, "we've had a few changes here at the station. Our afternoon drive host is Cupid, from the FM side."

"Cupid, huh?" He chuckled under his breath. From the tone of his voice I got the idea Detective Browne might have been a fan, albeit from a long time ago.

"Yes, but don't worry. I'll be doing the interview." I tried to sound reassuring. I didn't want him to think I'd be passing it off. "We'll patch you into the studio via a phone line. I just need to make certain both you and Miss Bixby are available between three-fifteen and three-thirty."

"Got a better idea. How about I pick up Leticia's grandmother and bring her down to the studio? I may have a little surprise for you or Cupid anyway."

I had no idea what Detective Browne had in mind concerning a surprise. I suspected either he, or perhaps Bessie Bixby, might have been fans and maybe had some memento they'd like to share from times past. Things like that frequently happened with listeners. Trouble was, I wasn't sure how Cupid would respond. But, given the circumstances, I was willing to gamble that Detective Browne's presence and that of Leticia's grandmother might be a good thing, helping Cupid to transition to the AM in the presence of fans. At least that's how I planned to position it. I gave Detective Browne directions and while I waited, Cupid's reply to my email appeared on my computer screen.

Sorry, babe. My contract requires I be at the studio thirty minutes before show time. Not sooner. See you then, Cupid.

*   *   *

Radio personalities seldom look like they sound. Cupid had a voice as smooth and sexy as a glass of amaretto on an autumn eve. But I knew better than to assume he really looked like the poster I'd seen of him—the Paul Newman lookalike—hanging in the hallway. The station had its own Hall of Fame with poster-sized prints of the FM jocks and AM personalities lining the hallways. All of the photos had been retouched and looked nothing like who they actually are, or probably ever were. The men had hair, the women were thinner and younger. Caricatures would have been better. The only thing I really knew about Cupid was that at one time he had generated enough ratings with his female audience—including my younger self—to make him a top jock in the market. But unfortunately things change, and some fool from corporate now thought that what remained of his fanbase might follow him to the world of talk radio.

I wasn't so sure, and when I walked into the dimly lit studio to meet with Cupid for the first time, I suddenly got why he had been reassigned to the AM. He looked like a wax figure from Madame Tussaud's that had been left out in the sun too long. He was paunchy, his once handsome face now round and putty-like, and he was drunk. Or at least he'd been drinking. In front of him, on the console, was an empty shot glass, and a bottle of Jim Beam lay between us.

"Wanna drink?"

I sat down and pulled the bottle towards me. The station had no rules about drinking on the air. A lot of hosts did, either openly, or discreetly. The fact that some of the talent were known to smuggle a small flask beneath a sport coat, or inside a purse, was not anything unusual. Management had decided long ago to look the other way. As long as the on-air host was reasonably sober and coherent, nobody cared, or said anything. I glanced down at the bottle in my hands; it was half full.

"You know, I called you once." I put the bottle back down on console between us. "Must have been nearly ten years ago now. You were on the air, and I needed a little advice."

He looked at me, his blue eyes heavily hooded, his lids drooping.

"It was a bad time in my life. And you talked to me, off the air." I doubted he remembered any of it, but I went on to explain how my ex and I had just separated. I had started working at the radio station and fallen in love with my job, while my ex had fallen in love with a younger version of me. It was a couple years after my son was born. I was lost and didn't really know what to do. "I remember calling the radio station, and you know what you said?"

He shook his head and reached for the bottle. I pulled it away.

"You played me a song. You told me you were going back in history a bit but that I'd get it. You know what the song was?"

He shook his head.

"*I Will Survive* by Gloria Gaynor. At the time you said you didn't think you'd played that song in nearly twenty years, but I'll never forget it. It was exactly what I needed, and every time I thought I was going to fall apart, I'd hear that song in my head. It saved me."

"So now you're here to save me, huh?" He reached for the bottle again. I didn't let go.

"No, I'm here 'cause I need your help."

He jerked on the bottle. I held tight. "I think I've given you all the help you need."

"I don't think so." I put the bottle beneath the console. Then I leaned forward into his face. "Look, I know you don't know me, and I know you don't want to be here, because you think the FM's kicked you to the curb. And maybe you're right. But I've got a job to do, and I just happen to believe it's important. So this is how it's going to be."

He looked at me, a smug smile on his face.

"Yesterday morning, the headlines in the paper were all about Monica Channing and the fact that LAPD's missing persons unit believed she'd fallen victim to a sex trafficking ring. You may have been too drunk to even remember, but it's important. 'Cause suddenly, guess what? Yesterday afternoon there's this earthquake. Nothing major, but enough to make the news. Then, right after that, there's a bunch of little kids celebrating a birthday party out in Manhattan Beach with a big bouncy house, and for some freaky reason, it dislodges from its bearings and everybody's afraid it's going to fly off into the ocean, maybe with a few kids in it. Fortunately, no kids were hurt. But the front page of today's newspaper has a picture of this flying bouncy house and people talking about how their glasses and ceiling lights shook when the earthquake hit. So now every news operation in town is chasing stories about bouncy houses and the earthquake and, oh, yeah, the fact that Lindsay Lohan's back in rehab. And you know what that means?"

He held his hands up to the ceiling and looked at me, like I expected him to care.

"It means this sex trafficking case just got bumped to the metro section, below the fold. That's where stories go to die, in case you didn't know. And to make matters worse, Chief Walker's not allowing anyone investigating the case to talk to the press, and I've got a grieving father slash federal judge that's not talking 'cause he doesn't want anyone to know his precious daughter was cavorting with some guy running a sex trafficking ring in Hollywood. So, unless you and I do something to keep this story alive, it's going to disappear. And so are a lot of other young, innocent women."

Cupid took the shot glass in his hand and for moment, looked like he was about to crush it. His eyes never looked up, the silence between us so strong I could hear the blood pulsating in my ears. I had less than five minutes to convince Cupid we needed to work together.

"Everything okay in here?" Tyler, with a hand on either side of doorframe, leaned his skinny body into the studio.

My eyes locked with Cupid's. *Are we okay?*

"Just hunky dory, boss." Cupid tossed the shot glass into the trash.

"Carol, your guests are in the lobby. You might want to show them in." Tyler waved one hand above his head and started to step out of the studio.

I got up to follow and when I reached the door, I looked back at Cupid. In his other hand, he had a copy of the notes I sent him earlier. He held them in front of his face, fanned them, and smiled. I wasn't certain if it was a sarcastic gesture or not.

"Hunky dory?" I asked.

CHAPTER 16

I met Detective Browne and Bessie Bixby in the lobby. Bessie was a frail, grey, grandmotherly looking woman, her light brown skin thin with age spots. She stood, holding a cane, next to Detective Browne, coming barely to his chest, and was dressed in what looked to be a secondhand purple pantsuit. On her head was a bright red fedora. She wore them both proudly. I stepped closer to her and noticed, pinned to the lapel of her jacket, was a small jeweled brooch with a photo of her granddaughter Leticia. I recognized her broad smile.

Bessie greeted me warmly, taking my hand and holding it gently against her heart. "Thank you so much. I hope you don't mind, but when Detective Browne told me Cupid would be in the studio, I asked a few of my friends to come along. We're all fans."

She pointed her cane towards the glass entrance, her hand shaking in the way that old people sometimes do. I opened the door, the cool breeze in my face. Just outside the station's tall wrought iron gates were dozens of red-hatted ladies, all dressed exactly like Bessie. From the street I could hear horns honking as commuters passed by. This small but mighty woman had formed a brigade and organized her own street demonstration. Outside the gates, an army of red hats waved posters in the air as the ladies walked up and down the street, shouting: "Help find our missing girls!"

"Ms. Bixby's a member of the Red Hat Society." Detective Browne smiled at me. "I assume you've heard of them?"

Up until that moment I wasn't familiar with the organization. Detective Browne explained that the red-hatted ladies were a group of mostly senior women who frequently got together for a good time. But today they were here for Bessie and the missing girls. And if possible, they'd love to say hello to Cupid. Most of them had been fans from when he first went on the air, forty years ago, and remembered him fondly for his late night Sweet Notes, messages he'd send out over the air from one star-crossed lover to another.

It was just the ammunition I needed. I picked up the lobby phone on the wall next to the door and called back to the studio. I told Cupid we had a few minutes before show time, and I had a surprise. Some of his fans were lined up outside the station and anxious to see him. No doubt they wanted to wish him well with his first show. I suggested he come join us on the front patio.

I then asked the guard if he'd open the gate and let the red-hatted brigade through. I watched as a group of maybe twenty senior ladies, some as unsteady on their feet as Bessie, others still vibrant in their stride, all entered the campus. Like a precision marching band, with their posters in their hands, they made their way towards the station's front patio.

Moments later, Cupid appeared from behind the station's double glass doors, wearing dark glasses, a sport coat and, most surprising of all, a baseball cap sporting KCHC call letters. Despite his pallor, he looked surprisingly natty, not half bad compared to the sallow figure of the man I'd just left in the studio.

Whether it was the sunlight or the fact that the ladies of the red hat society had instantly recognized Cupid, his ego-drenched transition was phenomenal. I stepped back and watched as they rushed him—not quite like screaming groupies maybe, but slowly and with an arthritic grace—and asked for autographs. I wasn't certain if it was their presence or that he'd read my notes concerning Hollywood's missing girls and decided he, or we, could make a difference. The only thing I knew for certain was that as we walked back to the studio, he was suddenly stone sober.

I opened the show and was in the middle of my on-air welcome, informing KCHC listeners there'd been a line-up change. T&T, our usual hosts, were taking a break. While in their place, we were happy to be welcoming Cupid from the FM.

I was interrupted.

"Carol, please let me be the one to say how happy I am to be here this afternoon. After all these years of spinning vinyl and talking shop about the top forty, I now have a chance to share with our listeners some of what goes on behind the scenes. And with the recent news about Monica Channing and Hollywood's Missing Girls, it couldn't be a better time for me to lend my voice and talents to helping us all to understand that beyond the glitz and glamor of Hollywood, there can be—for some anyway—a very dark side."

What a fabulous transition.

I thanked Cupid and moved on to welcome Detective Browne and Bessie Bixby. I explained Bessie was Leticia Johnson's grandmother, and that Leticia, along with her best friend Brandy White, had been missing for nearly two months.

Detective Browne spoke briefly about his role with LAPD missing persons unit, the number of cases they covered, and that fortunately most didn't end as Monica's had, tragically, in a homicide.

"But, because of Monica's murder, we've gone back and looked at a few cold cases involving what we thought at the time anyway, might just be teenage runaways."

"Like Leticia and Brandy," Cupid said, glancing at my notes in front of him.

"Exactly, and the more we looked into their disappearance, and that of a few other missing persons over the last several years, the more we began to think there might be a connection."

"I'm sorry, but it seems to me if a young girl goes missing in this city you would immediately suspect there was a connection. How is it the police didn't?" Cupid asked.

"That's a good question, but you need to understand this is a big city. We get about thirty-two hundred missing persons a year. I don't like to point fingers, but a girl like Monica Channing goes missing and everybody in the media knows about it. For days the press covers it, people talk. It's like she's the only one missing. Unfortunately, there are places in LA where the cops don't like to go and where people disappear and nobody reports it."

"But that wasn't the case with Leticia and Brandy," I reminded him.

"No, not at all. And I'm thankful you've given us time here today to discuss Leticia and Brandy's disappearance. Leticia's grandmother reported her missing right away. But, difficult as it may be for your listeners to understand, LAPD missing persons unit doesn't have the manpower or the resources to solve every missing person case, like they do on TV. It's just not that simple."

"But you have uncovered something that makes you think their disappearance may be related to that of Monica Channing?"

"We've been able to trace their activity to an internet café in South Central where they had been going after school supposedly to do research. We believe they met someone online and that person gained their trust, and eventually kidnapped them."

"Like Monica Channing?" I asked.

"I'm afraid I'm very limited in what I can actually say here today with regard to the investigation into Monica's death."

"And what about Gabi Garrison, Detective?" Cupid looked up from the report I'd given him. With a pencil in his hand he was making notes. "The Chief of Police said he didn't believe this case was connected. Do you agree?"

"With regard to the disappearance of Gabi Garrison, I can only say that we have a person of interest with whom we're speaking. Beyond that, I'm not prepared to comment. What I would like to focus on today, however, is the danger on the boulevard for young women, particularly those who may go out alone at night."

Detective Browne's statement was the perfect set up for my investigative report concerning Hollywood's active club scene. I spoke briefly about the popularity of the nightclubs and how I'd seen firsthand how easy it would be for a young woman to be drugged in the presence of friends and to disappear. I deliberately didn't volunteer that the young woman had been my daughter. I preferred to keep my personal experience and that of my daughter to myself.

I then introduced my first caller, Freddie Bleeker. I had tried to get Norma Jean, a.k.a. Holly Wood, to call in. I wanted her to expand on the nightlife, the attraction and the types of young girls who frequent the clubs, but she wasn't returning any of my calls. Freddie had been my second choice. I told him I didn't want to share my own personal experience with my daughter and that I wasn't planning on using him for any more than a few brief questions concerning his work inside the clubs. But he surprised me.

"Hey, I was probably one of the last people to see Monica Channing alive. I remember her coming into the club with an older dude, a regular. Looked like they were meeting up with someone. I don't know who. But the guy she was with, I've seen him around. He comes in from time to time. Fact is, I think I saw him with that pretty young black girl whose picture was in the paper Sunday."

"Leticia Johnson?" I hadn't expected Freddie to reveal anything like this, particularly during a live interview. I glanced over at Detective Browne, then leaned forward and put my hand on Bessie's shoulder, giving her a reassuring squeeze.

"Yeah, she was in a while back."

Bessie touched the locket on her lapel, her fingers gently rubbing her granddaughter's photo.

"Are you sure?" I asked.

"Pretty sure. After I saw those pictures in the paper anyway I got to thinkin' that just maybe she's with this same guy."

"You mean, the man you last saw Monica Channing with?"

"Could be, but I don't remember seeing that other girl. The one whose photo was in the paper with 'em."

"Brandy White? She would have been shorter, a little younger."

"Yeah. I don't remember her. Not at all. 'Course, that's not saying she wasn't there. I don't work every night, but I do remember seeing that other chick, Gabi Garrison. I recognized her 'cause she used to be on TV. I think she was a reporter or something. She was with her boyfriend. Least they were holdin' hands, so I guess he was her boyfriend. It was about a week ago now, and they were with this guy and some other dude, having drinks."

Freddie was a motor mouth. I wondered how much I could trust what he was saying. He sounded as though he was either nervous or just enjoying the attention.

I looked over at Detective Browne. I mouthed, *Did you have any idea?* He nodded, put his finger to his lips and then said, "Freddie, you said the man you thought you saw Monica Channing with was a regular, and that you believe you may also have seen Leticia Johnson and maybe Gabi Garrison and her boyfriend with this same man. Could you describe him?"

"Like I said, he's a regular, comes in from time to time. Always well dressed. Like some old Hollywood dude. You know what I mean. Got this small mustache, split in the middle and he's wearing this fancy suit. Oh, hell—"

I hit the seven-second delay button. Not that it mattered, *hell* isn't one of the FCC's seven forbidden words, but just the same, expletives didn't fit with the new light and friendly format and Tyler wouldn't like it.

"—could be he's even one of those fuc—*BLEEP*— impersonators, or maybe the real thing, a ghost for all I know. They're everywhere, and there are people 'round there who actually believe in 'em. Anyway, this guy, he always paid cash. Never used a credit card. So I don't know who he is."

We had to pause for a station break. I waited until I knew we were off the air then stood up.

"It's Clark Gable. The man Freddie saw. I saw him, too. The night of the pub crawl. I'm certain of it."

I felt certain Freddie had revealed the killer's identity. Browne scribbled a note in his pad as the station went to commercial break and said we'd talk later.

I opened the second half of the show and invited Bessie to

share some of what she knew about her granddaughter. She smiled at me graciously, adjusted the mic and pulled it towards her mouth. Her voice was raspy but surprisingly strong and deep.

"Before I begin, Carol, I'd like to thank you for allowing me to come on the show today. My granddaughter, Leticia Johnson, and her friend, Brandy White, have been missing for nearly two months, and it wasn't until you mentioned their names in association with the disappearance and murder of Monica Channing that the press started paying any attention to what we all know has been going on."

Bessie paused and looked at Detective Browne.

"I'm sorry, Detective. I know you're under orders not to talk about the case, but we need to call it what it is, and to address exactly why these young girls have been kidnapped. So, if you won't say it, I will. Carol, my granddaughter and her friend were kidnapped for the purpose of sex trafficking."

I looked at Detective Browne. He raised his hand and nodded to me that he wanted her to go on.

"I understand that the judge and his wife may not want admit that their daughter was caught up with a group that was involved in such a thing. Sex has a way of quieting people up. Culturally we don't want to admit when our daughters have been accosted or violated."

Wow. Bessie's words were hitting home. My own reaction to Cate's near abduction was suspect. Was it fear or shame that I didn't want to share what had nearly happened Saturday night?

"But the fact of the matter is, these girls—our girls—were targeted because men would pay to have sex with them. And the people of this city need to know there is a kidnapping ring for the purpose of selling young women into prostitution operating right here in Hollywood."

"Detective?" Cupid leaned into the mic. "If she's right, and there is a sex trafficking ring operating out of Hollywood, where are they? Why haven't we heard more about it? Why hasn't even one of these girls broken away and come forward?"

"Again, I'm sorry. I'm not at liberty to discuss an open investigation. However, in general, most women who become victims of sex trafficking rings are afraid to leave. In some cases, they may believe they're living better than they did, or might, without the protection of their captors. In other cases, they're blackmailed. Told if they try to make contact with their families, they, their parents, or their siblings will be murdered. Whatever it is they have on these girls, few of them ever try to escape."

Cupid glanced down at the switchboard. The inbound caller lights were blinking nonstop.

"Detective, since you can't really talk about the specifics of the case, perhaps we should take a few calls from our listeners. See if someone out there might know something about what Detective Browne's not able to talk about. What do you say?"

"Caller One, you're on the air..."

"Thank you, Cupid. I'm curious, Detective, just how does a business like this operate? I mean, there has to be a certain degree of secrecy among their clientele, or they'd be busted."

"You're right. It's a little like a private club—like the old speakeasies with a private password—and members of this club don't speak freely about it. The girls are frequently recruited online and once drafted into service, the more exclusive night clubs are often used as meeting grounds."

"Thank you, Detective. Caller Two, you're on the line."

The second caller said she lived on the Westside and couldn't imagine anything like human trafficking going on in her area and not knowing about it.

Detective Browne sympathized with her, then said: "You might be surprised to know that not far from where you live there's a twenty-four hour café and that young high school girls, from a well-known private school in your area, have been sneaking out at night and frequenting the café. Their new social high is taking turns getting into a stranger's cars and disappearing for hours at a time."

"I can't believe that. You're telling me they're prostituting themselves?"

"I'm telling you things go on in this city that most people don't even know about. Only difference is most of them don't end up on the front page of the *LA Times*."

The third caller was altogether different. He identified himself as a man of the world and he spoke with a muffled, husky sounding voice that caught my attention immediately. I suspected he was using some cheap voice-changer to disguise his voice.

"I've been listening to your show and, while I'm sorry to hear about Monica Channing and Ms. Bixby's granddaughter, I guess I got a different take on some of these websites."

"You've used them?" Cupid put his elbows on the console and leaned into the mic. "Visited these websites, seen girls for hire?"

"Why not? It's a free country. I mean this is between a man and woman, isn't it? Besides just like you said, Detective, some of these gals are probably living better than they would anyway. So far as I'm concerned, long as nobody's getting hurt, it's not a problem." Caller three hung up the phone, the dial tone droning out over the airwaves.

Cupid quickly filled the void. "Well, I think our caller, Mr. Man-of-the-World, is missing the point. These girls aren't acting of their own volition, they're—"

"Excuse me, but as the grandmother of one of these missing girls, I think what your caller forgets is that many of these girls had no choice. They were kidnapped. And if I might, Cupid, I'd like to say my friends with the red-hatted ladies society and I will be out on Hollywood Boulevard with flyers this Friday and every night until my granddaughter and Brandy White are found. I hope that you'll join us. Until then, we believe every young girl needs to know she could be a target. We may not be strong, but we will not go away until our girls, and the Gabi Garrisons of the world, are found safe and returned home."

CHAPTER 17

I left Detective Browne and Ms. Bixby in the studio with Cupid and returned to my office to find I had a message from a former client. Tony Domingo had called several times. In addition to a pink call-slip left on my desk marked urgent, I found another message from him on my voicemail. Curious, in that we hadn't spoken in nearly a year.

"Carol, this is Tony from Financial Futures. I need to see you. Right away. Tonight. It's about Gabi Garrison, and it's strictly off the record. Don't tell anyone, particularly the police. Meet me at The City Grill, Century City, eight p.m. and come alone. See you then."

His voice sounded strained, not at all like I remembered. And just hearing Gabi's name made me feel as though I'd just been zapped with an electric charge. I stared at the phone. The last time I had seen Tony Domingo was the day I'd met Gabi Garrison outside his office. The idea that he'd reach out to me now, with Gabi missing, made absolutely no sense. Unless—

I didn't allow my mind to wander. I had too much to do. I had one last top-of-the-hour news report to read before I left for the day and, as I stared down at the list of stories Tyler had pulled from the wire, I was furious. Attached was a note. *KCHC's new management team would like us to have a lighter, more friendly side to our news. Think chick-lite, happy news.*

The stories Tyler selected were nonsensical. IKEA had introduced a new catalogue, an old-fashioned print version. The slug on the story read *Back to the Future*. Brad Pitt and Angelina

Jolie had just made their relationship official and announced their marriage, and Sunday's earthquake had caused the waves off the Santa Monica beaches to swell. Twenty footers were breaking off the pier. Between the details of the Brangelina Wedding and the surf report, there was no time to include anything concerning the Hollywood Missing Girls.

I finished my report and left the studio in search of Detective Browne and Bessie. I wanted to catch them before they left the station. I still had questions for Detective Browne concerning the Clark Gable lookalike that Freddie said he had seen with Monica and maybe Leticia and possibly Gabi. I passed Tyler in the hall, nearly knocking him over in my rush.

"Have you seen Detective Browne?"

"He was headed towards the front door a minute ago."

I raced towards the lobby, hoping I still might be able to catch them. But I was too late. Detective Browne's car slowly cleared the gate as I reached the door.

My cell buzzed and I glance down at the caller ID. It was Sheri. The boys were back from their weekend football retreat with my ex and she was picking them up from school.

"Are you up for some spaghetti bolognaise? I thought it might be a nice welcome home."

I didn't want to say no. I was looking forward to welcoming Charlie home, hearing all about the game and spending time with the boys, but now, with Tony's call, and the idea that it might have something to do with Gabi's disappearance, I felt I just couldn't do both.

"Actually, I was just about to call and say I'd be late. I need to meet with a client."

"A client, tonight?"

"Yes, I—"

"Really, Carol, at this hour? Who are you kidding? You're not in sales anymore. Just who are you meeting, and where?"

I should have known better. I could hear the suspicion in her voice. I fessed up and told her about Tony's call, and that I was concerned he might have information concerning Gabi's disappearance.

"But you can't breathe a word of this. He said not to call the police. So promise me you won't. Not unless I suddenly disappear, and then, if I do, call Tyler. Have the station put out an APB. Spare nothing." I laughed nervously. I didn't want to think Tony might seriously have something sinister to do with Gabi's disappearance, but the idea that he wanted to see me alone had me feeling a little edgy.

"Wait a minute. You're telling me you actually think this Domingo guy might have something to do with Gabi's disappearance? I thought you said he was a client. Not some hit man for the mob."

"I said he was in finance, loans, re-fis, that kind of thing. I used to write his commercials. He'd sing them on the radio. Don't you remember? He sounded a little like Frank Sinatra, but I never said he was in the mob."

"Oh, Tony, the tenor?"

"You remember?"

"No. But that definitely settles it. After what happened Saturday night, I'll save the bolognaise for the boys and come with you. You're not going alone."

"Sheri, please."

"No way. You're not going alone, and we'll take my car. It's less *identifiable* than that red bomb of yours."

I wasn't so certain about that. Half an hour later, though, Sheri met me outside the station. She pulled up in her gold-trimmed, pearl-white Mercedes coupe, with the top down. Not exactly low profile.

I indicated with my thumb, pointing down, that she needed to put the top up, and as she did, she asked, "So where is it we're going?"

"Century City. The City Grill. But you need to drop me off. He's expecting me to come alone."

I explained I'd run in, find out what it was he wanted and then we could grab a bite afterwards. Sheri acquiesced, begrudgingly, but only after I promised I'd buy dessert.

Twenty minutes later, we pulled onto the Avenue of the Stars in Century City and were just about to enter into the Grill's parking lot when I saw something I didn't like.

"Stop!" With my hand nearly in front of Sheri's face, I ordered her to brake short of the entrance. A large black Rolls Royce was parked directly in front of the restaurant where the valets usually park late model, upscale cars. It looked familiar, in a very sinister sort of way, with its blacked-out windows and shiny, silver hood ornament of a woman leaning forward with her arms stretched out behind her like a bird about to take flight. "That's the car. I recognize the hood ornament. *The Spirit of Ecstasy.* It's exactly like the car parked in front of Holly's cottage where we went for the pub crawl. "

Sheri pulled to the side of the road and doused the Benz's headlights. We waited in the dark.

"That's the car I saw parked in the lot in front of the Holly Wood Tours cottage. The one the Clark Gable lookalike got into."

"You think it's a coincidence?"

I stared at the car, then back at the entrance to the restaurant. Three men appeared at the door.

"No, but I think it might be bad luck, at least for Tony. Look."

From inside the restaurant three men appeared at the doorway. All of them were dressed in business suits and approached the parked Rolls with their arms about one another like linemen for a football team. Two of them I couldn't identify. The third man, in the center of the other two, was Tony. He looked like he had been drinking, his hair mussed, tie loosened, coat open. The two larger men on either side of him ushered him roughly into the backseat of the Rolls, then slammed the door.

Neither of us said anything. Instinctively I slipped down into the seat, my eyes barely above the window, following the black Rolls as it sped past us. Then with a sound unusual for a Rolls Royce, the car screeched onto the street, running the light onto the

Avenue of the Stars.

"Did you see the plates?"

Sheri shook her head. "I'm not sure *what* that was."

"Dream Maker." I reached inside my bag for a note pad and quickly wrote down the personalized nameplate, the time and the date. "DRM MKR. The same plates I saw on the Rolls parked in front of Holly's cottage Saturday night."

Sheri tried to convince me as we drove home that Tony had been drunk, and that whoever the men were who were with him—probably friends—had put him in the car for his own safety and taken him home.

I didn't think so. Nothing about what we'd just witnessed appeared friendly. I kept thinking about his message. He had information about Gabi Garrison. He wanted me to come alone. Why? I checked my phone to see if I still had his contact information in my Outlook file. When I was in sales, I kept a detailed database, including birthdays, anniversaries, personal addresses, and phone numbers for all my clients. But since leaving that part of my life behind me, I had deleted my sales contacts and had nothing but Tony's cell number from my list of recent calls. I tried his cell. There was no answer.

My next call was to Detective Browne. I left a brief but urgent message on his voicemail, explaining I'd gone to meet a former client for dinner and had *maybe* witnessed a kidnapping. I wasn't sure. Only that I thought it might have something to do with Gabi Garrison's disappearance. I described the car, including the personalized plates, and hung up. There was nothing more I could do.

CHAPTER 18

The next day, Detective Browne called me first thing in the morning. He told me he'd listened to my message and I couldn't possibly have seen a kidnapping. Particularly since the car I described with personalized plates—Dream Maker—belonged to a civilian member of the police commission.

"Dr. Diamond," he said, "was appointed by the police chief himself, and he's a respected member of the community, a real estate developer who probably owns half of Hollywood. He supports a group home for at-risk children and, hell, I was in his suite at Staples Center last week for a Laker Game. Carol, I know what you *think* you saw, but if your friend looked anything like you say—falling down drunk—I'd interpret that as someone helping out a buddy, who maybe had a little too much to drink."

"Yes, but I was meeting him because he wanted to talk about Gabi Garrison." I explained Tony Domingo had been a client of mine and I'd met Gabi outside his office back when I was in sales. "I got the feeling he had information concerning her disappearance, *and* he asked me to come alone."

"Alone, huh?"

I didn't like the inflection in Detective Browne's voice. I could tell, based on the fact he believed Tony had gotten into some police commissioner's car, that he didn't think he'd been kidnapped.

"Look, Carol, I'll be happy to ask Dr. Diamond what he knows, but my hunch is that if you saw this friend of yours getting into Dr. Diamond's car, it's nothing. Least not what you think."

I let the innuendo that Tony's interest in me was other than professional slide and pushed harder.

"Yes, but he mentioned Gabi Garrison, like he knew something and wanted to talk to me specifically."

"Exactly, and the fact that he called *you*, and *not* the police, and asked you to come alone, makes me wonder if this former client of yours wasn't a little bit lonely. Maybe he's been following the story in the press and is looking for an excuse to get together."

Detective Browne may have been convinced, but I wasn't. Police Commissioner or not, I knew something wasn't right. I decided, as I hung up the phone, to drive by Tony's office. It was maybe an extra twenty or thirty minutes from the radio station, but after last night and talking with Detective Browne, I figured it was well worth the drive. I needed to settle my curiosity concerning Tony's wellbeing.

Tony's office, a small efficiency suite, was located inside a high rise on the corner of Glendon Avenue and Kinross in Westwood, just steps from the busy UCLA campus. I arrived and took the elevator to the twelfth floor. As the doors opened, I noticed the door to Financial Futures was ajar.

The office was empty.

In front of me, the receptionist's desk sat vacant. The drawers of her desk yawned open, their contents spilled out onto the floor. Pens, pencils and scraps of paper lay littered at my feet. I walked to the back of the suite where Tony's private workspace overlooked the busy campus below. The venetian blinds hung awkwardly at a forty-five degree angle as though someone had tried to close them in a rush and then given up. Dust had settled on the desk where Tony's computer had been, but it was gone. Everything was gone; the pictures on the wall of him singing, the phones, the computer, the files, and most of all, Tony. There was nothing left.

I reached into my bag for my phone. I was about to call Detective Browne when my cell rang.

"So did you find him? Was he at his office? Did he say what

happened? Is he okay?" It was Sheri, rattling off questions like a machine gun.

I laughed and started walking towards the elevator. Sheri knew without my saying anything to her that I'd try to track Tony down first thing this morning.

"No," I said. "In fact, I'm leaving his office right now, and it's empty. Everything's gone; phones, files, and there's not a trace of Tony anywhere. Looks like he left, and in a hurry."

"So what are you going to do? Call that Detective back?"

I thought about it while I waited for the elevator. I knew if I called Detective Browne and told him Tony's office was empty that he'd listen politely, but I doubted, after this morning's conversation, he'd take his disappearance seriously. He'd probably chalk it all up to some failed business deal, which might explain Tony's drunken appearance with Diamond. I knew he'd assure me he'd check it out. But I was beginning to feel our relationship, particularly since I'd mentioned seeing Diamond's car twice now, was beginning to wane. He didn't need to tell me, but I knew if I continued to harp on Dr. Diamond, the good will between us would evaporate like water on asphalt in the middle of a California heat wave.

"No, and I don't think I can tell Tyler, either. He's got his hands full with this new chick-lite format. I get the feeling sex trafficking and the kidnapping of young girls might not be exactly the type of story corporate would get excited about. In fact, they might get difficult and want to pull it—it doesn't exactly fit that lighter, friendlier form of news. But I do have another idea."

"And what's that?"

"LAPD's not the only one investigating this case. The FBI's working it too, and while they may have rules and regulations about talking to a reporter concerning an open investigation, there's no reason I can't talk to them."

"So you're thinking about calling Mark?"

"I am. If Eric were in town I'd be sharing some of my thoughts with him. No reason I can't talk with Agent Delfino. Let him know that I suspect Gabi Garrison's disappearance and that of my former client, Tony Domingo, may be connected to Monica's murder. And while I'm at it, mention that Dr. Diamond may be someone they'd like to talk to. LAPD sure doesn't seem interested."

The elevator arrived, and Sheri asked me to say hello to Mark for her. I suspected there was a dinner invitation in there somewhere, but decided not to pursue it. I promised I'd call later and hung up.

I was wrong about traffic. It took longer than I thought to get from Westwood back to the station in Culver City. The Santa Monica freeway, which should have been a clear shot mid-morning, was backed up, and the east-west thoroughfares, south of Wilshire on through to Venice, were all congested. Traffic lights were out everywhere. I tuned to KNX for a traffic report. A water main had broken off Overland and Venice, and streets in the area were being shut down, another story that would fill the midday news report. I selected an alternate route, weaving through surface streets and small neighborhoods peppered with stop signs, while I tried to call Agent Delfino. He wasn't in his office, and he wasn't picking up his cell. I left a message and asked him to call me, then tuned to KCHC.

Aaron Whitehall was a business news reporter Tyler was testing out. I caught him in the middle of his show, interviewing some developer. The topic seemed dry and I was curious how it fit into KCHC's new chick-lite, happy news format. I still had my finger on the dial when I heard the station's quirky sing-songy ID and got my answer.

*KCHC...Chick Radio...*A thirty-second sponsorship followed. *Everything old is new again. Live, play, and dine in the heart of old Hollywood...*

"Sellout!" I yelled at the station. Corporate may have wanted Tyler to program KCHC as a new, lighter, more feminine talk radio station, but if listening to Aaron was any indication, it was obvious if a host came through the door with a paid sponsor, KCHC could be whatever it needed to be for that hour.

Aaron welcomed back his audience. "So, in addition to your position as a member of the police commission, Dr. Diamond, you're a developer…"

I nearly rear-ended the car in front of me. *Doctor Diamond?*

"Actually, commercial real estate is my primary concern. Our mission with Diamond Developments is to reenergize old Hollywood."

"And you believe all this redevelopment…the gentrification of the old Broadway building, the Roosevelt Hotel and several of the others in Hollywood, turning them into lofts and business offices, will actually change the way we live in Los Angeles?"

"Absolutely. With the success of the subway, we're seeing a healthy resurgence in old Hollywood. Our goal is to encourage economic development and to promote and retain the entertainment industry. We hope to revitalize the area, bring back the historic significance, and provide new housing, not just for the well-to-do, but for all income groups. We want to meet the social needs of the area and make this a vibrant part of our city, like it once was. "

"That's a pretty big ticket, Doctor. You are aware, of course, the City Council refers to you as Dr. Mad, the Mad Mogul of Development?"

He laughed. "Yes, I've heard that. Actually, the initials of my name, Malcolm Andrew Diamond, spell out MAD, an acronym that's followed me my entire life. Perhaps that's why I pursued my doctorate, to validate myself. However, I'm not crazy. I consider myself a visionary."

"So you're not a medical doctor?"

"Absolutely not. My doctorate is in business. Diamond Development is an umbrella company for a number of different business ventures, everything from finance and commercial real estate to helicopters."

"That's right. You own Emergi-flight, the ambulance service in the air."

"As well as a transport service. I believe helicopters are the future for cities like Los Angeles. Emergency or otherwise. Just imagine a city where traffic was not a problem."

He had me. I couldn't switch the dial.

CHAPTER 19

I knew who the Mad Doctor Diamond was, I just hadn't realized he was also a member of the police commission. Diamond was a big man, a regular on the local Sunday morning television talk shows and a popular figure in Los Angeles. His picture would frequently pop up in the society sections of the Beverly Hills Courier, and it was rumored he owned a number of buildings up and down the Wilshire Corridor and Sunset and Hollywood Boulevards. If LA were a Monopoly board game, he owned the equivalent of Boardwalk, Park Place and Madison Avenue. Diamond wasn't just a developer; he was literally a pillar of LA's new skyline.

I arrived at the station to find Diamond's sinister black Rolls Royce with its personalized plates and sleek body parked directly in front of the patio entrance to the radio station, the engine running. Whoever was inside had avoided parking in the VIP visitors' section, and I had to walk around his car to get to the front doors. I strained to see if I could identify the driver behind the blackened windows, but it was impossible to see inside.

Eddie, one of KCHC's security guards, was standing behind the reception desk when I came in. I asked him if he was aware that a black Rolls Royce was parked on the sidewalk, blocking the entrance to the station.

"That's got to be against fire regulations," I said. "I had to walk around it just it to get through to the front door."

"Sorry, Carol, that's Dr. Diamond's car. He asked his chauffeur to keep the engine running. Promised me he wouldn't be long."

"Really," I said. "The man's on the air. Just how long does he think he'll be?"

Without waiting for a response, I went directly down the hall and stood in front of the large studio window. I crossed my arms and watched as Aaron continued to interview Dr. Diamond. I wanted to see him, up close, to compare his features to those Freddie had described as the *regular*, the Clark Gable lookalike that frequented the club, and the man I was convinced I'd seen with Tony just last night.

I was growing more and more certain the two were the same. I stared at him, mentally checking off the similarities: nice hair, square shoulders, same smile. The only difference I could see was that Diamond was wearing glasses, an expensive pair of thin, grey designer frames that flattered his square face. That, and his hair was different. He wore it slicked back, smooth and in place, with a lot of product that gave it a wet look, and there was no mustache. But still, he could be the same man, the Gable imposter I'd seen in front of Holly's cottage. I hadn't seen his face with Tony, but I did see the car. He had to be one and the same. This couldn't be a coincidence. He glanced up at me, adjusted his headphones, and then as though he recognized who I was, smiled broadly. My stomach knotted as I stared back at his big teeth. I felt a cold clammy chill run down my spine. I glanced at my watch. If I wanted to talk to Tyler before I went on the air, I had to hurry.

I found Tyler in his office, staring at a computer screen. He looked like he was involved in a game of mental chess. I didn't wait to be asked to sit down. I just sat.

"You know who that is, on the air with that new biz-whiz kid you hired, Aaron Whitehall?"

"That," Tyler said, "is Dr. Malcolm Diamond." Tyler's eyes didn't leave his computer. In front of him was a split screen with a digital read out of everything that was being said on the air. He read off Diamond's long list of accolades. "He's a member of the police commission, developer, entrepreneur, a.k.a. the Mad Mogul of Hollywood. I could go on, but why?"

"Because he's—"

I was about to say the man I'd seen hustling my former client into his car last night and the same man I suspected I'd seen in front of the Holly Wood Tour's cottage dressed like Clark Gable the night of the pub crawl. But I didn't get a chance. Behind me someone was calling my name.

"Carol Childs?"

I turned around to see Dr. Diamond in the doorway, his large frame completely filling the entrance.

"I thought that might be you. I asked Aaron when you passed by the studio window. I wanted to get a chance to introduce myself and say thank you."

He stepped into the room, his sheer presence nearly dwarfing Tyler's small frame as he approached the desk. Diamond was easily six-five, probably close to two-hundred and forty pounds, well dressed and with a quick smile, a political animal.

Tyler and I stood.

Diamond extended his large, fleshy, man-sized hand in my direction, expecting me to take it. I glanced nervously at Tyler then back to Dr. Diamond and gripped his hand firmly, hoping to hide my anxiety.

"Name's Dr. Malcolm Diamond." His eyes, like his hand, locked on mine. "I don't want to take a lot of your time. I know how busy you are. Just wanted you to know that as a businessman, I appreciate what you doing with your reports, Miss Childs."

He glanced over at Tyler, as though he wanted to confirm with my boss his appreciation. "Particularly that last report about Monica Channing and the pub crawls. Keeping this city safe is important for business."

Then he looked back at me, "But I do hope, Miss Childs, that you're being careful out there. A young female reporter like yourself, you never know. Things happen, girls—particularly young college girls—they disappear." He squeezed my hand incredibly hard. "But then, you already know that, right?"

An icy chill, like an electric shock, went from my hand to my heart. *Was he talking about my daughter?*

He dropped my hand, nodded to Tyler, then turned and walked out the door.

"Was that a threat?" I looked at Tyler. He sat down and leaned back in the chair.

"Tell me what you know."

CHAPTER 20

Tyler agreed, after I shared with him my suspicions concerning Dr. Diamond, that getting LAPD to look seriously at one of their police commissioners wasn't going to be easy. I had no proof. What I had was Detective Browne shooting holes in my theory. He didn't believe there could be any possible connection between my sightings of Dr. Diamond and the Clark Gable lookalike I'd seen outside of Holly's cottage the night of the pub crawl. Or that I'd witnessed anything other than the act of a Good Samaritan helping a friend home after I'd spotted him outside of the City Grill in Century City with my missing client. My accusations—both of them—despite my help with Bessie Bixby, appeared to have caused my relationship with LAPD and Detective Browne to cool drastically.

"But what really worries me is," I said, "based on what Diamond just said about girls disappearing—particularly college girls—is that he knows about my daughter. That she disappeared the night of the pub crawl."

"Cate disappeared?" Tyler sounded alarmed.

"I probably should have said something. But you were busy and I—"

I paused. Why hadn't I said anything? Did I think my silence might protect my daughter? Keep her from being exposed to the dangers of a news story she already knew too much about? All I knew was that I wanted her safe. I wanted her away from Hollywood, back at school, where she wouldn't be a target. Where no one might try and come back and kidnap her. And I wanted my professional life safe separate from my personal life.

"What happened, Carol?"

"Someone drugged Cate at the bar, when we were at Hemingway's. Nothing happened. Not really, but it made me realize just how easily she could have disappeared. I made a scene and evidently Diamond found out about it. I don't know how. He wasn't there. It didn't make the news, and I sure as hell wasn't talking about it."

Tyler got up and closed the door. Something I'd never seen him do. Tyler has a strict open door policy. I watched as he came back around to his desk without saying a word, and sat down.

"You know, of course, Detective Browne's close to retirement. He's probably got twenty years in, and he's not going to help you shine a light on a member of the police commission and do anything that might unsettle his pension."

I hadn't considered that, but Tyler was right. Detective Browne struck me as a good cop, a team player. Not someone likely to go looking to dig up dirt on a fellow member of the boys in blue, much less a member of the police commission.

"Meanwhile, the clock's ticking on these girls, and if you really think Diamond's your guy, you may have to find other sources for your information."

"Any ideas?" I said.

"Yeah, you might want to start here. Did you see this?" He handed me a copy of this morning's paper, the front section, folded and opened to an inside page. He pointed to a three quarter page color ad.

The advertisement was an announcement, a congratulatory ad for a fifty-thousand dollar contribution made by Dr. Malcolm Diamond to Tanya's Rescue Center in Hollywood. A picture of Diamond smiling with his arm about the founder of the center, Tanya Day, stared back at me.

"You know who she is, don't you?"

I looked at the photo and shook my head. "I've no idea."

"Her name was Sugar Lips. She's a former porn star."

I studied her picture again. She could have been anyone: schoolteacher, nurse, office worker. With her hair pulled back and very little makeup she hardly looked like she'd worked in the skin trade.

"The man's Teflon, Carol. He's got ads, like this one, in the paper nearly every day. Some of them for bullied youth. Veterans. The disabled. He gives hundreds of thousands of dollars to charity. And today, there's this one. Interesting, don't you think?" Tyler nodded to me.

"You think this is real? The money, I mean? A color ad like this in the *LA Times*, it doesn't come cheap, and then the donation on top of that. Just how much money does this guy give away?"

"Probably as much as he needs to make it look like he's being philanthropic...or maybe he's not really giving it away at all. Might be worth checking out."

I started to get up from my chair.

"Wait. Before you go, there's one other thing. Corporate's demanding we make another change in programming."

"Who is it this time?" I sat back down, expecting to hear they were cutting the news department.

"I wouldn't bother you with this, but it may be connected to your investigation, and you are a friend."

"Who?"

"Mr. King. KCHC's go-to legal guru. I was on the phone with him before you came in. Corporate doesn't think his legal show fits KCHC's new lighter chick-news format. I expected him to go all ballistic on me when I told him I was going to have to cancel his show, but he surprised me. Says he's been swamped with a case in federal court. And guess who his client is?"

I raised my hands, surrender style.

"None other than our good friend, Dr. Diamond."

"Diamond hired King for a case?"

Tyler nodded.

"Not only that, the judge on the case was Judge Channing. And..." Tyler pointed a finger at me. "Wait for it...he ruled *against* him. According to King, Diamond was furious with the ruling. Cost him a bundle. Swore he'd find a way to get even."

"What was the date of the ruling?" My eyes went to a large calendar Tyler kept on the wall with important dates and events.

"Tuesday, three days before Monica Channing's body was found up on Mulholland."

This time I did get up from my chair. I was due on the air in five minutes.

"You can't use that, Carol. It's pure speculation. But it might come in handy."

"Oh, don't worry. I don't plan to. Not for the newscast anyway."

I hurried out of Tyler's office, grabbed a stack of wire copy out of a basket marked chick-lite news, and headed down the hall for my report.

"Sorry, ladies, looks like George Clooney is about to be officially off the market...A great white shark has been caught off the Santa Monica Pier...and a La Canada Flintridge woman called police this morning to report two bear cubs were in her backyard. In other news, this is day six in the disappearance of Gabi Garrison, and police report there is no news concerning the whereabouts of Leticia Johnson or Brandy White."

Then, on a lark, I added, "However, undisclosed sources close to the investigation for Hollywood's Missing Girls announced today they plan to soon reveal the name of the kidnapper responsible for the abductions of Jessie Martin, Marilyn Ann Billings, April Hansen and a suspected number of other missing girls. This is Carol Childs, standing watch for KCHC and Hollywood's Missing Girls..."

I got up and left the broadcast booth immediately after my report, satisfied I'd sent a message to Diamond as much as he had sent one to me in Tyler's office. *Two can play at this game, Doctor. You can hide behind LAPD for only so long. But I know who you are, and I'm coming after you.* For the first time I wasn't worried Tyler would come looking for me—like he had so often when I'd gone off script—because I knew he wouldn't. I knew he'd be in his office, smiling.

CHAPTER 21

I walked out of the station with the newspaper in my hand and a growing list of people I believed each knew something about Dr. Diamond. If I couldn't lean on Detective Browne anymore, like Tyler said, I was going to have to come up with a few sources of my own. Off the top of my head I was certain Monica's best friend, Bethany, and Gabi's boyfriend, Dr. Ericson, each knew something about Diamond, and I was certain Holly Wood and now, Tanya Day, whose ad I'd just seen in the paper, probably knew another side altogether. Something that LAPD didn't. If I could combine those facts, based upon my strong suspicion, I just might be able to get a clear picture of who the mad Dr. Diamond really was and exactly how he was involved with Hollywood's Missing Girls.

I decided to start with Tanya.

I called Tanya's Rescue Center and asked to speak with their director, Tanya Day. She was busy, and I left a message with an assistant. I told her I was a reporter and wanted to talk with her about the center. I didn't mention anything about Dr. Diamond, only that I thought her program that helped young girls get off the street would make an interesting story.

I then hung up and headed over to the UCLA Medical Center. I didn't try to call Dr. Miles Ericson. I didn't want to give him a heads-up I was on my way. If Freddie Bleeker was right and he'd spotted Gabi and Miles inside his club and they'd been talking with someone, then Miles had lied to me. I needed to know why. I figured, based upon the time—it was almost noon—I had a better than fifty-fifty chance of catching him at the hospital, and that I'd probably find him near the Grab-and-Go where we'd met before.

He was standing at one of the vending machines when I came through the door. His back was to me.

"You didn't tell me you and Gabi met with somebody when the two of you went clubbing."

He turned around. The color of his face was white as his lab coat. He sighed heavily. "How did you find out?"

I nodded to the same small café table where we'd sat before. "We need to talk."

"Like I told you last time, I don't know anything. And I didn't kill Gabi, so why are you bothering me?" He sounded angry.

"I don't believe you." I sat down at the table and waited for him take a seat.

"Yeah, well, evidently the police don't either. They keep asking about her, like they think I've got her body hidden somewhere."

I leaned across the table and put my hand on top of his wrist. "Do you?"

"You know I didn't kill Gabi."

"Look, as I see it, the police have two separate issues here. Your girlfriend Gabi's vanished, and then there's Monica Channing, her murder, and a possible connection to a human trafficking ring. They don't think you're part of that. At least publically they haven't linked Gabi to Monica. But I do think they suspect you're trying to cover up Gabi's disappearance—that maybe you killed her—and that you're trying to make it look she was kidnapped by this sex trafficking ring and hoping you can get away it."

"That's ridiculous. It couldn't be further from the truth. I didn't do that."

"Then what is it? Because you're right, I don't think you killed Gabi. But right now the police do, and if Gabi doesn't reappear, real soon, or you don't do something to convince them you're not involved, things aren't going to go well for you. You're going to be spending a fortune in attorney fees, and you can forget about your position here at the hospital, because by the time the police, and unfortunately the press, are done with this story, nobody's going to want a doctor who was suspected of killing his beautiful, blonde girlfriend. It won't matter what I think, or that the police couldn't prove it, because you'll be guilty in the eyes of the public."

He hung his head and bit his lip. I noticed his hands, smooth like a surgeon's, grip his coffee cup. "If I tell you, and you say anything, or tell the police, they'll kill her."

"Kill her? Who would kill her?"

I listened as Miles explained that he'd been deeply in debt. His mother had become unexpectedly ill and he had maxed out his credit cards, paying for flights back and forth across the country, until she died. After that there had been funeral expenses and later, the move-in with Gabi had cost more than expected. The money problems had compounded and so had his relationship. Gabi wanted to help, but she had her own financial problems, and he had refused.

"Finally, she suggested I see someone. She had a client who she said could help. He made all kinds of loans; I think she'd taken a personal loan from him to consolidate some credit cards, and she knew he'd be able to figure something out. So I went to see him."

"Tony Domingo with Financial Futures?"

He nodded.

"At first it seemed pretty cut and dry. He asked me to fill out a few forms. Pretty standard stuff, and while I'm doing that, he asks what it is I do for a living. When I explained I was a surgical resident at UCLA, he suddenly got real interested. Came out from behind his computer, took his glasses off, and he started to talk to me like a real person, not just some cash-strapped financial applicant. All of a sudden, he's asking all kinds of questions. Wants to know more about what I was doing at the hospital, what kind of medicine I was interested in. That kind of thing. It seemed a little odd, but I figured he was just interested because of his relationship to Gabi. And then, he mentioned he had a friend, a doctor, he wanted me to talk to."

"Dr. Diamond?" I tried to mask my excitement.

"Yes. Dr. D. The mad Dr. Diamond."

Mad? I raised my brows. "And exactly what did Dr. Diamond want?"

"Well, to start with, he's not a doctor. Not a medical doctor, anyway. He's a PhD. Or so he claims. But I couldn't tell you from where or even if it's for real. He mentioned half a dozen different colleges and universities. His degree is in finance or international business, or maybe nothing at all. To tell you the truth, I think he's a scammer, but you have to understand, right then, I really didn't really care who he was. I was desperate. I just wanted to sign whatever paperwork he needed, get the money, and get out of there."

"Out of where?"

Miles exhaled deeply, as though he couldn't believe what he was about to say.

"A strip club. We were meeting inside a strip club near the airport. Tony had set it up. He said Dr. Diamond was on his way to catch a flight and we should meet there. That he frequented places like that and not to let it bother me." He looked away and shook his head. "Truth is, I think he owned it or at least he acted like he owned the girls who worked there. He even offered to have one his girls—you know—*visit* with me."

I tried to hide the surprise on my face. I nodded like I heard this type of thing every day. I didn't want the fact that I was shocked to cause him to stop and rethink what he was saying.

"Understand, at the time, I didn't have any idea what this was all about. All I knew is Tony had told me Dr. Diamond was interested in helping me. That he liked to help young doctors. He said he wanted to know if I'd be interested in changing my surgical residency and joining the transplant team at UCLA. I couldn't believe it. The man had just offered me a hooker and now he's talking about the transplant team? I figured the guy was nuts. A residency position like that can take years to get. And he was offering to pull strings to make it happen."

I reached into my bag for my notepad and started to take notes.

"So, Dr. Diamond arranges for you to join the transplant team, that's prestigious, I'm sure, but how's that help you financially? I mean you're still a surgical resident, working long hours and for not much money, right?"

"Except he says in exchange for my *agreeing to work* with the transplant team, he'll start paying down my college loans. He promises to funnel a stipend into my checking account every month from an offshore betting agency that won't raise any eyebrows. He'll arrange it so it looks like I'm winning a little at the track now and again. He said it'd give me enough to live on without being crazy. The idea was that when I completed my residency I'd be debt free and have a little money in the bank."

"Okay, so what's in it for Diamond? What is it he wanted you to do to in exchange for agreeing to work in the transplant unit?"

"He wanted somebody on the inside of the hospital working with the transplant unit." He paused and looked at me. "Because he's selling organs."

I dropped my pencil. I couldn't believe what I was hearing.

"He's been matching organ recipients with donors."

"Are you telling me, you think Dr. Diamond is somehow involved in the buying and selling of human organs?" This was beyond anything I'd imagined. Diamond really was a madman.

"No. I don't think he's buying. What I think is that Dr. Diamond is using the bodies of the young women who work for him as donors. I think he's selling."

He stared at me as I processed what he had said and took a long sip of his coffee before he spoke again.

"It all makes a nice little package. Don't you think? He's got these girls, he uses them, and then when they're no longer useful to him or maybe giving him too much trouble, he retires them. But he can't get rid of them. There'd be too many repercussions. How's a police commissioner explain he's involved in the skin trade? So he repurposes them. Kills them or has them killed. I don't know how and I don't want to."

"But how does he get the organs?" I picked up my pencil.

"He'd still have to harvest them, and like you say, he's not a doctor."

"That's just it, he doesn't have to. All Dr. Diamond had to do was make certain the girl had the same blood and tissue type as his client and a donor card on her when she arrived—near dead—at the hospital. After that, it's a done deal."

Miles explained that with organ transplants there were designated hospitals around the country, regional centers where if a patient died and had a donor card on them, their organs could easily be harvested. The centers were hooked into a national database and had information concerning persons waiting for an organ transplant. If a patient in Los Angeles needed a heart transplant and the donor died at one of the regional centers— usually within two hours of the recipient's hospital—the donor organs were harvested and loaded on one of Diamond's emergency helicopter transports.

"But what about next of kin and notification? Certainly somebody had to be notified."

"There are no next of kin. These girls all have fake names. None of them would have had a real ID. Cases like these, the hospital would have tried, but if there's no family available, the instructions on the card are implicit. It's a legally binding document. And time, in situations like this, is of the essence."

This was so beyond the scope of what I had imagined it took me a minute to process. I stared at the yellow pad in front of me, trying to piece together the framework of the mad doctor's menagerie of players.

"So this had to have happened more than once for you to get suspicious."

He nodded.

"At first I had no idea. Dr. Diamond called and said he had a friend whose wife was in the transplant ward waiting for a heart. He was all very casual about it and friendly. Said she'd come in from Hawaii and had suffered a devastating heart attack. Her own doctor had told her it was hopeless, that without a heart transplant she was living on borrowed time. But the husband wasn't giving up.

He insisted the family doc try to make arrangements for a heart transplant. The nearest place for that was Los Angeles and before you know it, she's making arrangements to come to LA and she's on the waiting list. Problem is, there's no shortage of patients needing hearts, but there is a shortage of available organs. So what I think happened is that her husband, a very wealthy businessman, learns that Dr. Diamond has this black market thing going. First I hear about it is when Diamond calls me and says he'd appreciate if I'd keep an eye on her. Make certain she stays healthy and is in good spirits. I didn't think that was anything out of the ordinary, just a friend looking after a friend's wife. Then this heart arrives a couple days later from Arizona. That's not unusual. Like I said, most of our organs come from either California, Arizona or Nevada. But I remember this particular case because the donor's heart was from a young female, and the match was unusually good."

"And after that?"

"The next couple of cases were all similar. Dr. Diamond would call and say he had a friend and ask if I would I look in on them. But what caught my attention was that the organs we received were all coming from young, female donors. Three in a row and just for his patients, none of the others in the unit." He paused and looked at me. "Just what are the odds of that?" He gestured, both hands, up to the ceiling. "It just wasn't possible. And then I started to wonder if maybe these organs might be coming from some of the women—girls really—like those I'd seen working in the strip club when I first met Dr. Diamond."

"And you shared this with Gabi?"

"I told her what I suspected and we agreed we'd go and talk to Tony. That's who we were going to meet with the night we went out, only Diamond was there and things got ugly. He said we better both keep quiet, or bad things could happen, and then he left. Tony got real uncomfortable and said Diamond had a bad side to him and warned us we better forget we ever said anything. But Gabi got irate and threatened she'd go to the press if he didn't do something. Next thing I know, Gabi's missing and I get a call on my cellphone from someone I'm pretty sure is Dr. Diamond. He warns me if I ever want to see Gabi again I better keep my mouth shut. So I make up this story that she and I have been arguing and that she took off."

CHAPTER 22

My cellphone had been quietly vibrating the entire time I was talking to Miles. I'd turned it off during our conversation so we wouldn't be disturbed, but as I hurried back to my car I pulled it from my bag and noticed I had three messages. The first was from Agent Delfino. And boy, did I want to talk to him. He'd gotten my voicemail and apologized for playing phone tag and would try back again soon.

The second message was from Tanya, or rather her assistant, telling me she'd be happy to talk about the rescue center, but her schedule was busy. Please call back. And the third was from Cupid. He sounded excited. He had an idea. Something to do with the Red Hatted Ladies and a station promotion he wanted to put together, Saturday Night on Hollywood Boulevard. He couldn't wait to see me. I was just about to call Agent Delfino back when the phone rang in my hand. I knew without looking it would be Sheri.

"So how's our investigation going?" Sheri sounded breathless. I could hear the rustling of paper bags and the ringing of a cash register in the background.

"Where are you? And what do you mean *our* investigation?"

"I'm shopping. You know, when I get nervous, I shop. And I figured since you didn't call me back, either Tony turned up or I'd better be getting a safe room ready for us." She paused as though waiting for a laugh, and when I didn't say anything, added, "By the way, do you like eggplant?"

"It's okay," I said.

I'm sure there are journalists who don't talk about their work, but between girlfriends and the fact that Sheri had been with me since I first started working the story, I found it difficult not to share some of what I knew. But not everything, not yet.

"Sorry to say, I haven't heard a word from Tony since his call. And no, you don't need to be prepping a safe room, at least not yet." I laughed, half joking.

"So, where is he then?"

"Hopefully not six feet under. But right now, Tony is the least of my worries. Turns out one of the men we saw with him in front of the City Grill is Dr. Diamond. And, get this, I just found out Diamond's a member of the police commission."

"Ah. So the plot thickens."

"He's also a man whose name keeps coming up with my investigation." I didn't want to worry her, so I kept the rest of the gory details concerning the transplants Miles had told me about to myself and switched the conversation back to something more palatable. "So this eggplant? Are you planning on cooking it for dinner tonight?"

"Could be. That is, if you and Charlie want to come by. I hate to cook a big eggplant lasagna for just Clint and me, and I know your schedule doesn't allow for anything that's not cash-and-carry. Particularly right now. Tell you what, I'll get the boys, and you bring dessert. Make it something sweet and sinful."

I agreed I'd bring something of the warm, chocolate gooey variety and told her I'd be by around seven-thirty and hung up the phone. Satisfied at least the part of my life dealing with the day-to-day of meals and family was not only predictable, but in order. I'd almost reached the station when the phone rang again. This time it was Detective Browne.

"Ms. Childs?" His voice sounded too formal for this to be anything but an official call. "I wasn't going to call you, but this hits too close to home not to notify you personally. Homicide just called. They found a body."

My heart froze. I pulled into the parking lot, gripped the wheel and braced for bad news, praying he wasn't going to tell me it was Gabi.

"Another girl?" I asked.

"No, a man." I expected him to tell me the body they recovered was Tony Domingo. Instead he said, "Freddie Bleeker. The fella you had on the air yesterday, when Miss Bixby and I were by the studio. The police got a call this morning saying there was a body floating in the pool at the top of the W Hotel and IDed him. Looks like he might have had too much to drink and fell in."

Freddie dead? That couldn't be an accident. "Was he murdered?"

"Too soon to tell. The coroner will have to determine cause of death. But according to one of the towel boys who worked the pool area last night, he was alone. Came up to the pool around eight p.m. Said he was drinking and told him he was there to meet with someone. Towel boy went home around nine. He said nobody ever came by and Bleeker was still sitting there when he left."

I sat silent and tried to process why Freddie would be at the W, particularly at that hour. It made no sense he'd be sitting around a pool when at that hour he should have been down the street working at Hemingway's.

I thanked him for the call and was about to hang up when he added, "Oh, by the way, I spoke with Dr. Diamond about your missing client, Tony Domingo. Turns out, you were right, he was with him at the City Grill last night. Says he ran into him at the restaurant bar, and just like I said, he'd been drinking. According to the good doctor, your client had suffered some pretty heavy business losses and had to close the doors. He was belly-up financially and he was in a bad way, nursing his wounds with a little old-fashioned Jim Beam. Diamond says he drove him home. You ask me, your client's probably like a lot of my missing cases, got in over his head financially, disappeared and doesn't want to be found. Debt'll do that."

I wasn't about to challenge Detective Browne on his theory. I had too many questions I needed answers to before I could tell him exactly how much I disagreed with him about "the good doctor." I thanked him and then asked if he had any news on Gabi.

There was an awkward silence, then: "Nope, not a word. But far as your client Mr. Domingo goes, I wouldn't count on him showing up anytime soon. Not until somebody's made him whole again and he's ready to reopen his doors. That's the way it usually goes with guys who go missing like this. They need to heal their wounds first."

"Yeah," I said. "Heal their wounds." I hung up and headed into the station.

CHAPTER 23

Tyler was in the studio with Cupid when I came in. In front of them, rather than the bottle of Jim Beam I'd seen with Cupid yesterday, were two Styrofoam cups of hot coffee, still steaming, and more than a dozen sugar packets scattered across the console. I could tell they'd been discussing Hollywood's Missing Girls. In Tyler's hand was a copy of the *LA Times* with pictures of Monica Channing. They looked up at me, startled, their faces prepped with questions, eyes wide and waiting.

"Where've you been?" Tyler asked.

"Freddie's dead." I dropped my reporter's bag on the floor. "Detective Browne just called with the news. He thought I should know personally."

Cupid let out a long, low whistle, then picked up his cup. "You think it's related to anything he said on the show?"

"The police don't know yet how he died, but my bet is the Mad Dr. Diamond didn't like what he heard yesterday and wanted to make sure Freddie didn't say anything else. I wouldn't be surprised if he had something to do with it." I took the stool next to Tyler and told them both I'd just come from meeting with Dr. Ericson.

"Freddie was right. He did see Gabi with Miles before she disappeared. They were at the club, just like he said, and they were talking with someone, only it wasn't Diamond. It was Tony Domingo. And Miles is afraid if he says anything, Gabi may show up dead."

"He thinks she's still alive?" Tyler asked.

"He's hoping she is." I explained Miles' financial troubles and how Gabi had suggested he go see Tony for a loan. "And once Tony realized Miles was a surgeon, he set him up with Dr. Diamond."

Tyler started counting on his fingers. "So now you've got Diamond, or a Gable lookalike, getting into a black Rolls Royce outside of Holly's cottage the night of the pub crawl. And we know from the plates on the car that it's registered to Dr. Diamond. Then you've got Diamond, again with his car, the night Tony disappeared outside the City Grill in Century City. And now Ericson's telling you Tony set him up to meet the Mad Doctor?" He held up three fingers and I nodded.

"Believe me, it goes a lot deeper than that. Diamond's into some real insidious stuff, and he needed a surgeon to help him with one of his business ventures. So, he pulled some strings at the university, maybe made some philanthropic donations to the center—not anything out of the ordinary, for the doctor anyway—but just enough to get Miles transferred from his surgical residency inside UCLA to the university's transplant team."

"Damn." Cupid stood up and emptied another of the sugar packets into his coffee and shook his head. "This is so much more interesting than spinning records."

I ignored the comment and continued. "Which he did because it just so happens that one of Dr. Mad's business ventures is, in addition to the kidnapping and trafficking of young women," I paused, "the selling and transport of their organs."

There was silence in the studio. Both men looked at me. Stunned.

Tyler was the first to speak. "You're telling us Dr. Ericson told you Diamond is involved in the buying and selling of human organs?"

"Not the buying," I said. "Just the selling. He's got all the organs he needs."

Cupid nearly choked on his coffee. "You mean he's—"

"Murdering the young women who work for him," I said.

I explained how Miles started to get suspicious when Diamond asked him to look in on certain patients and noticed that those patients were all getting organs from young, female donors.

"As for how Diamond found his patients, I think he did it the same way he found the young women he's using. He sets up a website. Only this time, it's for people desperate for black market organs. People not willing to wait and who will pay any price for what they need. Then, he suggests his client enroll in an organ transplant program somewhere in the country. The centers are geographically located throughout the US, and if his client is accepted—meaning healthy enough for surgery—they're put on a waiting list until a suitable organ is available. After that, all Diamond's got to do is ensure one of the girls, who he's already matched for blood and tissue type, has an accident. The girl arrives at the hospital, most likely brain dead or close enough that she's beyond hope, and coincidentally, she's got a donor card with a fake ID in her wallet. After that, an attempt is made to contact her next of kin, and, of course, none is found and her organs are harvested."

"And time is of the essence," Tyler said.

"Exactly, and once the organs are harvested, they're immediately transported to the nearest hospital, which in our case just happens to be the transplant center where Diamond's client is ready and waiting."

"Dammit," Tyler said. "He's even got the helicopter service to help with the transport."

"That he does," I said.

"So let me see if I've got this straight." Cupid put his cup down on the console. "Miles tells Gabi what's going on and she goes to Tony and tells him she suspects Diamond's up to no good, and 'fore you know it, she's off the radar."

"Which explains why Tony called me," I said. "He's a former client, and he probably heard my broadcast about Monica Channing's disappearance. And with Gabi gone and Diamond sitting on the police commission, he knows he can't go to the police—not without word getting back to Diamond—and he's starting to get worried, so he calls me. Figures maybe the press can help."

"And Miles is afraid if he says anything, he'll get his girlfriend back...in pieces." Cupid picked his cup up again and took a long swig of his coffee. "Maybe in an organ transplant box. Signed, sealed and delivered. Gruesome."

I put my elbows on the console, my head in my hands. The pieces weren't fitting. I still had questions.

"Okay, let's just say, for lack of a better word, Diamond is *recycling* his girls and selling their organs to the highest bidder. Then why not Monica? Young healthy girl, you'd think her heart and lungs would bring a good fee. So, why then did her body show up in Stone Canyon last Friday?"

"Maybe 'cause she wasn't."

"What? You don't think Diamond kidnapped her and was planning to use her as part of his sex trafficking ring?" I shook my head and explained how the coroner had found a tattoo on the inside of Monica's wrist. "The police believe whoever's trafficking these girls uses it to brand them. For all I know it might indicate their blood and tissue type. Monica had one, right here." I pointed to the inside of my wrist. "The police didn't want that information made public and the judge wasn't about to dwell on his daughter's connection to any human trafficking ring. So it was hushed up."

"I didn't mean she wasn't kidnapped, or a victim of some sex-trafficking ring, for that matter, but maybe she wasn't all that healthy." Cupid reached for the newspaper and spread it out on the console. "Maybe the reason Diamond didn't use her body was because she wouldn't have made a good organ donor. Look at this."

Cupid pointed to a black and white photo of Monica, at three years old, sitting on a tricycle in front of her family home. "It says here, shortly after this picture was taken, Monica was hit by her mother's car as she was pulling out the drive and was hospitalized in critical condition for several weeks. What if something happened back then? Maybe something her family's kept secret? Could be she had a blood transfusion, or maybe she even had an organ transplant. Maybe contracted something that would have made her high-risk and Diamond knew he couldn't use her. Things like that happen. It might explain why her family's been so protective of her."

"And...it might explain the virginity pledge." I hadn't meant to say it aloud. Both Tyler and Cupid looked at me.

"What?"

I shared how I'd met Monica's friend Bethany at my son's game and that she had confided in me about Monica's affair.

"That is, if you can call it that. She said Monica had met someone online. I'm pretty sure it was Diamond, and that he met her and thought she'd be good for business. Pretty girl, maybe not too smart, but who's definitely making herself available to him. He wines and dines her. Exactly like Freddie said. Brings her down to the club, shows her off in front of couple of men. Only she gets serious and confides in him. She tells him that she's ill. I mean, the girl had daddy issues and suddenly she's in love with him. Or at least she thinks she is. But he dumps her and then..." I paused. Something Tyler had said this morning fit perfectly.

"What is it, Carol, what are you thinking?"

"Oh my God. This is perfect. It was what you said about King representing Diamond in a case before Judge Channing. King said Diamond was upset with the verdict and blamed the judge. Maybe he figured a way to hurt him. He couldn't use Monica, not like he had wanted. He couldn't use her as a sex slave and later murder her and harvest her organs. She'd be too high-risk. But he could use her to get to the judge. She landed in his lap, perfectly. Coming back to him, right after Judge Channing hands down his verdict and—"

Cupid stood up, and staring at the newspaper, stirred his coffee. "Oh, that's beyond cruel. Can you imagine? Diamond loses a case before the girl's father. She probably doesn't know anything about it, and he tells her something like he's going take her away. Romances her a bit. Gets her into that helicopter of his and then flies her out over her folks' home, opens the chopper door and out she goes."

He dropped the stir-stick from above his head and Tyler and I watched as it landed on the console.

Splat!

Tyler looked at me. I could see he was weighing his options. Considering carefully how he wanted to proceed. I knew corporate had been on him to dial back on hard news, and that he'd been covering for me, pushing me to get as much as I could on the air about the missing girls. I didn't want this to be the reason he pulled back, not now.

I stood up, my hands in front of me. "Don't say what I think you're going to say."

"Carol, I need you to take some time off."

"No way," I shook my head. "I'm in the middle of an investigation. We're getting close. You can't possibly expect me to stop what I'm doing, not now."

Tyler put his hand up to stop me. There was no point in arguing.

"I'll fill in with Cupid for the next couple of days. We'll issue a statement. Explain that you've been working too hard, that you're suffering from exhaustion. That you're taking some much-needed time off. It'll give me some breathing room with corporate anyway. And who knows down the road, a report like this might lead to an award. Something I might like and the station needs."

"But—"

Again with the hand, this time closer to my face.

"Look, yesterday Diamond comes in my office and says he wants to thank you and then subtly says something about your daughter. You and I both know he was sending a message. What we need to do is send one back. Let him think you're scared. That you don't plan on pursuing Hollywood's Missing Girls. That after yesterday's news update you went off the deep end, suffered a breakdown. I'll put out a press release, something about your taking a little R&R time, and fill in with a bunch of crap about the station's new direction. Our new lighter, friendlier chick-lite news and talk format, while you go home and—"

"But—"

"Don't worry. LAPD's not issuing any updates on the

investigation. They've got a blackout on anything to do with the story and until they're ready to talk, nobody else in town is doing anything with it. There's too much else in the news to cover. So we'll just let this die down a bit."

"But I can't just go home. Not really. Not now."

"Hear me out. The police—far as we know—don't suspect Diamond; he's one of their own. But the FBI's doing their own investigation and I wouldn't be at all surprised, close as you are to them, if you haven't found a way to funnel a little inside information concerning Diamond's involvement."

"I left a brief message. It's not quite the type of thing I could go into on a voicemail. What was I supposed to say? 'I think Dr. Diamond, a respected member of the police commission, is really more of a Dr. Jekyll and Mr. Hyde, and we need to talk, 'cause LAPD's sure not returning any of my calls.' I don't think so."

Tyler stood up and began to pace. "It'll take some time for the FBI to sort through things. Even if they suspect Diamond, they're not going to just run over and make an arrest, they'll need evidence. But in the meantime, if Diamond thinks you're not working the story, he may try to clear up a few more loose ends, like he did with Tony and Freddie. And, if we're lucky, he'll get careless. In the meantime, you could continue with your investigation, under the radar, without anyone either here at the station or inside LAPD knowing what you're up to. With you out of sight and off the air, nobody's going to bother you."

"And me?" Cupid pointed to his chest. "What am I supposed to do? What about my idea for a station promotion with my fans, the Red Hatted Ladies, and the march down on Hollywood Boulevard Saturday night? We're supposed to pass out flyers with Leticia and Brandy's photos on them."

"We'll still set up a station tent Saturday night. I'll get promotions on it, and you and your Red Hatted lady-fans can pass out flyers, march, do whatever you like. But I need you to make this a station promo, not just about Hollywood's Missing Girls. Give out keychains, t-shirts, signed photos of yourself and some of the other station personalities. Think you can do that?"

"Not a problem." Cupid smiled and lifted both hands as though they were cuffed and he were surrendering. "Long as I got my Red Hatted Ladies with me."

"You're going to bury this," I said.

"No, not really. In fact, nobody's going to think we did anything more than follow our new corporate strategy for lighter, friendlier chick-lite news and talk. And far as your promotion goes, Cupid, I'll have Kari Rhodes sit in from the studio Saturday night. She's good on entertainment news, and she can cut to you for updates, interviews from fans on the boulevard and that type of thing. But beginning today, I want you to start to wean yourself away from this missing girls story. Mix it up with a little Hollywood gossip." Tyler walked over to the computer screen next to Cupid and pulled up a list of news stories. "Look, we got a story right here. Be perfect for you. There's a woman out in Thousand Oaks, got herself stuck in some guy's chimney. Man says he met her online and she's been stalking him. Do something with it. I don't care what, but by the time Saturday night rolls around I want this Hollywood's Missing Girls story to be just one of the stories we're covering, not *the* story."

Tyler started to walk toward the door. We were done.

"Wait, don't go. What exactly do you want me to do? You can't just leave me out in the cold. Where do I start? What do I do?"

He stopped at the door, and in his best Clark Gable impression looked at me and winked. "Frankly, my dear, I don't really give a damn."

"Ha. Very funny," I said. "But you don't really think I'm going to go home, do you?"

"Carol, I know you better than that. You're not capable of it. I'm just hoping Diamond doesn't know that."

CHAPTER 24

I couldn't remember when I'd left the station early enough to actually get home *before* dinner. The fact that Tyler was sending me home was really a good thing. I hadn't had much quality time with my son since he'd come back from his college-bound football trip with his dad, and I was looking forward to a nice quiet dinner and the chance to catch up with him about the game and the trip.

But I was troubled. As much as I wanted to focus on home and Charlie, I couldn't stop thinking about the investigation. Tony was missing. Freddie dead. And both of them on the same night. If Diamond was responsible, how did he do it? It was impossible to think that he could have been in two places at the same time.

I drove up Fairfax and stopped in at Dupar's, next to the Farmer's Market, and picked up a chocolate cream pie. It qualified as the decadent, chocolate, and gooey dessert I'd promised to bring Sheri in exchange for her making dinner, and with a little luck it would serve as a diversion. I decided I wasn't going to say much concerning the investigation, or that Tyler had sent me home. I figured what they didn't know at this point wouldn't hurt.

What I didn't know was just how helpful our dinner conversation might be. The four of us were sitting at Sheri's dining room table, having just polished off the last of the eggplant lasagna, and I was about to get up and bring in the chocolate cream pie when I overheard Charlie and Clint talking about the USC/Boston College game.

"It was fake right, fake left." Clint sounded enthusiastic.

"Yeah, Mom," Charlie looked at me. "You should have seen it.

SC's down by three, and everybody's standing up thinking the quarterback would throw the ball down the field but—"

"He handed the ball off to the tailback and he ran with it. He was wide open. Made a forty-yard touchdown." Clint was gleaming with pride.

"Awesome play!" Charlie raised both his hands in the air, a victory salute.

"Fake right, fake left, huh?" I got up, cleared the dishes. I wondered if that's what Diamond had done, faked me out with a fake right, fake left kind of play.

Sheri followed me into the kitchen as I went to retrieve the dessert. She was like a heat-seeking missile, on my heels, right behind me. She knew something was up.

"Okay, so what's happening? And don't tell me you can't talk about it 'cause you're never home this early and you're obviously thinking about something. So what is it?"

"Nothing," I said. "Just thinking how great your eggplant was. I never would have imagined the boys would clean their plate like that."

"Stop it." Sheri put her hand on top of mine. "Fess up, what's on your mind?"

I took the pie out of the box. "Where's your pie cutter?"

Sheri pointed the knife at me, blade first. I wasn't taking it from her without an answer.

"It's Freddie Bleeker," I said. "He drowned last night."

"No!" Sheri looked like she was about to fall over and balanced herself on the counter. "Did Diamond kill him?"

"If he did, he did it within an hour of kidnapping Tony. And I don't see how that's possible."

I explained the timing. How we'd been parked outside the Century Grill at eight p.m. when we witnessed Tony being pushed into Diamond's black Rolls.

"Thing is, I can't figure out how he kidnapped Tony and, on the same night, got all the way across town and killed Freddie an hour later. The towel boy at the W says Freddie was alive when he left him around nine, and the coroner's report says he drowned sometime shortly thereafter. I know he did it, but with traffic and no witnesses, it just doesn't seem possible."

"What if Diamond didn't drive to the W, but flew?"

"You mean by helicopter?"

"Exactly. Think about it, Carol, the man's a developer, he owns a helicopter service. My father used helicopters all the time to scout movie locations. He could be anywhere within minutes. Most of the old buildings in LA were built with helipads for emergencies. They're all over the city. He could have taken off from Century City, from the pad on top of the Wells Fargo building, and landed on top of the W inside of fifteen minutes."

I knew Sheri was right. The station had recently run a story about LA's new fire codes. The older buildings in LA had flat roofs and, with new improved emergency services, the city felt the old codes weren't necessary anymore and was approving an exciting new skyline with peaked roofs and rooftop gardens.

"You're right, and once he's inside the helicopter, he changes identities and assumes his Clark Gable disguise, then lands in Hollywood and nobody's the wiser. He's just another impersonator on the way to some gig. It's brilliant. I like it: a real fake right, fake left play. I would have never thought of it."

I ran my finger across the side of the pie and licked the chocolate. Sweet as it was, it left an odd taste in my mouth, and not because of the chocolate, but because of something I was thinking. If Diamond knew I had seen him with Tony, I'd be the perfect alibi. I felt as though I was being drawn into some game of chess I hadn't signed on for, and suddenly I'd been checkmated. Nobody would believe me if I said I suspected him of Freddie's murder. I'd look ridiculous. He couldn't possibly be in two places at once.

"You all right?"

"Yeah, I'm fine. I'll mention this to Tyler in the morning."

I didn't tell her Tyler had sent me home. I didn't want to worry her. I wanted to leave work at work. After all, home was my safe place. Instead I said, "How about some pie?" Then taking the pie back out to the table, I asked Charlie if he'd tell me a little more about his game. But my mind was still thinking about Tony. Was he dead, or had Diamond faked his kidnapping to throw me off?

The following morning I began my research with Tanya Day. Tanya's rescue center was tucked up next to the Hollywood Freeway. It was a small campus, a scrappy piece of property Diamond owned in the middle of an industrial district off Van Owen in the valley. I had researched it, and found it had originally been developed as a short-term rehabilitation center for the elderly, and later converted to a non-profit home for girls. Outside the ten-foot high concrete walls was a sign that read simply, "Tanya's Home."

"Tanya will be with you in a moment, Ms. Childs. Please have a seat."

I couldn't help but wonder about the young girl who showed me into Tanya's office. She was dressed conservatively, in a uniform, a blue skirt and white blouse, and was maybe sixteen years old. She wore her dark curly hair atop her head, away from her pretty face. Her slim, tapered fingers held the back of the thin wooden chair as I sat down.

"Is there anything I can get you? Coffee? Water?" She smiled. From beneath long lashes her blue eyes sparkled against her smooth, satin, cocoa-colored skin.

"No. I'm fine, thank you. I'll wait."

The small room was illuminated by the light coming in from a single window behind my head. It cast a grey bar shadow onto Tanya's desk. Wrought-iron bars had been installed to keep the riff-raff out and the girls safe inside. On top of the desk, pens and pencils were all bound together, books neatly upright and organized by their size and in descending order. A large, potted plant sat on the corner of the desk, providing the sole color for the otherwise plain room. The leaves traveled down one long leg and nearly reached the floor. For all its austerity, Tanya's small quarters provided a peaceful and quiet respite from the world outside the rescue center.

"I'm sorry I'm late." Tanya entered the room, her hands full of notebooks. She looked twenty pounds heavier and older than the photos I had seen of her online. I estimated her to be in her mid-forties. She was dressed in black, and looked more like a nun in a no-nonsense knee-length dress than a former porn star. She went directly to her desk, sat down, and smiled as though she were switching gears and used to doing it.

"So, what can I do for you, Ms. Childs?"

"I'm working on a story for KCHC—"

"Yes, I know, about sex trafficking." She sat back and folded her arms. From her body language I could see she didn't think my report was going to make any difference.

I didn't want to tell her I agreed with her. That I knew one reporter filing one story on one radio station might not make any difference in a world I knew she knew more about than I possibly could.

"Actually, I'm not here about that. I'm here because I want to talk to you about Dr. Diamond and the donation he made to your center."

I pulled a copy of the ad from my bag, placing it on the desk between us, and noticed the color in her face drain as she looked at it. Reaching into the desk drawer she took out a handful of hard candies.

"If you think I'm going to comment on that ad, you're crazy. One thing I don't need to is to have Dr. Diamond upset with me. I've already got enough of that."

"Really?" I was surprised. I hadn't imagined someone in receipt of so much money would react that way.

"You don't do what I do without a few critics." She unwrapped one of the candies, popped it in her mouth and offered me one.

I shook my head. "I'm afraid I don't understand. Critics? I'd think people would be happy about the work you're doing here."

"You forget, Ms. Childs, I was a porn star. I don't have a

problem with that, but a lot of people do. What I did was, and is, legal. In my opinion, if a girl's of age, and wants to make a living shooting sex videos, that's her business. What I *have*," she accented the word heavily and paused, "is a problem with the pimps who kidnap young girls and have 'em working hot-sheet motels and truck stops. Most of 'em end up livin' beneath some freeway overpass or crashing in some abandoned building, and the only thing more frightening for them than their next trick is facing their pimp empty-handed, or getting arrested and going to jail. Believe me, those pimps out there consider me an eyesore. They'd like to see me go away. And as for all those other good, well-intended people, who you seem to think should happy about what I do, I'm afraid they're few and far between. I'm afraid I'm not very popular."

"Look. I'm not here to judge." I raised my hands, palms forward, and shook my head. "My job is just report the facts, and—"

"Yeah, well, the facts in this case won't do me any favors."

"I guess I don't understand."

"You're assuming I knew Dr. Diamond. That maybe we had some kind of personal relationship? The fact is, I didn't, and I don't. Diamond contacted me five years ago. Like you, he was responding to something he saw in the paper. An article some hotshot reporter wrote about me rescuing girls, giving them a bed and a room in my home. Back then, I was trying to do exactly what I'm doing now, only on a much smaller scale. Then I get this call from Dr. Diamond. He says he's got a rehabilitation center in the north valley and was about to close it. He wanted to offer it to me. He thought I could use it to rescue more girls. Beyond that I didn't look a gift horse in the mouth. I wasn't about to ask questions then, and I won't now."

"Okay, but I still don't get it. Why wouldn't the fact that Dr. Diamond made a fifty thousand dollar contribution to the center be a good thing?"

"Off the record?"

I nodded my head, "Yeah, off the record."

"Because he didn't. That's why. He never donated fifty

thousand dollars. It's a scam. He puts a few thousand bucks in an account and promises he'll add more later. But he never does. I'm sure it's the same with all his charities. Everybody thinks he's this big rich guy, who's got his picture in the paper all the time, giving money away. Believe me, nobody's talking. Everybody wants to believe he's going to come back and make another deposit. But I'm not about to say anything. I do and he'll evict me. And then where would I go? Back to my apartment with two tiny beds and a leaky water closet? I don't think so. I keep my mouth shut, and I imagine his other charities do as well."

I shook my head and reached for one of the candies. I had what I needed. Diamond was a fraud. I didn't have to expose Tanya as my source; I could easily follow a paper trail of money transfers and expose him.

"How about you give me a tour of the center, and I'll see if I can't find a way to tell our listeners what it is you're doing here. Don't see why I can't include some word about the good work you're doing rescuing kids off the street. Maybe a little profile story here and there. Talking about how you're helping them get their high school diplomas, find jobs. You might have more supporters than you know."

CHAPTER 25

I should have known I couldn't keep a secret from Sheri. The fact that I managed to hide out at home, going about my business, quietly below the radar without making too many waves, exactly as Tyler liked, was bound to backfire. And it did. Friday afternoon, Sheri appeared at my doorstep. She had a bag of groceries in her arms and a look on her face reserved for naughty dogs and rebellious kids.

"Why didn't you say something?"

Sheri had been in the car, on the way to Gelson's, one of LA's upscale supermarkets, when she heard Tyler on the air, doing my usual midday news report. In addition to the news, he deliberately let loose the fact he was filling in for me temporarily. I knew he was going to do that. Tyler knew he was going to do that, but Sheri didn't, and when she heard I wasn't at work, that I was taking some much-needed time off due to exhaustion, she made a beeline for my front door.

"How do you think I feel, suddenly hearing my best friend is home sick or God forbid—knowing what I do about what you're working on—even worse? I raced right over. What's happening?"

"Short story?"

"Just tell me, Carol, and don't spare me the details. I'm a big girl." Sheri shifted her groceries from one hip to the other and walked past me and into the kitchen, her patience growing thin.

"Okay. Tyler sent me home to investigate. On the QT."

I told her I hadn't been exactly one hundred percent honest

with her about Diamond. I didn't want to worry her or discuss what I knew in front of the boys. But that once I had told Detective Browne I suspected Diamond *might* be involved with Monica's murder and Tony's disappearance, things between us deteriorated. He stopped returning my calls and LAPD closed ranks.

"All of a sudden, I can't get so much as a call back from anyone selling tickets to the policeman's ball, much less any of the detectives investigating the missing girls."

"Are the police riding Tyler? Trying to stop to your reports?"

"No. But what I found out about Diamond you won't believe."

"Try me."

"Okay, brace yourself. Diamond's not only involved in the selling and trafficking of young women." I took a deep breath. "He's been selling their organs, as well."

"You're kidding! And I thought he was just your run-of-the-mill pimp with bad makeup."

"Ha! Ha! Very funny. No, I'm serious."

"Oh, my God, so you're home because—"

"He threatened me."

Sheri stepped back and hugged the brown paper bag full of groceries closer to her. Her mouth open, the look on her face like she was about to say something, but nothing came out.

"And Gabi Garrison?" I said. "She *is* connected to this case, and in a big way. Turns out her boyfriend, Dr. Ericson, just happens to be on the UCLA transplant team. And the reason why? Dr. Diamond pulled some strings over at the university. Only thing is, Gabi and her boyfriend started to get suspicious about the donors and, guess what? Suddenly Gabi disappears and Miles shuts up. He's afraid if he says anything, Diamond will kill his girlfriend."

"Oh my God."

"Plus, I'm pretty sure I've found evidence to prove Diamond had it in for Judge Channing. He didn't kill Monica because she wouldn't cooperate, but because he was upset with a verdict Judge Channing handed down in a case that Diamond had before him the week earlier. So he *shoved* her out a helicopter."

Sheri dropped the bags on the counter.

"And all those ads Diamond runs in the *LA Times*, showing him making some huge donation to charity? Fake." I reached for the coffee pot. "Coffee?"

"With what you just told me, I think I need something stronger. You have anything open?" Sheri put her groceries down and headed towards the bar where I had an open bottle of red wine and poured herself a glass.

I followed, watched her take a large gulp and waited for her to hand me one. When she didn't, I reached for my own. "Don't mind if I do," I said.

"But why come home? Why not go to the pol—"

"Because what I have isn't hard evidence. It may have been good enough to scare Diamond into thinking I'm getting close. But that's all it is, and Tyler thinks Freddie's murder may be Diamond's way of sending a message."

"To you?"

"Me, or maybe the station. I think Diamond was afraid Freddie was starting to talk too much. He described the man meeting with Monica Channing the night she disappeared as an old actor-type with a thin mustache. It could have been any of a number of old actors: Errol Flynn, Douglass Fairbanks, William Powell. He didn't use his name, but I suspect Diamond didn't like what Freddie was saying. That he was getting too close to describing Clark Gable and he had to silence him."

"You think he might try to kill you?"

"No, but after that little episode with Cate at Hemingway's, I do think he believes he can scare me. Get me to stop my investigation and that in time, this will all blow over. And since there's really no news to report and the police are sitting tight on the investigation, Tyler thinks it makes sense for us to pull back. So, right now, that's exactly what Tyler wants him to think. That the station's given up on the story and I've gone home to rest."

"And you *knew* this last night and didn't say anything?" Sheri sounded agitated.

"No, not everything." I crossed my arms and tried to look reassuring. "I didn't know Diamond's donations to charity were all phony until this morning."

Sheri got up and walked into the kitchen, scoured around for a bag of potato chips from the cabinet, then came back to the bar.

"So, let me get this straight," Sheri said. "You see Diamond, or this Clark Gable lookalike who you think is Diamond, the night of the pub crawl and then again the night Tony Domingo disappears. But how does he know you saw him?"

I took a sip of wine and tried to imagine why Diamond might think I suspected he was involved. I'd never mentioned any suspects in any of my reports. I'd only reported on the facts of the missing girls and how the police thought they were lured to Hollywood via the internet because they fit a certain profile.

"Holly Wood had to have mentioned to him that I was there the night of the pub crawl. She was upset with me when she realized I had Cate with me and that she wasn't twenty-one. She went back inside the cottage to get a pink scrunchie for her to wear because she was underage. Diamond must have been inside and come out after he thought we left. That's why I saw him on the porch and when he saw me. As for Tony, he may have told Diamond he called me and that we were planning to meet at the City Grill the night he disappeared." I paused and tried to connect the dots. "All I know for sure is that the other day, when Diamond was at the station doing an interview with our new business guy, he certainly seemed to know who I was. In fact, he made a point of coming into Tyler's office to introduce himself. Both Tyler and I got an uncomfortable feeling about him. That's when I told Tyler I thought he might be threatening me."

"And then, Freddie dies and—"

"And Tyler takes me off the air. Like I said, he wants me to continue the investigation, quietly, behind the scenes, while the station starts to pull back from the story until we have something more concrete to report. He's convinced Diamond's egocentric and that once he thinks we've given up, he'll start to get careless."

Sheri downed the last of her wine. "So, what's our first move?"

I looked at Sheri. There was no way I was going this alone. I sighed and weighed my options. On the positive side, two would be better than one. Sheri might help to provide a diversion, and I could trust her. On the other side of the coin, there was the Mad Dr. Diamond and his body-parts business. I didn't like to think about that, but I definitely liked the idea of Sheri's company.

"Alright, to start with, we need to find out exactly how Diamond's operation runs. We know he uses the internet to attract young women. But where is it he's keeping these girls, and how does he get around town? Could be he uses a helicopter. Flies the girls from wherever he's hiding them to various hotels or even out of state. We know there're a handful of high-rise hotels that have heliports and that W is one of them. Plus, he met Freddie there. So I'm thinking, Diamond has an apartment inside the W's residential towers and keeps the girls hidden somewhere close by. Maybe there or inside one of the other hotels or..." I paused. The idea was chilling. "Or possibly beneath them. In a type of underground prison no one knows about."

A while back I'd done a series of reports on old Los Angeles. Back in the time of Prohibition many of the old hotels had speakeasies, private clubs for a discrete clientele, hidden in their basements. A password was necessary to obtain entrance, and once inside, the world was wine, whiskey and wild women. And because much of what went on inside was illegal, many had escape passages that led to a tunnel beneath the street, allowing those visiting to come and go without being detected.

"Suppose he's got them hidden in some old speakeasy or an old basement cellar of some kind. It'd be the perfect hideaway, or maybe just a way of coming and going from inside a hotel without being detected. Some of those tunnels were pretty elaborate."

"Except the W's a new hotel," Sheri said. "It was built just a couple of years ago. If there were a hidden club or any kind of tunnel there before it's not there now."

"But the Roosevelt down the street's not new. It's nearly a

hundred years old." I needed to do a little research on the hotel's history, and I asked Sheri to call the W and see if she could find out if Diamond was a resident.

"But I'm afraid it's not going to be that easy," I said. I had already checked with their front desk and they had a strict policy about revealing the identities of their residents. "It's very high end. They pride themselves on their chichi clientele—superstars, athletes and the like who maintain a residence at the W when they're in town and value their privacy."

"Well then." Sheri poured herself another glass of wine. "You've asked the right person. That's easy. Celebs are my expertise. Hand me the phone."

Sheri's father, the source of her worry-free lifestyle, had been a major player in the movie business going back nearly forty years. She'd grown up around Hollywood stars and knew every paparazzi scheme anyone ever pulled.

"Trust me." Sheri stood up and tossed her scarf over her shoulder. "Places like the W have interior designers running in and out like ambulance chasers with chemise sheers thrown over their shoulders, like their clients were in need of life-saving surgery."

What? I was beginning to think Sheri had too much to drink.

"CC." I started to rise and she pointed at me to stay seated. "I've got this covered. Who's to say we're not there to measure Mr. Diamond's flat for something?"

I listened as I continued to Google the history of the old Roosevelt Hotel, while Sheri placed a call to the W. She explained she was a decorator, doing some work for Dr. Diamond. Her voice took on an immediate lilt, a very affected tone.

"Hi-i-i, this is Karen Fine with KFA Interiors. I'm sure you're familiar with our firm's work. We've done several penthouse suites in the tower, and I'm working on a project for Dr. Diamond; he's one of your tenants." Sheri paused, looked up at me with a hopeful gleam in her eye and motioned for a refill of her wine glass.

"Yes, yes, that's him. Tall. Good-looking. A little Clark Gable-ish." She rolled her eyes. "But with glasses and without the mustache, of course." She paused and listened to the person on the end of the line, then squelched a laugh as I refilled her glass. "Oh, please. I know. He's quite the cad, isn't he?"

Sheri had made a connection. Whoever it was on the other end of the line knew exactly who Dr. Diamond was, and judging from Sheri's response, had been quite charmed by his manner.

"Yes, well, you see, I've been doing some work for the doctor, and, silly me, I left my cellphone inside his apartment when we were measuring for his new étagère. I had my assistant call, but you know how difficult it is to get help today, and I'm afraid your front desk couldn't find Dr. Diamond's name among the list of residents. I simply must get my phone back as soon as possible. I'd call the doctor myself but his contact information's on my phone, and as you can tell, I'm lost without it. I thought perhaps you could help."

Again another pause, then laughter. "Ah, but of course, no wonder. It's listed under his business's name. Dream Maker, Inc. How could I forget that?"

Sheri looked at me. I gave her a thumbs-up. Dream Maker. Of course. The same name he had on the Rolls. Finally, I had a connection.

"Just one more thing." Sheri smiled at me like a Cheshire cat. "Any chance I might come by this afternoon with my assistant? I need to pick up my phone; as I said, I'm lost—totally lost—without it. I realize you could just give it to me, but I was hoping while I'm there, we might go in and measure the master bedroom, one more time. Dr. Diamond would be fine with it. He gave me a passkey, but, wouldn't you know, it's on the table with my phone." Sheri put her wine glass down on the bar and traced the stem with her index finger while she waited. Seconds seemed like hours, then, "Yes, yes, of course, that would be fine. Thank you."

I could tell from her enthusiastic tone she had done it. She picked her glass up and tipped it to mine. "They're expecting us within the hour. If we leave now, we could be back in time for the boys' game tonight."

I grabbed her wine glass. "I'll drive."

CHAPTER 26

My cell rang as Sheri and I drove into Hollywood. Caller ID identified the caller as Agent Delfino. I knew he'd be very careful with what he could share with me concerning the investigation, and I didn't want to share with him what Sheri and I were about to do. I had little doubt he'd try to talk me out of it. And besides, some of what I had in mind I knew wasn't legal. I let the call go to voicemail.

Our first stop was the old Roosevelt Hotel.

We left my embarrassingly dirty Jeep, the windows streaked with grime, with the valet and then entered the hotel through the grand lobby. The Roosevelt is an old, historic Spanish Colonial, dating back to the early part of the twentieth century. Overhead a gigantic wrought iron chandelier hung from intricately carved wooden beams two stories above. Beneath our feet marble floors were surrounded by a colonnade of gently domed columns that opened onto sweeping hallways leading to dining areas and smaller rooms for receptions. The hotel was the site of the first Academy Awards Show and rumored to still be haunted with the ghosts of Marilyn Monroe, Cliff Montgomery, Errol Flynn, and of course Clark Gable and Carol Lombard. The front desk kept a record of mysterious phone calls from nonexistent rooms and guest sightings—apparitions—of former residents. I grabbed Sheri's hand and we headed directly through the lobby to a bank of elevators, their doors polished like satin.

Inside the elevator, brass buttons indicated the number of floors. Twelve floors up, including the penthouse, and three floors down. The markings for those down indicated LL for lower lobby,

LB for the Library Bar, the current hot night spot, and a third button, marked LLB. I assumed LLB meant lower level basement, and I knew from my research that this had once been the location for the Roosevelt's original speakeasy. But on top of the button marked LLB, someone had placed a piece of silver duct tape with the words "temporarily closed" written on top of it.

I glanced at Sheri. *You ready for this?* She nodded and I pushed the taped button on the elevator wall and we descended to the lower level basement, somewhere beneath the hotel. With a slight shudder, the elevator stopped and the shiny brass doors opened on to a dimly lit construction site.

In front of us, a bare cement floor was dusty with the smell of concrete and damp earth. Yellow tape marked caution in big black letters blocked our entrance. Directly behind it was a workmen's bench. A hardhat and tool bag lay on top as though someone had just wandered away. It was difficult to see beyond the bench. A small shop light above the bench provided what little light there was, but not enough to indicate what lay beyond the yellow-taped area behind it. From what I could see, with the exception of a number of support girders and concrete pillars laced with overhead ducting and wires, the space appeared empty.

I lifted the tape, and using my cellphone to light the way, we ventured further into the darkness. I was determined to find some evidence of a tunnel. My idea that Diamond might be hiding the missing girls here was clearly out of the question.

Nobody could possibly be living here. It was cold and damp with a thin layer of concrete dust everywhere. I shined my light down on the floor. Evidence of footprints showed everywhere in the dust. But not the heavy patterned soles from that of a construction worker's boot, but rather the smooth sole of a man's dress shoe. A large sized print, and with it was that of a woman's high heel, a small, narrow toe-box with a tiny dot behind it. I'd seen imprints like this, dozens of times, just feet above my head on the Hollywood Walk of Fame. But these weren't the prints of famous stars. These were the footprints of a couple, rushing through the basement, coming from the direction of the W hotel, directly east of us.

I tried to flash a picture with my phone, but the light was too dark, the image blurry. It was no use. I moved farther into the darkness. A cold whisper of wind rushed past me. I looked back at Sheri. A tunnel entrance maybe? She shook her head and pointed at my feet. There lying on the ground was a red feather. Like something that might have been affixed to a ladies evening gown or maybe a costume. This had to be Diamond's tunnel. This was how he secreted his girls from one hotel to the other without being seen. Perhaps he came through here, dressed as Clark Gable, with one of the missing girls, and maybe the red feather was from a costume one of the girls had worn. Maybe they were all dressed as impersonators, Diamond as Gable and the girls as Carol Lombard, or Judy Garland, or maybe Marilyn Monroe. It would be the perfect disguise. As a builder and developer Diamond would know the service elevators, the hidden staircases the hotel no longer used, the back-end entrances to the clubs and restaurants. Nobody would stop a Clark Gable or Carol Lombard passing through a lobby. They would assume they were impersonators on the way to a gig and allow them to pass without incident. Or perhaps, if their presence surprised residents in the hallway, they'd think they'd seen ghosts. No wonder the hotel had a reputation for being haunted.

I grabbed Sheri's hand and we were about to venture farther into the hotel's cavernous underpinnings when I heard a voice.

"Someone back there?" From behind us a construction worker approached. He was dressed in yellow overalls, carrying a wrench in his hand and wearing a hard hat. "You ladies lost?"

I whispered to Sheri, "Play along." I put my arm around her shoulder.

"I'm so sorry. We must have gotten off on the wrong floor." I tried to sound a little tipsy. "We were looking for the club. The old speakeasy? I'm afraid my friend's had a little too much to drink and pressed the wrong button."

"Ah. You want the Library. Next floor up. You shouldn't be down here; let me call the elevator." He pushed the button, waited for the car to arrive, then watched as Sheri and I got in. "You two have a nice night now, and take it easy on the martinis." He tipped his hat and smiled as the door closed.

On the ride up I told Sheri I was convinced, whether we'd seen it or not, that there was a tunnel running beneath Hollywood Boulevard from the basement of the old Roosevelt to somewhere either beneath or close to the W Hotel. LA's new subway had a station right next door to the W. "It might even connect into that," I said. "But one thing I do know: that red feather we saw on the floor, it had to belong to one of the girls Diamond's hiding." I felt like I was getting closer.

From the Roosevelt, Sheri and I walked down the street to the W. It was a little less than a mile, and I reviewed my options, questioning the wisdom of exposing my best friend to any unknown dangers.

"You're certain you're up for this? I mean, you don't have to go along. I'm fine doing this alone. Nobody's going to know I'm not the decorator or your assistant for that matter, stopping by to get your key."

Sheri stopped mid-step and looked at me.

"You think for two seconds anyone at the W's going to believe *you're* a decorator and let you into Diamond's apartment? I don't think so. Look how you're dressed."

Sheri was right. I didn't look the part. I was dressed in my mom jeans, flats, and a standby blue blazer I had grabbed earlier that morning for my interview with Tanya. My sensible outfit made me looked like I'd been outfitted at Target, hardly designer-like. Sheri, on the other hand, never left the house if she wasn't dressed like she was prepared for a photo op—the result of growing up with a famous father—and today was no different. She had on a smart-looking little black felt fedora and shawl, and with her jeans tucked inside a pair of soft burgundy leather boots, she shrieked attitude.

"Besides, I know this world," she said.

We left my Jeep at the valet and headed into the residential tower. Fifteen stories of opulence with a separate grand entrance from the famed hotel of the same name. It was clearly in a world of its own.

Sheri led the way to reception.

From twenty feet away I watched as she plopped her large Hermes bag—a gift from her father—on the counter and introduced herself. I stood back in awe. All those acting classes she had taken as a child were paying off, big time.

"Hi, I'm Karen Fine, the interior designer. I spoke to one of your people a few minutes ago. They're expecting me. I need the key to the Dream Maker suite." She held out her hand, palm up. There was no question she expected the young, inexperienced girl behind the counter to hand her the key.

Which she did.

Sheri turned back to me and finger-waved like I was some lowly assistant, then smiled. "Follow me."

Like a scribe I followed Sheri with my head down. Not that anyone might recognize me, but I wasn't taking any chances. I shuffled, feet behind her, as she sidled up to the elevator, like some diva in her overly large dark glasses, and punched the button impatiently for the fifteenth floor.

Alone, inside the elevator, we high-fived each other and laughed nervously.

"You could still back out. I've no idea what we might be walking into." I was relatively certain, since it was almost mid-morning, that a busy man like Diamond wouldn't be there. *But what if he were?* I didn't want to subject my best friend to anything dangerous. "You could wait downstairs. I just need a minute to go in. Look around. See if I can find anything to connect Diamond to the missing girls."

"How about I stand guard and hold the elevator? In case we need to make a quick run for it."

"Not a bad idea." I took the key from Sheri's hand and headed down the hall towards the Dream Maker suite, my heart pounding.

Suite fifteen-oh-one. I knocked softly. Just to make sure nobody was home. Waited. Then inserted the key. I had never done anything like this before. I could feel beads of perspiration on my brow. My head felt warm, the brass knob, cool in my hand. Nerves, dammit. I took a deep breath and turned the key. I could feel the pins click into place. The lock released. Then, suddenly, without any effort, the door swung open.

"Hello, Carol."

I looked up to see Dr. Diamond standing in front of me.

CHAPTER 27

I was arrested.

Diamond had outsmarted me. Not only that, he must have had the police on speed dial, because I wasn't inside his apartment for more than ten minutes before they arrived.

Fortunately, I didn't have to spend the night in jail. I was allowed one call, but the arresting officer told me I probably didn't need it. My attorney and someone from the radio station would be along shortly.

I knew without a doubt that Sheri must have realized as soon as Diamond had pulled me into his apartment, something was wrong. She immediately alerted Tyler, and Tyler did exactly what I expected. He called Mr. King, the station's attorney.

As a courtesy to the radio station, I was told they were not taking me back to a holding cell. Whatever that was. I envisioned a jail cell full of transients and worse. I was thankful they decided instead to cuff me to a metal chair in the administrative area. I was allowed to sit there with the desk sergeant as my monitor until Mr. King and Tyler arrived. It was just now six p.m.

I could see King through the bulletproof glass doors as he came lumbering into the Hollywood Police Station. He was winded and mopping his brow, his tan trench coat wrinkled and stretched across his thick middle. He looked at me sternly as he approached the counter.

"I don't think I need to remind you, Carol, not to say anything."

I responded with my eyes glued to his, my lips tight.

"But you need to understand, I'm here officially for the radio station—not for you. Much as I like you, Carol, Dr. Diamond is a client of mine, and as such, I am here only because the attorney I'm going to assign this case to is unable to be here right at this moment, and I don't like the idea of your spending the night in jail."

For the next few minutes, there was a nervous exchange between King and the arresting officers. I got the feeling, based on the fact I'd been cooling my heels here for well over three hours, that they had very little patience for anyone stupid enough to break into the personal residence of one of their own. Particularly the residence of one of LAPD's police commissioners. I could see King was doing his best to keep them from transferring me down to the city jail. Then, just when it looked like he was about to convince them to release me into his custody, Tyler walked in.

Tyler was outraged. His presence was like adding fresh kindling to a smoldering fire. He was dressed in skinny jeans, high top sneakers and a yellow t-shirt that read, "Question Authority!" He started yelling that the police had arrested me on some trumped-up charge and demanding I be set free. For a moment I thought there might be a scuffle. Several officers approached Tyler, but King quickly got between them and ordered Tyler to take a seat.

Since I had no priors and there had been no physical damage to Diamond's apartment, I was hopeful King would be able to negotiate bail, and I'd be released on my own recognizance. I watched, my lips sealed, not saying a word, as King continued talking to the arresting officers, then returned to Tyler.

"You bring the check?"

Tyler nodded, mentioned the radio station had agreed to post bond, then reached into his backpack for a slim envelope.

"Five thousand dollars?" King held his hand out. "Certified?"

Tyler nodded again and handed King the check. Five thousand dollars seemed like a lot of money. I was relieved and breathed a sigh of relief.

A date for a preliminary hearing was set for Monday morning, three days from now, and I was unceremoniously allowed to stand and be un-cuffed. My wrists ached.

"In the meantime, Ms. Childs," the booking officer looked at me like he was about to stamp my deportation papers, "you need to go home. Go directly there, and do not pass go." He paused. *Was that a joke?* I looked at King. He stared stoically at me, his eyes steady. *Do not respond.* "And most importantly, do not attempt to make any contact with Dr. Diamond. You got that?"

"Yes, sir." I rubbed my wrists. If felt as though my hands had been in a vise.

"And you're not to do anything that would bring you anywhere within five hundred feet of Dr. Diamond or his residence. You got that?"

"Yes."

"Because, in addition to filing charges against you for breaking and entering, Dr. Diamond has also filed a restraining order."

What?

King grabbed me by the arm. "Not a word, Carol. Tyler will drive you home. We'll work out the details of your arraignment later. "

Tyler had the top down on his small MG as he drove me home. The wind in my hair made the silence between us almost bearable. Several times I tried to explain what it was I was doing, but each time he shifted the gears, causing the roar of the engine to drown out any attempt I made to speak. Finally, when we got to my building he jammed the car in park and turned to me.

"Just what the hell were you thinking, Carol? You could have gotten yourself killed. Maybe you really do need to be on leave."

I got out of the car and slammed the door. I didn't need to be lectured. "You know exactly what I was doing. You know what's at stake."

"You're crazy, Carol. You've got a kid...two kids. You need to be careful. We need to talk about this more—later." He gunned the engine and drove off, and I watched the red taillights as far as the corner, then went into the house.

I was too keyed up to sleep. I had no idea how I was going to explain to my son why I'd missed his game. Hopefully Sheri, my sister in crime, had covered for me, but it'd only be a temporary fix at best. How long could she keep this up, and at what cost? I made myself a large pot of coffee and checked my voicemail. I had a message from Sheri. Just as I had expected, she'd called Tyler, then driven my Jeep home and picked up the boys. *Don't worry. They're fine. I didn't tell Charlie about the arrest. He thinks you're working late. Talk to you in the morning.*

Maybe Tyler was right. Maybe I was crazy. But I couldn't, both as a reporter and a mother, let go of this case. I took my notebook from my bag and reviewed my notes. Monica Channing was dead and there were six missing girls whose disappearances may or may not be related at all. Captain Walker, at Judge Channing's press conference, had said LAPD believed there may be as many as a dozen young women who had been kidnapped, *perhaps* by the same person or persons who'd taken Monica. But beyond their initial report LAPD had issued nothing new concerning their disappearance. Due to the fact this was an open investigation, any information released prematurely could interfere with the success of the operation. They needed to play it safe, but I didn't. There wasn't time. I couldn't wait on LAPD, or until I could talk to the FBI and tell them what I knew about Diamond. The story sounded preposterous, parts of it even ghoulish. By the time they checked it out, Gabi might be dead. Her life, and those of the other girls— Jessie Martin, Marilyn Ann Billings, April Hansen, Leticia Johnson and Brandy White—hung in the balance. I spent the night weighing my options, analyzing the facts. I was in the kitchen, making another pot of coffee, when the newspaper arrived at five a.m.

I stared at the headline: "Radio Reporter Arrested for Breaking and Entering." I was furious. Diamond hadn't just outsmarted me; he was using the media to discredit me, to humiliate me. It was right there on the front page of the *LA Times*. The article read: "Los Angeles real estate developer Dr. Malcolm Diamond believes KCHC radio reporter Carol Childs to be stalking him." It went on to question my mental and physical stability, reporting that the radio station had sent me home to recover from extreme exhaustion brought on by work-related stress.

The phone rang before I finished the story.

"You're home." It was Sheri.

"I am." I sighed heavily, thankful to hear her voice. "It was awful, but King thinks we'll be able to kick the breaking and entering charge. Says it's totally preposterous. Particularly since Diamond pulled me into his apartment after I *knocked* on the door."

"*Knocked* on the door?" Sheri laughed. "So that's what we're going with?"

"Why not? King seems to like it. Plus he says Diamond knew somebody was trying to get into his apartment *before* I got there. He told the cops someone from the hotel had called him saying his decorator wanted to come by to retrieve her phone, that she'd left it there while taking some measurements, and that he we suspicious it was a prank."

"Oh, boy. So we were busted before we even got there." Sheri sighed.

"Yeah, but that's not the worst of it," I said.

"There's more?"

"Diamond filed a restraining order against me. I'm not to come within five hundred feet of him." I poured myself another cup of coffee.

"So how are you doing?"

"Frustrated. You see this morning's paper?"

"I threw it in the trash. I didn't want to the boys to see it. But we can get to that later. Were you able to get anything when you were inside the apartment?"

I explained that I was more convinced than ever that Diamond was involved. "He's nothing like the man we see, from time to time, on the news—who looks a little like Clark Gable—and who we hear talking about all the new developments he's involved with in Hollywood. He's like an optical illusion. The man in public is nice looking, smooth talking, but the man in Diamond's apartment, he was odd, scary odd. It was like I was seeing someone totally different. The expression on his face was gaunt and tough. And his eyes, they were dark and distant. Like there's evil behind them. He's creepy. Like a Jekyll and Hyde."

"Did he try to hurt you?"

"No, but he stood right in front of me, so close I couldn't move, and he's too big for me to have tried to escape. I was trapped with the wall behind me."

"Did he say anything?"

"It was gross. He put his hand on my cheek and told me I was much prettier than I sounded on the air. And then he took a step back and looked at me and said I must have been a young mother. That I probably wasn't much older than Cate is now when she was born. I wanted to spit at him. I told him he had no right to talk about my daughter—that I knew he had something to do with her being drugged that night on the pub crawl—and he smiled this really weird, awful smile with those big teeth of his and said he could do anything he wanted. He could find Cate Childs anytime, anywhere."

"Cate Childs? He said her name just like that?"

"Exactly."

Sheri paused. "Then he doesn't know."

"And he's not going to." I said. Few people knew Childs was my maiden name, and that both Cate and Charlie went by their father's last name. And for right now, I planned to keep it way. I wasn't about to share it with anyone.

"What did you do?"

"What could I do? I was trapped, and by then he'd called the cops and they were on their way. But before they got there, I had a chance to observe the front rooms. They were neat. I don't think he's living there. I don't think anyone is. But it looked like someone was at the bar in the living room having a drink, maybe the night before. There was a lipstick-stained wineglass, along with two other empty glasses on the bar, and an ashtray with a couple of cigarette butts in it. Diamond smokes. I think he's funneling girls through there for *meetings*. You can define that anyway you like."

"Okay, let's say you're right and he is using his apartment to set up rendezvous, introducing his clientele to his girls. Just how's he getting them in and out without anyone noticing? Particularly now that the police know the names and identities of some of the girls missing?"

"I think he's using the helipad on top of the building, and he's probably got the girls so disguised nobody would know who they were if they did see them. But the fact that he has an apartment inside the W in Hollywood, and that it's close to the nightclubs, is really no big deal. It's leased to the business, and Diamond Developments, for all practical purposes, is legit. He probably owns the building. He has every right to be using the helipad and coming and going as he pleases. And I can't get him arrested just because I suspect he's bringing women to his apartment. Unless I can prove Diamond has a connection to the missing girls, I'm out of luck. Until then, I don't have any proof."

"Not yet, you don't."

I stood up and was about to get myself a fresh cup of coffee when I paused and looked back down at the paper. I hadn't even glanced at the sports section. The results of the boys' game would be inside. "How was the game?"

"We lost. Twenty-eight to seven."

I groaned. This wasn't going to be a good day. Charlie had been certain the Vikings would crush the visiting team, and I couldn't even remember who it was. My mind wouldn't let go of Diamond. I couldn't get the vision of him out my head, standing in front of me with the large, floor-to-ceiling plate glass window and a view of the Hollywood sign in the background. The man was a real life Jekyll and Hyde, and I felt certain I was the only one who really knew it.

"Don't worry. It's going to be a marathon college football viewing day anyway; USC's playing Arizona at ten and UCLA's playing Oregon at four. I've got the fridge stocked with colas and we've got plenty of snacks and burgers for the grill. Why don't you plan on coming for dinner?"

I agreed and told Sheri I'd be by around four. I wanted to take a nap and read through my notes again.

"Just promise me you're not planning on pursuing Diamond."

"Not today, but I am planning on going to the station's promotion tonight. Cupid's going to need me." I didn't have time to explain. My cellphone was ringing. I told her I'd be by around four and hung up.

Caller ID indicated it was Eric. *Back already?*

I took a deep, cleansing breath and answered. Eric spoke before I could say hello.

"Hey, I understand congratulations are in order. You're officially on LAPD's watch list."

I laughed. "Guilty as charged."

"You okay?"

"I take it Agent Delfino told you about my arrest? Either that, or, you're home, reading the paper."

"Not home, not yet. But you're right, Mark called and told me. I'd tell you to back off, take it easy and let the detectives do their work, but I know better."

"You don't need to worry. The fact that Diamond made my snooping around public makes me think he's not going to do anything more than try to discredit me. And, with the radio station behind me, he'd have more trouble than he'd like if I suddenly disappeared. Besides," I joked, "I'm hardly his type. He's into young girls. Not finely aged, full-bodied, mature women."

Eric laughed. Exactly the reaction I wanted. In the background I could hear the sound of the wind whipping through the *Sea Mistress's* sails. I had a vision of Eric standing behind her wheel, tall, tan and warmed by the sun. It calmed me. "Sounds like a good bottle of wine. And, just so you know, I happen to be particularly fond of this particular, finely aged, full-bodied version. So take care of yourself. Don't take any unnecessary chances. We're making good time. I'll be home soon. Miss you."

CHAPTER 28

I let myself in Sheri's back door. It was unlocked, and I followed the sounds of her voice and those of the boys to the family room. I found them in the middle of a popcorn bash. Charlie and Clint were each sitting in one of Sheri's leather recliners with bowls of popcorn on their laps. In front of them, to the sides of them, and on the floor, everywhere, were popped kernels that looked as though they'd been tossed, like shrapnel at the TV and at each other. Sheri, standing between the two, had a mouthful of popcorn, and laughed when she saw me, as though she'd just been busted by the junk-food patrol.

"You're here." Sheri waved with a handful of popped kernels and then tossed them in the direction of the boys.

"Hey, Mom." Charlie glanced momentarily in my direction, dodged the incoming kernels and then looked back to the TV.

SC scored a field goal, and all eyes were immediately diverted to the excitement of the impending victory. Any chance I had of making apologies for missing last night's game were suddenly lost.

"So much for being missed," I said. I nodded to Sheri and grabbed a cola off the counter. I was about to sit down on the couch next to the boys when Sheri indicated she wanted me to follow her. With a drink in her hand, she led the way down the hall towards the back of the house and the master suite.

"You still planning on going to KCHC's Hollywood promotion tonight?"

"Yes, why?"

"Charlie doesn't know about what happened last night. I spoke with his teacher and asked her not to mention anything, and you know the boys, they don't read the paper—unless it's the sports section—so you don't have to worry. I think it's better that way. And besides, with all the wall-to-wall football going on this weekend, I don't think Charlie will miss you not being here. I told him you were working and he could stay with us this weekend. He's fine with it, and tomorrow it's the Jets and Chargers game, so go and do what you need to do. Just don't get yourself arrested, okay?"

"Believe me, it's not my intention."

"Good, because I think you need a disguise if you plan on going tonight. And I have a closet full of possibilities."

Sheri's master bedroom included a room-sized walk-in closet that would rival the wardrobe department of any Hollywood back lot. Many of the items she hoarded included pieces from shows her father had produced, plus an assortment of her own she'd never worn. Things she'd bought and held onto in hopes of one day returning to her once, impossible-to-maintain, size zero.

"Think of it as camouflage," she said. "A little guarantee that if the station sets up their promotional tent anywhere on Hollywood Boulevard, Diamond won't spot you and accuse you of stalking him, and you won't end up back in jail."

"Or front page news for tomorrow's paper," I said. "So, what magic have you got in mind?"

"This." Sheri pulled a purple pantsuit, a la Hillary Clinton style, off one of the racks that lined the mirrored walls. "Go on. Try it on. Let's see if it works."

While I dressed, Sheri slid a long wooden stepladder along the floor-to-ceiling shelves to where she had hatboxes, dozens of them, stacked above the racks. She climbed up, removed a box marked *Brunette* from a top shelf, and handed it to me.

"And this too." Inside was an assortment of wigs, all lengths and styles. "Believe me, nobody will recognize you with dark hair."

I tried on a short pageboy, turned around and looked into a full-length mirror and scarcely recognized myself. Staring back at me was a face I didn't know.

"Perfect," Sheri said. "And, if I might, a little, ah, pièce de résistance." From behind her back Sheri took a red hat and placed it on my head, then stood back and, like the famous costume designer Edith Head, admired her work. "You look fabulous, darling, simply fabulous."

"Ha! Doesn't do a thing for me." I stared into the mirror. The word frumpy came to mind.

"Here, try these. They're your size." Sheri handed me a pair of red heels. Ironically, despite her being barely five-two and me nearly seven inches taller, we were, albeit our different proportions, the same exact size, shoes and all.

I wiggled into the shoes and took another look. "Not bad. The entire look is more Chanel than what I saw Bessie Bixby wearing the other day. But...good enough." I smoothed the pants with my hands, did a cursory rearview look in the mirror and figured nobody would recognize me.

"Yeah, well let's hope 'good enough' keeps anyone from recognizing you. It just might save your life if Diamond's there," Sheri said.

I knew she was right about that. I couldn't risk running into Diamond. Not again. Not after the restraining order. I looked back in the mirror and adjusted the hat.

"Look out, Dr. Diamond. Two can play at this game. You want to be Clark Gable. I can be a red-hatted Lois Lane."

Sheri gave me one last look. "Wait a minute, before you leave, take this."

From one of the high top dresser drawers, Sheri took out a watch and put it on my wrist.

"What's this?" I asked. On my wrist she had placed a red, digitalized plastic sports watch.

"It's mine. I think it might come in handy. I bought it in a weak moment when I actually thought I might enjoy working out. It has a GPS device built into it. Do me a favor and wear it. It'll send a digital readout of your heart rate, plus your location, back to my computer. At least, if something happens, I'll know where you are, and if you're still breathing."

"Oh, thanks for the vote of confidence." I took the watch and fastened it to my wrist, assuring her that she had absolutely nothing to worry about. I'd learned my lesson. "Believe me," I said, "I'm not about to do anything foolish. Tomorrow night, it's my place for dinner. You can count on it. No excuses. I promise."

It was almost nine-thirty by the time I parked my car behind the Pantages Theater and hurried down the street toward the corner of Hollywood and Vine. My feet were screaming at me. Sheri's selection of footwear, while the right size and appropriate-looking, was anything but functional. Pointy shoes have no place at a stakeout. I stopped, adjusted one shoe, and with the other in my hand, hopscotched over Neil Patrick Harris's star on the Walk of Fame, then continued down the boulevard, one shoe on, one shoe off. I was running late. There was a cool snap in the air, a sense of excitement.

Any other time I might have actually enjoyed it. The street was crowded with people, the sound of music vibrating from within the clubs and the smell of hotdogs wrapped in bacon with grilled onions from street vendors. But tonight I knew there was danger in the air. Like at the beach when there's a red flag warning for high surf or a shark sighting. Somewhere out there in the darkness there was a great white, swimming silently just off the shore, waiting to grab some innocent beachgoer and disappear into the depths.

KCHC's tent was set up on the north side of Hollywood Boulevard in front of a nightclub called Déjà Vu Showgirls. Outside the club, a neon sign advertised it as a hot spot for nearly nude, barely-clad dancing young divas. It was situated directly across the street from the W with a perfect view of the hotel's residential tower and farther down the street, Hemingway's, the nightclub where Cate had nearly disappeared. And where I also suspected Diamond was setting up his meetings between his girls and his heat-seeking clientele.

I reached the tent, a four-poster with a blue-canopied awning sporting KCHC's call letters on top. In the dark of night, the station's logo was almost impossible to see, but beneath it, illuminated by high intensity lanterns, I could see a flurry of activity and Cupid. He was sitting in the center of the tent behind a broadcast table, surrounded by a swarm of ladies wearing their red hats. A group of them were grabbing flyers off the table and pressing them into the hands of anyone who passed by.

In my purple pantsuit and red hat I blended in flawlessly. None of the ladies looked twice at me. I was one of them, a nameless volunteer, from one of the countless groups, responding to Bessie's urgent request for help. I took one of the flyers off the table and stared at it. *Help Us Find Hollywood's Missing Girls.* Beneath the headline were pictures of Leticia and Brandy. Even in the dim light, their smiling faces beamed out from their black and white photos. Beneath their photos were smaller pictures of the other missing girls: Jessie Martin, Marilyn Ann Billings, April Hansen and Gabi Garrison. A brief description and quotes from several of my news reports were included. "Police believe a major sex trafficking ring operating in Hollywood is responsible for the kidnapping and disappearance of these girls, and possibly more." At the bottom, a warning in bold letters advised women to be on the lookout for predators and asked for anyone with information on the whereabouts of the girls to call LAPD's missing persons unit.

Outside the tent on the sidewalk, I noticed Detective Browne with Bessie Bixby. The two were talking to a group of leggy young coeds in spiked heels and short dresses. I watched as they listened wide-eyed to Detective Browne, then giggled and shook their heads. Innocents, I thought. A herd of forever young, invincible twenty-somethings. I hoped they were right.

I slipped beneath the awning of the tent, hoping not to be seen, then leaned over and bumped shoulders with Cupid. "May I have your autograph?"

Without looking up, he reached for a black and white glossy of himself, started to sign and then paused. "Name?"

"Carol Childs," I whispered in his ear. Now he did look up. His eyes blurred with confusion as he studied the dark wig beneath my red hat, then putting two and two together, smiled. Putting my index finger to my lips, I slowly shook my head. "Don't say anything."

I pulled up a chair and watched as KCHC's promotion staff bumped shoulders with the red hatted ladies and their flyers, while they handed out keychains, t-shirts and autographed copies of Cupid's photo. It was like a fish feeding frenzy with people grabbing for freebies.

"Have you been able to get any time on the air?"

"Very little." Cupid had to yell above the street noise. "Tyler's got Kari Rhodes on and she's doing her thing, going on about Brad Pitt and Angelina's wedding like she was a guest or something. It's a big deal, and I can't get a word in."

It was exactly what Tyler wanted. Just enough to make it look like the station was following up on its story about Hollywood's Missing Girls, but not so much that it became the main focus of the broadcast. To anyone listening, including Diamond, it would sound like the station had moved on to other news.

Between the background din of Kari's broadcast, the activity on the street with KCHC's promotional staff, the red hatted ladies, the street performers, tourists and those looking to go clubbing, the area in front of Déjà Vu Showgirls was a circus atmosphere. Everywhere there was activity, and not just on the sidewalk, but on the boulevard as well. The street was jammed with everything from bicycles weaving in and out between high-end European imports, to double decker tour buses. We were absolutely blocked in. In front of us it was impossible to see anything but the upper floors of the buildings above us and across the street.

Then suddenly, *crash!* There were horns and the screech of brakes. A jaywalker had jumped in front of a tour bus, and a long white stretch limo slammed into the back of it. The jaywalker, oblivious to the accident, scurried away, unscathed and unconcerned. But the wreckage, one limo fender locked beneath that of the bus, blocked cars east and west, providing a momentary break in the traffic. The end result was a perfectly unobstructed view, directly in front of me, of the buildings across the street. It was as clear and visible as a big screen at an IMAX theater on a Saturday night.

A group of gathering rubberneckers across the street stood two and three deep straining to see who it was in the long white limo that had been hit. Several people were starting to get out of the car, and from across the street, folks were pointing, thinking they recognized someone.

I didn't take my eyes off the crowd. Whoever was down the street wasn't nearly as interesting to me as who I saw directly in front of me. In the center of the group, across the street, was a man. He was taller, by a good four or five inches, than the tallest in the crowd and he was staring directly back at me. His silver hair was slicked back against his head, the collar of his coat jacket turned up slightly, accentuating his broad shoulders, a thin mustache, a rakish smile. I punched Cupid.

"Tell me that's not Diamond."

Cupid studied the man across the street. He'd only seen pictures. Saturday morning after my arrest I'd emailed photos to him, side-by-side comparisons of Dr. Diamond and old publicity shots of Clark Gable. I wanted him to see the similarity.

The crowd started to disperse, the fender-bender down the street no longer an issue. But Gable, or Diamond, stayed and stared back at me. Despite my masquerade—my brown hair and red hat—I could feel his eyes penetrate my own. He knew exactly who I was. I could feel it in my bones. Diamond knew I was there.

Then as though he'd been cued by some offstage director, he nodded to us both, turned and walked back towards the W.

"If that's not Diamond," Cupid said, "then the ghost of Clark Gable really does haunt the boulevard."

CHAPTER 29

KCHC's Hollywood promotion didn't end until well after midnight and I was too keyed up with the sighting of Diamond to even think about going home. Cupid suggested we grab a bite to eat at Musso and Frank's, a classic old Hollywood eatery famous as much for their star sightings as their menu. He teased, as we walked down the boulevard, that with a little luck, Mr. Gable might even join us. That didn't do much to calm my nerves, but the fact that the place probably hadn't changed much in the almost one hundred years it'd been in Los Angeles, had a nice calming effect. Musso's is a real old-fashioned New York style steak house with white tablecloths, red leather booths and waiters in tuxes. Cupid ordered their Saturday night classic, braised short ribs with mixed vegetables. I ordered an omelet.

"What you need to find, Carol, is a reason why Diamond would get involved in sex trafficking in the first place. Find that and people may start to see what you see."

"How about money...or maybe the lack of it?"

"The man owns buildings all over LA. He gives away millions to charity. He's a billionaire. I don't think he's got financial problems."

"What if I told you I wasn't so sure about that? That I think the sex trade was maybe subsidizing his developments?"

"I'm listening." Cupid picked up his fork and started in on the braised short ribs.

I explained I'd done a little online research that afternoon. After Tanya Day had shared with me that Diamond's gift to Tanya's rescue center was really more of a down payment, I pulled up a bunch of old newspaper ads, a dozen in all, announcing his generous donations to various charities.

Tanya was suspicious he had made deposits into various charitable accounts in exchange for publicity, and I wanted to track his record. What I found was that in the last year alone, Diamond had given away nearly a million dollars. That in itself wasn't out of line for someone like Diamond, whose net worth according to *Forbes* was well over two billion dollars. But if Diamond had recently suffered a financial loss due to a court case he had before Judge Channing, and he was angry enough to kill the judge's daughter over the ruling, he might not be as well-heeled as he liked to project. Plus the last couple years had been brutal in real estate.

The idea intrigued me. The market was just now coming out of its huge slump. The Great Recession had resulted in not only the loss of property for many, but jobs as well, and there was hardly anyone in California that hadn't been affected. My guess was Diamond had been hurt financially and had been looking around for a way to recoup his income, and the sex trade, with its multi-billion dollar tax-free income opportunity, was ideal.

"All this is good, Carol, but uncovering a trail like that takes time. Diamond's probably got that money laundered six ways to Sunday, and until you tie the money to the girls and to Diamond, you don't have a smoking gun." He cut off another piece of meat and stuffed it in his mouth.

"And if I can't do that?"

He put his knife and fork down.

"I don't want to scare you, but after what I saw tonight, if you don't strike first, he just might."

Cupid's comment wasn't the best note to end the night on, and as a result, I decided I'd take a shortcut home, up Laurel Canyon to the valley, rather than the freeway. Even at this hour an accident on the 101 could result in a backup and a lot of rubbernecking, and I wanted to be home. There was nothing more I could do tonight. I wanted to be away from the craziness of the boulevard, the nightclubs, the music, the screaming fans yelling at stars as they got in and out of their limos.

I wanted to go home, back to the quiet sanity of my own life and condo. I was maybe halfway up the narrow canyon when I noticed a set of headlights in my rearview mirror. At night the canyon was dark and the road very twisted, steep against the hillside. At first I thought I might be imagining something. Another lone car on the road headed home, not a big deal. But within minutes of my spotting it, the gap started to close between us. I concentrated on the approaching headlights, my eyes riveted to my rearview mirror.

They were low, square and with their bright-white, halogen glow, unmistakably that of a Rolls Royce. I sped up. I tried to increase the distance between myself and the black Phantom Rolls behind me. Whoever it was, they stayed on my tail, just feet from my bumper.

My heart started to race.

There was nothing I could do. I was alone, it was dark and I couldn't think of anyone I could call. The police couldn't get here in time, and even if I called them what would I say? How could I explain seeing Diamond when I had a restraining order preventing me doing just that?

At the top of Laurel Canyon there's a stoplight at Mulholland. The light turned red and I pulled a hard right onto the shoulder of the road and paused momentarily. I don't know what possessed me to wait, but I did.

My hands gripping the steering wheel, my foot ready to hit the gas. The black Rolls pulled slowly up beside me. I hit the automatic lock on my door and watched as the darkened window of the car next to me slid slowly down.

Inside sat Diamond, staring straight ahead. Like he didn't even know I was there. I wanted to yell out, but before I could say anything the light turned green and the black Rolls with its personalized plates—DRM MKR—rolled slowly ahead of me and disappeared into the valley below.

* * *

Sunday morning felt like a hangover. Like the low hanging fog I could see from my kitchen window, cloudy and depressing. I had risen early to get the newspaper. Hopeful I might find something in the paper about the Red Hatted Ladies' vigil and their march down Hollywood Boulevard in their effort to bring awareness to Hollywood's Missing Girls. If nothing else, I thought it might make for a good photo op: the ladies in their sensible shoes, walking the boulevard, amidst all the glitz and glamor of the short-skirted younger set.

But there was nothing.

Gabi's trail was beyond cold, and my vision of Diamond, appearing as Clark Gable and staring at me from across Hollywood Boulevard and again at the top of Mulholland, sitting in his car, was there every time I closed my eyes. I felt as though I couldn't clear my head any more than I could clear the fog from the San Fernando Valley. I was stuck, and I wasn't about to sit at home.

Trouble was, I didn't know what I was supposed to do. Sometimes when I was stumped—like I was now—doing mindless busy work helped to clear my head.

I called Tyler and told him I needed to get out of the house. I was desperate, so much so that I volunteered to clean out the station's storage closet, a kind of Fibber McGee's catch-all for old radio paraphernalia. Inside was everything from stacks of old vinyl albums to things the promotional staff no longer used. He told me he'd alert the guard at the front gate that I was there to pick up some boxes, but that I should come through station's rear emergency exit. He'd leave the door unlocked. Even though it was Sunday, and most of the staff was gone for the weekend, he wanted to reduce the chances of anyone seeing me, thinking I might be back to work. We needed to stick to our story.

I agreed and pulled on a pair of skinny, white jeans and heels— not exactly a work duty outfit—but the closet was more messy than dirty, and the heels were my standbys: comfortable and confidence building. Something I felt I needed right now. I topped it off with old KCHC polo shirt that had a station ID on the breast pocket: a microphone surrounded by the words, "Chick Radio–Something to Cluck About," and headed out the door.

The station was quiet when I arrived, the hallway like a vacated bowling alley after hours, dim and hollow. I passed the production studio, expecting it to be empty, and glanced at my reflection in the window and stopped. I felt as though I'd just hit a brick wall. There, on the other side of the glass, standing in front of a microphone, was Tony Domingo.

"Tony!" I charged into the studio. Both Tony and Ted, the production assistant, looked up at me as though the Wicked Witch of the West had just entered the room. I must have looked a fright. "What are you doing here?"

Tony looked at me, the deep tan lines around his mouth vanished instantly into a broad, confident smile. He stood up and, pushing the microphone away, approached me.

"Carol." As he held his hand out, a thick gold bracelet on his wrist, matching a chain on his neck, caught my eye. "I didn't expect to see you."

"See me? What are you *talking* about?" I backed away. Tony was a big man, squarely built, not tall but broad with an extra thirty pounds around the middle. He looked tanned and relaxed. I lowered my voice and stepped forward, my back to Ted. I wanted to keep my conversation with Tony private. "You're supposed to be missing," I whispered.

Tony laughed, put his hands on my shoulders and gently shook me. Then raising his voice just enough so that Ted could hear, said, "Oh, Carol, I've missed you. I'm sorry to hear you've had a difficult time lately. But, really, I don't know what you're talking about. Missing? Do I look like I've been missing?" He laughed again and stepped back, arms wide, and gestured to his well-fed belly. "I've spent the last several days on a friend's boat, fishing, while I had my offices moved. I really don't know what you're talking about."

"Oh, yes, you do know what I'm talking about. You know very well what I'm talking about, and even better, you know why." I blurted it out, like bullets from a machine gun.

I looked at Ted. I wanted to yell at him, too—to tell him I knew what he was thinking, that everything he had read or heard about me wasn't true. But his eyes were focused on the controls in front of him. He was obviously avoiding eye contact with me.

His fingers traced the knobs of the soundboard. I had no doubt that he'd read Tyler's memo, announcing to the staff I was taking a temporary leave of absence due to work related stress, or that he'd read the *LA Times* article. It hadn't done me any favors. Then there was the fact that I had reported Tony missing. Nobody else had reported that, just me. There was nothing in the paper about his disappearance. I had reported it to Detective Browne and nothing had come of it. And now, here I was, charging into the studio like a crazy person. I was sure Ted thought I really was nuts.

I turned back to Tony.

"You called me. You were worried about Gabi. You set her boyfriend Miles up to work with Dr. Diamond. You knew something had happened to Gabi and wanted to talk. You know where she is. I know you do."

Tony looked over at Ted and shrugged like he had no idea what I was talking about and then back at me with a look of pity in his eyes.

"Gabi? Carol, Gabi Garrison hasn't called on me in over a year. I can't imagine why you think I'd call you about her. I called Ted this morning because I wanted to start working on one of my new commercials. You know, just like you used to do for me, where I'd sing a few bars. I've got a new one. *My Way*. Would you like to hear it?"

I turned back to Ted. "Did you call Tyler? Does he know Tony's here?"

He didn't answer.

It didn't surprise me Tyler didn't know. The production facilities weren't next to the newsroom, and the production guys were always doing odd jobs on the side. Tyler probably had no idea.

Tony tried to put his hand on my shoulder. I backed away.

"Carol, why would Ted call Tyler? Ted always cuts my spots. He doesn't need Tyler's permission. I pay him on the side. That's why I'm here on a Sunday."

I backed out of the studio. Ted looked relieved to have me retreat. I left the station the exact way I'd come in, through the emergency exit door. I was reeling at the shock of seeing Tony in the studio and wanted to get away. I needed to clear my head.

I got in the car and I started to drive. I didn't care where I went, I just needed to think. I headed south down La Cienega Boulevard as though on autopilot, then right on Pico and west to the ocean. I wanted to feel the fresh sea air on my face and clear my head of the shock of seeing Tony alive. I knew Diamond was behind Tony's sudden reappearance. It was perfect. Everything Diamond was doing made me look like I was losing my grip. I was playing right into his hands, no matter what I did.

I wondered what Tyler would think when he realized Tony was alive and in the studio, right under our noses. I knew he'd be shocked. But what if that shock led him to question whether I'd really been correct about Tony's abduction? I needed Tyler to believe me, but now? What if he started to think I really was messed up? That maybe Monica's murder, and my daughter's attempted kidnapping, had sent me over the edge? We had barely spoken since my arrest. Maybe the reason he wanted me to come in the back door today was because he really had lost faith in me.

Dammit, Diamond! I didn't like the questions rattling around in my mind. I was beginning to doubt myself.

The only thing I knew for certain was that Diamond had gotten to Tony. That after Gabi had disappeared, Tony had reached out to me, but Diamond had gotten to him first. He had to have known Tony was getting nervous, and he set him straight before I even had a chance to see him. And now that I'd been arrested, Diamond was getting exactly the story he wanted.

Crazy reporter stalking real estate developer, making up

stories about sex trafficking and people disappearing. What better way to discredit me than to have Tony suddenly reappear? Diamond was probably even paying for the studio time so that Tony could cut a new commercial. And tomorrow, I wouldn't be at all surprised if there were even an ad in the business section of the *LA Times* announcing the reopening of Financial Futures.

The blows just kept coming.

CHAPTER 30

I could hear Tony's soft tenor voice, crooning in my head, as I drove west with the rising sun behind me down Pico Boulevard. How appropriate. *My Way.* I knew exactly how Tony's new commercial spot would sound. I used to write all his ad copy. In fact, I was the one who got him started in radio. Up until then, he'd been plugging away with newsprint with bored-looking black and white ads that blended into every other ad in the paper. In radio, the best advertisers all have something special, some gimmick or a key phrase, that separates them from the rest of the noise on the air. I call it an earmark. And when I discovered Tony, I thought I found just the thing that could make him a star.

I had been cold-calling financial clients when I walked into his office and saw a keyboard in the corner. On a lark, I asked if he could sing. I must have literally struck a chord, because for the next hour Tony sang, or perhaps, a more adequate description would be, he serenaded me.

Tony had a voice like Sinatra and an ego to go with it. But unfortunately, there wasn't room on the music charts for another Sinatra sound-alike, and the closest he was going to get to being on the radio was crooning his way into his clients' hearts. So I suggested he sing. I wrote out a few commercials and very quickly, not only did his business take off, but so did my account billing. Tony became one of my biggest accounts, mostly because he loved to hear himself on the radio and bought lots of spots, and partly because nobody else was selling financial packages and singing about it. The script always went the same way. He'd open with a few lines from a favorite song, then stop and say something like, "Financial debt causing you to lose sleep? Credit cards keeping you from living the life you could be living? Call me, Tony Domingo at Financial Futures and let us help." Then he'd end with a few more bars from the song and a voiceover would air the phone number.

I glanced at the watch Sheri had given me. It wasn't yet ten o'clock. I had to do something. I couldn't just go to the beach, wander aimlessly up and down the boardwalk, and hope I'd come up with an idea. Monica was dead. Gabi still missing, and, while I didn't know where they were, I knew Leticia and Brandy and the other missing girls were being held by Diamond somewhere. And now that Tony had reappeared, it was as though Diamond was taunting me. I couldn't help but feel that time was running out. Something had to happen.

Cupid was right. What I needed was a smoking gun, something that would tie Diamond and his Clark Gable persona directly to Monica. And it had to be indisputable. I figured since the cops and the FBI had confiscated Monica's computer, any email exchanges she had with her abductor would have revealed a name or at least an identity. Since Diamond's name hadn't come up, it was likely he was using an alias, and any IP address or reference back to one of his computers clearly had not revealed his name. In fact, it could well be that I was the only person who did know that Dr. Diamond and the Clark Gable lookalike were one and the same.

Except for Holly.

Holly had been upset with me the night of the pub crawl. Initially, I thought it was because I had brought Cate with me. But maybe it was the fact that I had seen Diamond getting into the black Rolls Royce outside of her cottage that upset her.

She must have told him I was the reporter who had covered the discovery of Monica's body. And when Holly went back inside the cottage to get a pink scrunchie for Cate, she must have added that my underage daughter was with me. But Diamond probably wasn't worried I would know who he was. Why would he be? He could have been any of Holly's impersonators. The cottage was where they came to get their checks and maybe their assignments. His big mistake was getting into that black Rolls Royce in front of me. If he hadn't done that I might never have put Diamond together with his Clark Gable lookalike. And neither would anyone else.

With its blackened windows, he could drive anywhere—day or night—and, unless he lowered the window like he had with me up on Mulholland, the night of the pub crawl nobody would know who was in the car. Once inside, all he'd have to do to switch identities would be to take off his glasses and don Gable's trademark mustache. He had the upper hand.

He had me right where he wanted, a reporter with a young, beautiful daughter whose safety he could hold over my head. He must have started plotting that very night. If I got too close to him, he could scare me, threaten me, or he could discredit me. The cards were all in his favor. No wonder Holly had been so evasive when I asked who he was.

And why she wasn't returning any of my calls.

I started to pull a U-turn in the middle of Pico Boulevard. I wanted to head back to Holly's to confront her. To let her know I knew exactly who Diamond was and that I knew she knew, too. I was midway into the turn when my phone rang.

"Carol, it's Bethany Richards, Monica's friend. Can you talk?" Bethany's voice sounded thin and strained. "I probably should have called yesterday, when I saw the article in the *LA Times* about your arrest. I think I know who Monica was meeting."

I pulled over to the side of the street and parked in front of Bibi's Bakery, a favorite of mine. Any other time, I might have dashed inside and picked up a dozen sugar cookies and brought them home for dinner. Instead, I took my cell off speaker and held it tight to my ear. I didn't want to miss anything she might say. "Talk to me, Bethany. I need to know exactly what you know."

"Monica sent the man she was seeing an audio file. I'd forgotten all about it. It was a copy of Judy Garland singing *You Made Me Love You.*"

"You mean, *Dear Mr. Gable?*" My voice must have gone up an octave. I remembered the movie. It was a favorite of my mother's. We used to watch it together when I was a little girl. In it, Judy Garland, who was barely sixteen, was writing a fan letter to Clark Gable. It had to be a clue. "You're sure?"

"Yes. She was always looking for ways to surprise him. When I read the article in the paper, about you and the arrest, it got me thinking about the interview you did on air with that Freddie guy. He described Monica and this man she was with as looking like an old Hollywood star with a thin mustache. And then I remembered the tape and I thought, what if it's Clark Gable? And this man you're accused of stalking...from the picture in the paper, he kind of looks like Clark Gable, but with glasses. What if it's him?"

I wanted her to be right, but without something concrete, I had nothing.

"The police must have a record of this. Do they know?"

"No. And I don't want to talk to them. The newspaper said the man you were stalking is a member of the police commission and I don't trust them. What if it is him, and he comes after me? I'm not talking to them. I'll talk to you, but that's it."

"Okay, but the police have access to her computer and her credit cards. Wouldn't they know about her purchase of an audio file and be able to trace it to whoever she sent it to?"

"That's just it. She didn't pay for it." Her voice cracked. She sounded as though she were about to break down. "I did. I paid for it. And it wasn't on her computer. We were in the library on a public computer and Monica had left her purse in the car. So I told her not to worry, that I'd pay for it. So I did. I used my credit card to pay for it online."

"Did Monica tell you if he kept the file? Maybe saved it on his phone?"

"I don't know. Like I said, Monica was very secretive about him. All I know is that she said he had two phones. That he was some big businessman and he told her he used one for work and one for pleasure."

"So then you don't think the police know anything about this?"

"How could they? Like I said, I paid for it, and Monica sent the file over the internet from a computer in the library. There's no record connecting it to her."

"But *you've* got a record, right? And you remember being there when she sent it?" I felt like I were coaching her, but I needed to know.

"Yes. She sent me a copy, because she thought it was so cool. I kept it on my computer."

"And the phone she sent his copy to was—"

"The one she and this man always used to communicate. His second line."

"You mean his pleasure phone." I couldn't help the sarcastic remark. "Which is probably a burner phone, and why the police haven't connected it to Diamond. But...if he's still using it and, if he's got Judy Garland's song saved on it, it just might prove a connection to Monica. Will you do me a favor?"

"Yes."

"Call Cupid at KCHC. Tell him you spoke to me, and I asked you to email him the file you just told me about. Tell him to hold on to it. That it's the song Judy Garland sang to Clark Gable in the movie, Broadway Melody, *You Made Me Love You.* I'll text you his number. Tell him it's not quite the smoking gun we need, at least not yet. But it just might be the breakthrough we're looking for."

CHAPTER 31

My cellphone rang before I reached Holly's cottage. The caller ID read Cate. I answered instantly.

"You okay?" I must have sounded worried. I could feel my heart beginning to beat faster as I waited for her reply. Seconds seemed like minutes. I gripped the phone, praying the next words out of her mouth would be, *I'm fine, Mom, don't worry.*

But instead she pulled one those mother/daughter reversals on me and in a very parental tone, said, "I think the question is, are you okay?"

"I'm fine. You don't need to worry."

I had phoned Cate immediately after my arrest to give her a heads-up on what had happened with Diamond. I didn't want her to hear about it on the news. But mostly, I think I called her because I needed to hear her voice, to assure myself Diamond hadn't tracked her down at the university. That she was safe.

"I spoke with Aunt Sheri. She told me you're still on the case."

"On the QT," I said. "Tyler sent me home after the incident with you at Hemingway's, and I've been pursuing a few leads behind the scenes. Nothing terribly exciting." I didn't want her to know the truth. Parents are supposed to protect their kids. I figured it best she not know everything.

"The guy's a real perv, Mom. You need to be careful. With what Sheri was telling me, he's playing a lot of mind games with you, using the press to make it sound like you're losing it."

"It's nothing you need to worry about. Tyler's got my back, and the station's not about to lose a good reporter. "

"Yeah...Just like CBS wasn't going to lose Gabi Garrison." The sarcasm in her voice hit me like a wet rag in the face.

"That's different. She wasn't reporting for them when she disappeared, she—"

"Mom—"

"Trust me, Cate." I tried switching the topic. "Have you called your brother? He's the one you should be worrying about. The Vikings lost Friday. He could probably use a little cheering up."

"Where are you right now?" She wasn't letting me off the hook.

"I'm headed over to see Holly Wood," I said.

"I think she knows more than she lets on." Her quick response caught me by surprise.

"Really?" I paused, silently hoping she wasn't about to tell me she'd had contact with her. "What makes you think so?"

"That night of the pub crawl, some of the things she said. She kept talking about college, how expensive it could be. She said a young girl could really make a lot of money in Hollywood. She knew girls who got apartments, had their tuition paid, everything. Made it sound like all they had to do was go to dinner with some old guys. No big deal. But there was something about the way she said it that made me think there might have been something more, that she might have been part of the life." She paused. "Mom, tell me you're not going over there alone."

"How about I promise I'll call when I leave Holly's, and in the meantime, you promise me you won't answer any unsolicited emails or phone calls with unfamiliar numbers." Cate promised, and I hung up.

I circled the block around Holly's cottage. I wanted to make certain Diamond's black Rolls Royce wasn't anywhere in the neighborhood. I didn't want to be caught visiting Holly, certainly not by Diamond. Fortunately, I didn't see signs of his car anywhere. Nor did I see a place to park my own car.

Up and down the street in front of Holly's cottage a production company was in full swing, preparing to film some hot new Hollywood release. Crew trucks and Star Waggons—mobile dressing rooms, named after the founder, actor Lyle Waggoner—were double parked in front of any available parking signs, leaving me no choice but to park in the lot surrounding Holly's cottage. Behind the chain-linked fence the lot stood empty.

The entire property, not much bigger than a McDonalds drive-through, looked out of place in the neighborhood, surrounded by larger, more modern looking office buildings. Holly's cottage stood like a reminder of days gone by, in the center of the concrete parking lot with weeds growing up through the pavement. In the light of day, the small white Craftsman appeared very different than it had the night of the pub crawl.

The wood-framed structure looked almost abandoned, the front steps, dry and cracking, the white paint chipping and yellowed with age. Rusted security bars covered the cottage's dark windows.

I decided my red Jeep would be less obvious if I parked behind the cottage. I drove around the back. A dusty black Mini Cooper was parked next to the steps leading up to the back door. It was a nicer car than I expected Holly might drive, but then I noticed the personalized plates, BTFL DMR. Beautiful dreamer. It had to be hers. The connection to Diamond was obvious. I parked my car next to it.

I decided to try the back entrance off a small utility porch rather than walk around to the front. The steps creaked, and the wooden railing felt unsteady in my hands. Like the house it was old and in need of a repair. At the top of the stairs I found a metal security screen unlatched and the back door wide open.

That seemed strange in a big city like Los Angeles, but I knocked anyway.

The screen rattled against the doorframe. From inside I could hear movement. It sounded like someone was shoving heavy boxes across the floor.

I knocked again, a little louder this time, and waited.

Moments later Holly appeared. I wasn't sure who was more startled, Holly to see me standing on her doorstep, or me, staring at a whole new Holly. She had totally redefined her look. Her round faced was rouged and dark hair was cut short and spiked with red tinted ends that glowed iridescent. She was dressed in denim overalls, cuffed at the bottom and wearing a pair of beat up old cowboy boots. A single suspender over one shoulder left the bib partially open, revealing a banana-top barely covering her ample breasts. She placed one hand on the door.

"What are you doing here? You were arrested, and Tony's back, so why ya bothering me?"

"How did you know Tony's back?"

She walked away from the door. "I just do. Okay? Now go away."

"I need to talk to you...about Dr. Diamond. I believe you know him."

I opened the screen door and stepped inside the room. It was a large, narrow, open area, separated from the front of the house, where the office was, by a white paneled wall that looked like something out of the early sixties. The floors were old and wooden and badly stained, and like the steps outside, creaked. There was a small kitchenette to my left with an island counter that divided the kitchen area from the rest of the room. A big screen TV was on the center wall directly across the room in front of me, next to a door leading to the office. The door was padlocked shut. A staircase anchored the far end of the room, leading to what I assumed must be bedrooms upstairs.

I glanced at the staircase and asked, "You alone?"

"Why wouldn't I be?" She sounded irritated and turned her back on me and walked towards the kitchen. "You'll have to excuse me. I'm in the middle of something, and I've got work to do. You shouldn't be here."

In front of me a Louis Vuitton bag lay on the floor. On the island counter, open cardboard boxes were stacked, and spilling out of them and onto the floor were sundry negligees. Bras, panties, corsets, boas, G-strings, all sizes and colors, were scattered everywhere. It looked as though she'd raided a Fredrick's of Hollywood, bought one of everything, and was trying to pack it all away, quickly.

"What are you doing?"

She leaned down and picked up a small red-fringed whip off the floor. The type found in a sex shop. Hardly a defense, if that's what she was thinking.

"What does it look like I'm doing? I'm leaving."

"Why? Where are you going? Are you in trouble?" I stepped closer to her and reached for the whip. But she twisted away. I grabbed her arm. A dark leather wristband she'd been wearing, spiked with metal studs, fell to the floor. Quickly she pulled her hand back and held it against her. I grabbed it again and realizing she was trying to hide something from me, I pulled her closer to me.

"What is it?"

"Nothing," she said, twisting in my grip.

"Then let me see. What are you hiding?" I turned her hand over so that I could see her slim wrist. There, against her milky white skin, was a tattoo, a small triple diamond pattern, interlinking, with an initial in the middle of each; M.A.D. I wondered if this was same pattern the coroner had found on Monica's wrist. M.A.D. Malcolm Andrew Diamond. Proof she was one of Diamond's girls. "Is this his tattoo?"

She didn't answer. She looked at me. Frightened, like a trapped animal, shaking. I pulled her back to the table and sat down, my hands still firmly on her wrists. She was clearly terrified.

"I want you to tell me what you know about Dr. Diamond. Everything. And I want to know how you know about Tony, too. And I'm not leaving until you tell me how you're connected to all this, and what you're doing."

She tried to pull back from me, but it was useless. I wasn't letting go.

"What do you *think* I'm doing? He owns me, Carol. If I don't do what he says, he'll kill me. Just like he killed Monica."

I gripped tighter. I didn't know if she'd run or perhaps hit me and take off. "Tell me what you know or I'll..."

"Or you'll what? Call the cops and tell them I'm turning tricks? I don't do that anymore. I do this. It's how I survive."

Cate was right. Holly had been part of the life. She explained how she'd met Diamond, exactly like he met most of his girls, online. She'd responded to an ad for aspiring actresses and he'd promised to help her. Told her he would set her up with the right people, pay for her headshots, acting classes and living expenses. And then when things slowed down, like they always did, Diamond explained she needed to help out with the expenses.

"I did it all, okay? Everything. You understand what that means? I danced in seedy nightclubs. I flirted with men old enough to be my grandfather. I let them touch me. I stripped. I had sex with whoever he told me to and however they wanted it. I did it until I couldn't take it anymore. I was going to run away, but there is no getting away. Nobody gets away from him. He's got a GPS on my car, and I have a younger sister who I love. He told me if I ever left, he'd find her, and that it wouldn't go so well when he did. She's only ten. I wasn't going to take that chance."

"So you helped him."

"What else was I going to do?" She paused, and I released my grip. "You ever hear of a Judas horse?"

I shook my head.

"He's a traitor to his own. I know 'cause I grew up in the desert outside Reno. There's a large herd of wild horses up that way. Every year the BLM does a roundup. Supposedly it's for the horses' own good. But most of them eventually end up going to slaughter. The Judas horse is the one the wranglers use to lead a feral herd into the corrals. It's what I do. I'm the Judas horse, Carol. I collect the girls he spots in the streets and thinks would work. The rest he does online."

She diverted her eyes from my mine and stared at the floor.

Like she couldn't look me in the eye and there was something more...something even more terrible she needed to say.

"What is it?"

"That's what I was doing the night your daughter disappeared."

I felt like she'd just punched me in the stomach.

"Then it was you. You were trying to recruit Cate!"

"I didn't, okay?" Her eyes snapped back to mine. "Diamond just wanted to scare you."

"Scare me!" I wanted to strangle her. "How did Diamond even know I was there?"

"He heard your report on the air the day Monica's body was found, and—"

"That doesn't explain how he knew who I was."

"He knew you'd be at the Walk of Fame. The station announced you'd be there that morning. Kari Rhodes was talking about it. I was there with the Marilyns for the flash mob dance, and Diamond wanted me to make sure I met you and that I gave you my business card."

"But how did he know I'd call?"

"He didn't. But I'd made the connection. And if you didn't call me, I was supposed to call you."

"But why me? Why did he come after me?"

"All those reports you did about Hollywood's Missing Girls, you made them personal. And he wasn't happy about it. He said it was bad for business. People were starting to worry about the clubs and boulevard. The police had issued warnings to young girls about going out alone at night. And then the morning Monica's body was discovered you kept harping on the dress she wearing. That red dress and her high heels. You said it looked like she'd been dressed to go clubbing. He wanted to see who you were. He wanted to make sure he could get to you."

"And then I called you and set up a tour." I shook my head. I'd fallen into his trap. "Exactly like he wanted."

"He knew you'd do that. Don't ask me how, but he's pretty

good at figuring out what people will do. As for me, I was just supposed to show you around. Honest. Get you into a few hot clubs. Give you a sense of the crowd, the vibe. I knew he'd be watching. I never thought anything was going to happen. But then you showed up with your daughter and—"

"And suddenly he had a different idea about what he wanted to happen that night." I was beginning to understand just how frighteningly erratic the Mad Dr. Diamond's mind could be, and the depths to which he would go.

"You never mentioned you were bringing your daughter. That's why I was so upset. He was on the phone with me when you saw him on the cottage porch that night. He was giving me instructions, what he wanted to have happen."

"So he orchestrated the whole thing, step-by-step."

"I slipped a roofie, a sedative, in her drink when she was at the bar. She was never in any real danger. He just wanted to establish that you were vulnerable and emotionally unstable. And when Cate disappeared, you'd go crazy and allow your personal feelings to color your report. That you couldn't be trusted to cover a story like this."

I paused and considered what Diamond had done. How he had managed to stay a step ahead of me the entire time.

"And Tony, how do you know him? How's he fit into the picture?"

"I introduced Tony to Dr. Diamond. He used to own this strip club in Vegas. That's where we met. It wasn't on the main drag or anything, more of a dive with a steady clientele of drunks and hookers who came in to clean up. I don't think Tony much cared, long as it paid the bills. Back then, all he wanted to do was be a singer, but nothing was happening. And by then, I'd met Gabe, Dr. Diamond, online. That's what he called himself. Later I learned it was short for Gable, that he fancied himself a Clark Gable ladies' man. Believe me, I didn't care what the man called himself, or who he thought he was. All I knew was that I hated dancing in some seedy club and was looking for a way out, and Diamond was it."

Holly explained Diamond ended up putting money into Tony's club, turned it around, and it became one of the places he'd showcase his girls in Vegas. It was just far enough off the strip to not attract too much attention.

"Tony and Dr. Diamond were in business together. Eventually he moved Tony to LA and got him focused on the finance business. Tony's job is to launder money for Diamond. Most of it, I think, is through the clubs, and maybe some it is in the form of the loan packages he puts together. I don't know for sure. But I do know Tony introduced Dr. Diamond to Gabi's boyfriend."

"Dr. Ericson?"

"Yeah, but I don't know much more than that, only that Tony told me Gabi was upset about something and threatening to go to the police. Next thing I know, Gabi's disappeared and so has Tony. I don't ask questions. I know better."

"But you knew, the morning we met, that the body up on Mulholland was Monica's and that Diamond had killed her."

Holly swallowed and nodded her head yes. "He didn't know much about her at first. She was just like every other girl he had met online. Pretty. Fun. She probably believed everything he told her. But then he found out she was sick."

"Sick? What do you mean, sick?"

"I don't know what it was. All I know is she had a lot of health issues. She kept it a secret, but when Dr. Diamond found out, he was furious. She told him when she was a kid she'd been in an accident and was in the hospital."

My mind flashed back to a small picture I'd seen in the paper with Monica on a tricycle and the conversation I'd had with Cupid and Tyler in the studio. Cupid was right. Monica was ill. It explained a lot: her father's overprotective custody, Monica's conservative lifestyle.

"The girl was naïve, or maybe she was just soft in the head. I don't know—whatever. But she believed everything he said. She really thought Diamond loved her. To tell you the truth, I thought she was out of the picture. Once he knew she was sick, he dumped her. He told her not to come back around. The girl was home free. But then, two weeks ago, stupid girl, she comes back. Surprises him at the Roosevelt Hotel, and the next thing I know she's—"

I stopped her. "Did you know Diamond had a case before Judge Channing?"

"No. Why?"

"Because I think you were right, Monica was home free. Diamond didn't want her, but he had a score to settle with Judge Channing."

"I knew when she came back, she was in trouble. I didn't want to think it, but I knew."

"But he couldn't use her, could he? Not like he has the others, when he's finished with them." I paused and waited to see if I saw a reaction. She pinched her eyes shut, like she was trying to block what I was about to say. "You know about the others, don't you, Holly?"

"I told you. I don't know. I don't want to know." She shook her head.

"Diamond doesn't let his girls go, Holly. Ever. It's why he befriended Dr. Ericson. He works on the transplant team at UCLA. Did you know that?

Holly wasn't looking at me. Her hands were clasped in front of her. She was biting her nails.

"Diamond wanted Dr. Ericson there, to oversee his special projects, to make certain when an organ came in that it went to the right patient. Organs are difficult to come by. There's a long waiting list, unless of course, you have money. And do you know where those organs came from, Holly?"

"Oh my God!" Holly paled and sank back in the chair, hugging her shoulders. "You have to believe me. I didn't know what he was doing. He said certain girls weren't working out anymore, and they'd just disappear. I thought he just sent them away somewhere. Like I said, I didn't ask. And far as Monica went, I didn't know anything about Judge Channing, or that Diamond was going to kill her. All I know is I was with her that last night. We were at the apartment he keeps inside the W, and she was all dressed up 'cause they were going out. She seemed happy. The last I saw her, they were walking out the door and up to the helipad. I figured, the way she was dressed, maybe they were going to Vegas, or something. He does that a lot, flies girls back and forth in his chopper. I didn't think he'd push her out. I couldn't believe it. But when I heard the news, the report you did about the body up on Mulholland, I knew. I just knew. That's why I asked you the morning of the Walk of Fame celebration if they had identified the body. I kept hoping I was wrong."

I felt like I'd been kicked in the chest. Knowing I'd been right about Monica's death all along felt awful. The vision of Monica, all dressed up and walking out the door with Diamond, getting into that helicopter, trusting him and then realizing, at the last second, what he meant to do. It must have been horrifying. It was difficult to breathe.

I forced myself to take a deep breath. "So where did he keep her until that last night?"

"Same place he's got all the others," she said.

"And where's that?" I asked.

"On his boat."

"His boat?"

She stood up and started to close one of the boxes on the table. "That's where I'm headed now. He wants me to bring all this extra stuff for the girls. He's getting ready to sail, tonight. But I'm gonna get it there before he does, and after that, he'll be too busy getting ready to leave to go after me, or my little sister, and I'll disappear."

CHAPTER 32

Just my luck. Diamond had hidden his girls on a boat. The one place I had no stomach for. Even the thought of it caused me to feel seasick. I stood up and picked up the small velvet whip off the floor, tapping the fringed laces against the palm of my hand. I couldn't believe what I was thinking, or the words coming out of my mouth.

"You've got to get me on board."

"You want to go with me?" Holly looked at me with disbelief, her eyes and mouth both wide open. "Are you crazy?"

"Why not? Diamond's not there, is he?"

"Not yet. He told me he had some business to wrap up, but he'll be there later."

"Good." I slapped the palm of my hand with the whip. "'Cause with a little luck, we could get in and out, and he'd never know I was there. All I need is proof the girls are on the boat, and Diamond will no longer be a problem. I promise."

Holly looked at me, then back at the Louis Vuitton bag on the floor and stood up. "You're insane. You know that, don't you?" She grabbed a few loose garments off the floor and threw them into the bag. "He'll kill us both if he thinks I took you there. There's no way I'm taking you."

I grabbed her wrist again.

"Then consider this. There's no way you're going without me. You leave here. I follow you. You try to lose me, I call the station. I describe your car with those personalized plates of yours to our on-air traffic reporter and tell him I just witnessed a hit-and-run. You won't make it as far as The Beverly Center before some cop picks you up. Believe me, I'm not letting you out of my sight. Not until I have proof of where he's hiding those girls."

Once a month, Holly explained, Diamond arranged for a nurse, an illegal from the Philippines he'd hired in exchange for her silence, to check on the girls. Her job was to look for any signs of communicable disease, plus colds, runny noses and that kind of thing.

"Except when there's a new girl," Holly said. "And then the nurse does a complete physical."

"Including blood test?" I asked.

She nodded, reluctantly. I didn't want to think Holly really knew what Diamond's cruel end-use plan was for his girls. But if Diamond had used a nurse to get blood samples, it was easy to think he could send them out to a lab—perhaps in the Philippines— and get the results he needed, and nobody would be the wiser.

"So what do I need to do?"

"Can you read a thermometer?"

"Yeah." My quick response surprised even me.

"Then I doubt anyone will know the difference. I've got an old nurse's cape and hat in the bag here. One of the girls uses it for dress-up. With your white jeans and heels, it just might work. I'll tell the guards you're filling in and believe me—old-fashioned cape or not—they won't notice. They're like me, they don't ask questions. Nobody does. "

I tossed her the whip. "Then what are we waiting for? Let's go."

My first big mistake was allowing Holly to drive and to take her Mini Cooper. Not because I was worried Diamond might have placed a GPS inside of Holly's car. He had instructed her to clear out the cottage and was expecting her anyway. But because the Mini Cooper, with the front seat moved forward to make room for all the boxes and the Louis Vuitton suitcase stuffed in between us, was so tight that there wasn't room for my long legs. My second mistake was leaving my red Jeep parked behind Holly's cottage. It hadn't occurred to me until we were halfway down the Harbor Freeway that Diamond had probably installed security cameras in the lot, and at that very moment may have been monitoring the area. I might as well have taken a photo and posted it on my Facebook page, telling the world I was in Hollywood visiting Holly.

I tried to put the thought out of my head. I was being paranoid. I pictured Diamond seated in front of a bank of computer screens, monitoring his various properties, and seeing me, or at least my Jeep, parked behind Holly's cottage. I imagined him ordering up one of his helicopters and that it'd come swooping down on me like some drone or giant bird of prey. I took a deep breath and exhaled. This was ridiculous. And, there was nothing I could do about it, not now. Instead, I continued to push Holly for more information about the boat, how big was it and who was onboard.

"Does Diamond have Gabi Garrison on the ship? Is she there with the other girls?"

Holly's eyes shifted nervously to me then back at the traffic ahead. We were headed west on the ninety-one, toward the marina. She didn't answer.

"Is that where Diamond's hiding her?" I pressed.

"I don't know! I don't know, okay? I mean, maybe. Like I said, I don't ask questions. All I know is he told me they're shipping out and to bring all this stuff for the girls."

Her hands gripped the wheel, her small frame leaning forward against the steering column as we weaved our way in and out of traffic. She nearly sideswiped an airport shuttle van as we raced toward the end of the Marina freeway and took the final exit on to Lincoln Boulevard on two wheels. I got the feeling Holly wasn't just nervous; she was petrified of being late.

"Where's the boat, Holly? Is it docked here at the Marina? Or," I crossed my fingers, "twenty-six miles across the sea, in Catalina?" I didn't think my stomach could handle a boat ride to Catalina. I could already feel it starting to churn. Just the thought of rocking in the water had me feeling nauseous.

"It's anchored in the harbor, just outside the marina. Diamond's got a couple of goons. He calls them his goon-squad. Overpaid flunkies who work for him. They guard the boat and keep it ready to go. There'll be a dinghy and a pilot waiting behind the Chart House."

I considered trying to call Tyler and telling him what I was up to and that he should call the police, but as I reached for my cellphone, Holly put her hand on top of mine.

"Don't. I know you want to, but I don't trust anyone, Carol, particularly the police. You don't know who Diamond's connected to. He's on the police commission. He knows everyone. I'm not taking any chances." Holly's eyes locked on mine like a trapped animal. The fear in them was almost palpable. I put my phone away and grabbed the nurse's cape from inside the bag.

"I guess I should put this on now."

The cape was a rare vintage blue and red wrap. I imagined one of Diamond's girls had worn it with not much else. I pushed the thought from my mind and put the cape over my shoulders, thankful for the warmth. The cool sea air was starting to come in and the temperature fell. I held the nurse's hat in my hands.

"Look, once we deliver this stuff, I'm outta here. Anything happens between now and then, you're on your own," Holly said.

I glanced back at my watch, thankful Sheri had thought to loan it to me. If I weren't home in time for dinner tonight, I'd be up for bad mother-of-the-year. But, thanks to the watch's internal GPS tracker, at least Sheri would know exactly where I was, and just how fast my heart was beating.

"Come on, Holly, what could go wrong?" I tried to sound reassuring. "We get on board, you introduce me as the nurse, I meet the girls, pretend to take a few temperatures, sneak a couple of pictures with my cellphone, and we leave. Simple as that. Besides, Diamond's not going to be there, and even if he was, what do you think he's going to do, make us walk the plank?"

CHAPTER 33

Holly was right. The faceless man piloting the dinghy didn't seem to care who I was or why I was there. He had a scarf wrapped around his neck and wore a Dodger baseball hat low on his forehead, as though he was trying to keep his identity a secret as much as I was my own.

Without so much as a hello, I climbed into the dinghy, a motorized inflatable not much bigger than my bathtub at home, and pulled the nurse's cape close around me. Whether it was the cold chill coming off the water or my nerves, I wasn't sure, but I craved the security of the wrap about my shoulders. I moved as far forward as possible and sat down, unable to stop shivering.

Holly and the pilot quickly unloaded the boxes from the back of her Mini Cooper until the entire craft seemed to almost sink beneath its weight. By the time they were finished, I could easily dip my fingers into the ocean without leaning over and my stomach was beginning to react to the up-and-down motion of the boat.

I closed my eyes and put my head between my legs. I tried to imagine Eric with his arms around me. When I'd feel seasick aboard the *Sea Mistress*, I'd lean up against him and we'd look out at the water together. In his arms and beneath her big white sails swelled with the wind, I felt like I could almost tolerate the motion of the water slipping beneath us. But even the thought of Eric holding me wasn't working now. I stared out at the horizon and wrapped my arms about my body. The biting sea air whipped against my face and stung my eyes. My head felt dizzy, my stomach like a yo-yo, bouncing and bobbing, as the boat sped away from the marina. I tried focusing on the horizon, not the rolling waves coming at me. With enough willpower, I could maybe mentally walk myself through the worst of this.

I forced myself to concentrate. Tyler always said a good reporter follows the facts. He loved to lecture me. *Don't wait for the story to come to you, Carol. No matter where the facts lead you, follow them.* I laughed to myself. I was doing that just now. Too bad he didn't know. I wished I'd called. I thought of the sign Tyler hung above his desk. GOYA/KOD. Get off your ass/knock on doors. Well, here I was, Tyler, seasick and headed out of the harbor. *How about that for knocking on doors?*

I focused on the missing girls. Their lives depended upon my finding them. If Diamond moved them before I found them, I might never reach them, and they'd be gone forever. I had no idea what I was I was getting into. I didn't even know if I could trust Holly. But I had to do something.

Up until Monica's death, it had never occurred to me that sex trafficking was something that actually happened here in the United States. I always thought things like that happened elsewhere, in third-world countries, where women were little more than chattel. But after Bessie Bixby bravely announced on the air that she was certain her granddaughter, Leticia, and her best friend, Brandy, had been kidnapped by sex traffickers, it blew open an entirely new discussion. Detective Browne, who couldn't talk about Monica's case specifically, spoke in generalities about what he feared was the very real problem of sex trafficking in Hollywood. The girls he believed were all targeted based upon their looks, their desirability, and just how easily they could be kidnapped and in most cases, forgotten.

"Runaways," he said, "girls escaping abusive situations, girls from poor sections of town, didn't get the attention of the media like a rich girl from west side of town might."

Girls like those he believed had been targeted weren't working some hot-sheet motel downtown or some sleazy brothel. Girls in the trade were most likely housed, fed and clothed in a safe house.

For the first time in their lives, they may have had better accommodations than they had ever known. Suddenly they were in the company of rich men, going to fancy parties, wearing expensive designer clothes and traveling in circles they never dreamt possible. And it was likely, he said, they wouldn't run away because they were either too afraid, or convinced they had a better life with their captors.

I had no idea what Diamond's boat might look like, but as we slowed, I was awed. Ahead was a massive four-story white cruiser, twice the size of the *Sea Mistress*, maybe a hundred and fifty feet long. It looked like a party boat, the type of craft people rent for weddings and office parties. But I knew better. This was no amateur operation. On the top of the boat was a communications tower with a satellite antenna that looked like it could have relayed signals from here to Mars. On the side, in large black letters, was the ship's name, *Sweet Dreams*.

I had a basic understanding of ships, but it was very limited and only what Eric had taught me. The top deck, or the sundeck, was located directly beneath the bridge. Multicolored flags hung from the ship's masts to its railing, as though to welcome its visiting clientele.

Beneath the sundeck was the mid-deck. It included a series of small French balconies, obviously leading to staterooms, where I assumed the girls were being held. The doors were all closed and the windows darkened. At the end of the mid-deck, or at the ship's stern, was the poop deck. This was a ridiculous term Eric told me had nothing to do with one's bodily functions, but on ships like this, frequently provided a play area.

I could see a small sauna and jet skis with a lifeboat tucked neatly to the side of the ship. Beneath the mid-deck was the lower deck, or what I assumed from the smaller, round, portal windows, was the crew's quarters. Below that was the orlop deck, or the bottom of the ship, where the ship's cables are stored. I wondered if that's where I might find Gabi. It'd make an ideal prison. My heart sped up at the possibility.

I looked back at Holly. "So this is it, huh?"

She leaned towards me, the sound of the motor and the wind whipping though our hair, nearly drowning her voice out.

"Yeah, this is it. No matter what you think about Diamond, the ship's amazing. Used to be an old World War II minesweeper. He completely redid it. You'd never know. It's like a floating nightclub."

"Only it's not," I said.

"Yeah, it's not."

We pulled up alongside. I don't know what I expected, but a rope ladder definitely wasn't it. From above me, someone had tossed the ladder—a rope with wooden steps—that rolled down the side of the ship, like a venetian blind, into our dinghy. Our pilot grabbed it, then tossed another rope up to the top deck, maybe forty feet above my head, and waited for it to be secured. Then he nodded to me.

"Climb."

CHAPTER 34

Climb? I looked at Holly. *This is it? This is how we get onboard?*
She grabbed the Louis Vuitton bag, like it was no big deal, and
started up the rope.

"Really, I'm supposed to do this in high heels?" I hollered.

"Just don't look down and, whatever you do, don't look back."

I had no choice. I buttoned my nurse's cape, secured the cap
on my head and carefully grabbed the rope in front of me. It was
damp with seawater. I took a deep breath and placed a very
unsteady foot onto a slim wooden foot-bar and focused my eyes
solely on Holly's cowboy boots just inches above my head. I tried as
best I could to dodge the oversized Louis Vuitton bag that was
nearly hitting me in the face as I followed her up the ladder.

When Holly got to the top, she screamed. I watched helplessly
as two sets of tattooed arms leaned over the railing and lifted her
out of sight.

I stopped. I was too afraid to move. I stared helplessly up at
the empty steps above me then quickly down at the ladder behind
me. There was no escape. The dinghy pilot had moved the small
inflatable boat as soon as Holly reached the top and black water
formed small whirlpools where the boat had been. The ladder, with
only me on it, bounced aimlessly against the side of the boat. It was
too far to jump. Swimming would be impossible. The water too
cold. The distance too great. I had nowhere to go but *up.*

*   *   *

Slowly I put one foot in front of the other, then just steps from the top, two pair of strong arms reached across the railing, exactly as they had with Holly, and roughly pulled me aboard, depositing me on deck like a piece of unwanted baggage. I hadn't even gotten my bearings; my legs were still crumpled beneath me when I heard my name.

"Carol, my dear. Again?" Diamond grabbed me by the arm and pulled me to my feet, then wrestling with my wrists, turned me around to face him. "We really have to stop meeting like this."

I struggled helplessly to free myself from his grip. My nurse's hat came off and fell like a wounded bird back toward the water. My eyes followed it, then I looked back at Diamond.

"Nice to see you too, Doctor."

"I'm sure it is." He pulled a nylon rope from his pocket and started to bind my hands together as he spoke. "You shouldn't look so surprised. I can be anywhere I want to be inside of forty minutes. But then, I'm sure you know that." He nodded to the chopper sitting atop the helipad behind the control tower, its rotor blades barely visible. From the angle we had approached the big ship, I hadn't seen it. "It's the future, Carol. Certainly you've heard me talk about it. Too bad you won't be around to enjoy it."

Then securing the knot with a heavy yank of the cord, he ran his heavy hand down the lapel of my cape, coming to stop just above my heart. "A nurse, huh? You couldn't have done better than that?"

Next to me, Holly was struggling. A man, twice her size, had his arms around her small frame. She was no match for his strength.

"Why does that surprise you, Doctor?" I could feel my body quiver in the cold air, or maybe it was his touch, but I refused to let him see me shake. I stood up straighter, my voice stronger. "I would think with your penchant for disguise, *Mr. Gable*, you might appreciate that."

"Actually, I do like the blue and red nurse's cape, Carol." He stood back and taking one side of the cape in his hand, held it out from my body, studying me. "It does something for you. A little like Red Riding Hood."

"And I suppose you're the Big Bad Wolf?"

"Oh, we could have fun with that now, couldn't we?" He put his other hand on the back of my shoulder and pulled me close to him. His head just inches from my own.

I spit in his face.

"My, my, well now, it's quite obvious as a nurse you don't follow instructions, do you?" He pushed me away and took a handkerchief from his back pocket and wiped his cheek. "Too bad you just didn't stay home and recuperate. I could have sailed away with my cargo and been gone, and you'd never find me or my girls. In certain parts of the world, what I have to sell is considered exotic—bringing an even better price than what I'm getting now. But now that you've interrupted me, I suppose we have to see how good of a nurse you really are. Perhaps we should start with the sight of blood."

He laughed and nodded to two of his cohorts. "Get their cellphones, and take Holly down to the hold. As for Miss Childs, escort her to my suite, and make sure the door's locked from both the inside and out. I wouldn't want Red Riding Hood here to get out and get lost. She and I have some things to discuss." Then turning back to me, he said, "I can't wait to hear your story. I'm sure I'll find it quite amusing. Too bad no one else will ever hear it."

I'd hidden my cellphone, best as I could, in the front pocket of my jeans and Diamond's henchman had no trouble patting me down and finding it. I yelled as he took it from me and handed it to Diamond.

"You want to know something about cellphones, Doctor? It's why you're never going to get away with this. Monica's friend has a copy of an audio file she sent to your cell. *Dear Mr. Gable.* Sound familiar?" I paused and waited for some sort of recognition on his face. He glared back at me, his eyes narrowed.

"She sent it to your cellphone. The one you used to talk with her...for pleasure...Monica told her you had two. One for business, and the other one for...what did she say? Fun?" I laughed nervously. "I had a copy sent to the station. Monday morning, it'll be all over the air, along with Monica's friend saying how Monica sent it to you right before you took her out and killed her. Pushed her out of your helicopter, over her parents' home, 'cause you wanted to settle a score with her father."

"You mean this phone?" Diamond took a cellphone from his pocket and held it out over the side of the boat. "You think I'd be stupid enough to save something like that? Well, not anymore." He tossed it overboard. We both watched as it hit the water like a rock and sank. "Now get them out of here."

I watched as Holly was hustled down below the main deck. My last visual of her was her eyes—big and terrified looking back at me as though I were her final hope. With my hands bound in front of me I tossed my head confidently, a nod of camaraderie. We were in this together. I hated this guy and hoped my fury inspired her to know we weren't going down. Not without a fight.

If there were any of Hollywood's Missing Girls on board, I didn't see them, as I was escorted down the steps from the top deck. Daylight streamed in through the ship's windows to the deck below, illuminating a large open club-like area.

At the far end of the room was an elaborate wooden bar with crystal glasses hanging above it and a fully stocked shelf of wines and liquors behind it. In the center of the room were cocktail tables surrounding a large stage, and in the middle of the floor—I couldn't believe it—was Marilyn Monroe's star. He'd stolen it. With all his money, he wanted her star here on his ship. And surrounding the star were three, long slim, floor-to-ceiling poles. *Pole dancing?* I didn't get a chance to ask.

I was hustled through the room and down a long hallway toward the front of the boat to Diamond's suite, where I was shoved through the door.

I tripped over my own two feet as I stumbled into the room

and fell into a small swivel chair. Behind me, I heard the door pulled shut and the lock click into place.

I glanced down at my hands, bound with white nylon cord and nearly laughed out loud. *Diamond, you fool.* In his haste to bind my hands he had tied a loose fitting clove hitch instead of a more secure constrictor knot. I knew the difference instantly. Charlie and I had spent one summer studying various knots and their uses for a Boy Scout's program.

I had easily impressed Eric with my knowledge of knots. While I knew nothing about sailing, I did know my knots. Wiggling my wrists I was able to loosen the slim nylon rope, and with my teeth I pulled the cord through the knot until it slipped free. The ease of which it came off made me wonder how often Diamond might have used this same cord before and with whom. I shuddered to think of the consequences and tossed off the nurse's cape, leaving it to fall in a heap on the floor, and went immediately to the door behind me. It was locked. A doubled-sided keyed lock, the likes of which I'd seen used on security gates around the radio station.

I surveyed the room. I had to find a key, or something. Bobby pins. Nail file. Anything I might use to pick the lock.

The stateroom was neat, a white-on-white décor with a minimal amount of furniture. In addition to one of the small chairs that I'd crashed into, there was a desk, a big screen TV and a full king-sized bed.

Across the room, a pair of French doors opened up onto a large, private balcony. I tried them and, realizing they were locked, started to shake them, hoping I might jar one loose, but it was no use. They were secured with the same type of double-sided lock as the entry door.

Next I searched the desk, pulling out the drawers, turning them upside down, dumping the contents onto the bed. There had to be a key somewhere. But still, nothing. *The bathroom.* It looked as though it had recently been used. There were water spots in the tub and the towels were damp. I opened the vanity and found a number of pharmaceutical prescription bottles all with his name on them. Abilify, Depakote ER, Risperdal. It was a virtual pharmacy. This was Diamond's crash pad. It had to be. The apartment inside the W was for business purposes only. I closed the cabinet door and looked at myself in the mirror.

Behind me, hanging on the door, was a plush white terry bathrobe. I took it off the hook and ran my hand instinctively from the collar to the one of pockets, feeling for something. A phone, a key, anything that might help.

If he were here recently, maybe he left a key in the pocket. I've left things in the pocket of my own robe: my reading glasses, my cellphone. Just maybe he might have done the same thing. I reached into the pocket, praying I'd find something. Anything that might help me escape, or get word back to the station, or Sheri. I was desperate. And then I felt it: a long slim, piece of metal.

I took it out and stared at it. In the palm of my hand was a key, and not just an ordinary key, but a master key for the ship's doors. He must have kept it in his robe so that he could wander into any room onboard, at any time he wanted. I didn't want to even think about why he'd left it in the pocket of his robe, or whose room he'd visited the night before. Only that I was in luck. I had the key. I had my freedom.

I glanced at Sheri's watch on my wrist. It was just almost five o'clock. Outside the sun was beginning to set and the sky was growing grey. Any time now Sheri would be wondering why I hadn't called her about dinner. I had promised I'd be home. With a little luck she'd try to call me, and when I didn't answer she'd realize I was missing and check her GPS locator on her computer. Once she discovered my position—in the middle of Santa Monica harbor—she'd know, beyond a shadow of doubt, that I was in trouble and wasn't coming home. But until then, I was on my own.

I held my breath and put the key into the lock of the bedroom door and felt the tumblers fall into place. I breathed a momentary sigh of relief, opened the door, and glancing cautiously to my right and back to my left, entered the hall. It was empty. Carefully I tiptoed towards the clubroom, hugging the wall, praying no one would discover me. I was about to slip down a second set of stairs to the deck beneath me when I heard the ringing of ship bells.

I leaned against the wall and held my breath. When Holly and I had boarded, or been pulled aboard, I heard a series of bells that appeared to alert the crew to our arrival. I suspected it had been a warning, some type of security alarm, sending the girls back to their quarters. I knew this wasn't the traditional ringing of bells to mark any change of shift for the crew. This was something else. Moments later Diamond's voice came over the PA, asking for the ship's captain and crew to join him on the upper deck. Immediately.

I took that as sign that the coast was about to be clear, at least for the moment. I slipped down the steps to the middle deck. I remembered as Holly and I approached the ship that this was the deck where the staterooms were and where I hoped I might find Leticia, Brandy and the other girls Diamond had kidnapped. I glanced down the hall. The doors were all shut. I tried the door closest to me. It was locked. I tapped lightly. I knew behind the door was some young girl, probably frightened, waiting for the all clear signal and afraid to say anything.

Quietly, I tried my passkey in the lock, and when it released I pushed the door open.

There on the bed like a frightened child, clutching her knees to her chest and looking at me as though I might be a hostile intruder, was Leticia. I recognized her instantly from her picture, her high cheekbones, her big eyes. She was too afraid to speak.

"Don't be afraid." I put my finger to my lips, *shush*. "I'm a friend, Leticia. I know your grandmother. I'm here to help."

She didn't move. I came over to the bed, sat down next to her and put my arms around her. In her lap was a small portable radio, the earbuds still in her ears. I took them out and whispered. "It's going to be okay. Trust me. You're going to get out of here. You're going to be fine."

Even as I said it, I wondered how I could promise such a thing. There was no phone in the room, no way I could call for help. She was a prisoner, and so was I.

"You know Nana?" Her voice was shaking, her hands trembling. Tears started to roll down her face.

"Yes, yes, and she's looking for you." I wiped a tear from her face and held her head between my hands and told her I was a reporter. But before I could explain how I knew her grandmother, the ship's engines started to warm up. The heavy sound of the motor began to churn, like a thrashing machine, and the entire ship started to vibrate with noise. She fell into my arms and started to cry harder.

I grabbed her earphones. "What are you listening to?"

She told me she was listening to KISS, a favorite station with kids her age.

"You know what station your nana likes? She's a big fan of Cupid. He's on my station, KCHC. Why don't we try and see if we can find it? You could listen to it."

I quickly dialed the station's frequency then turned the radio up so we could both listen.

I was shocked.

Sheri was on the air with Cupid. I could hear Cupid's voice, loud and clear.

"So, you're saying your friend, and our reporter, Carol Childs, is missing?"

"Yes. She's been working on a story..."

I stood up and kissed the watch on my wrist. "Thank you, Sheri!"

Leticia looked at me like I was crazy. "What is it?"

"It's Sheri, my friend. She knows where I am. Help's on the way! Trust me." I explained how Sheri had given me the watch and that there was GPS tracker in it. "And if she's called the station, that means she's also called the cops and the FBI, Eric's friend, Agent Delfino and—"

I could see I was confusing Leticia. She had no idea who Agent Delfino was, or that he was Eric's best friend, or who Eric was for that matter, or why that was important. But I did, and now I needed one more miracle.

I went to the French doors and unlocked them with the passkey. They opened onto a small balcony. It was too far to jump. I scanned the horizon.

The last time Eric and I spoke, he said he'd be home early, that he was running ahead of schedule. If Sheri had called Mark, and he had been able to reach Eric, and if Eric were close enough, there was a chance that the *Sea Mistress* might be coming into port right about now. And if she were, she'd have to sail right through this same channel to get to the harbor. Just maybe we might be lucky. We only needed a little help. Just enough time to stall Diamond from leaving before the cops could get here to rescue us.

I focused on the horizon. The setting sun was making it difficult to see. Staring directly into it burned my eyes. But I refused to leave the balcony until I knew.

Like a black dot on the horizon, I could see the outline of a ship approach. I squinted, my eyes watering as I stared into the sun trying to make out the size and shape of the approaching vessel. *Come on Eric. Please, God, let it be the Sea Mistress.* But as it came closer, I could see it wasn't slowing. Its port beam aimed directly towards shore.

A loud ship's horn blared as it passed. My heart sank, but I refused to give up hope. The channel's like a flight path. Maybe the next ship. I waited, my hands gripping the balcony, my eyes steadfast on the horizon. I never wanted to see the *Sea Mistress* so badly in my life. And then I saw her. In all her glory, with her sails full. The *Sea Mistress* was headed in our direction. My heart soared.

"Do you have a flashlight?" I turned from the door and looked at Leticia. I knew there had to be a life preserver with a flashlight and a whistle in the cabin somewhere. It's a law all vessels carry lifejackets, and most include some type of flashlight with them.

Leticia got off the bed, ran to the closet and took out an orange life vest. Attached to it was a small flashlight, not much bigger than the size of my hand. But it was enough. I grabbed the light and began signaling.

S-O-S. S-O-S.

I was never so thankful that I knew Morse code. Never in my life did I actually think I'd need it. To date it had merely been a fun exchange of coded messages, little flirtations between Eric and me. Like that he sent for my birthday, *miss those long slow curves.*

But now, I knew it was a matter of life and death. Agent Delfino may have been able to get word to Eric that we were in the harbor somewhere. But where? We weren't the only ship out here, and I couldn't count on Sheri's watch being that accurate. I flashed the signal, three quick flashes, followed by three long flashes then three quick flashes again. I continued until I saw a light flash back.

"Leticia, you think you can do this?"

She nodded and I gave her the flashlight.

"Keep doing this until I come back. And don't answer the door. Not for anyone."

I was about to hand her the radio. I knew she'd find comfort listening to Cupid. What I didn't expect was to hear was Cupid, with a direct message for me.

"And Carol, if you can hear this, you'll understand why this song's for you." I paused and listened. *I Will Survive.*

The song buoyed my spirits like a rocket. I told Leticia not to worry and left her in the room, frightened, but capable. Then locking the door behind me, I proceeded down the hall toward the stairway and into the bowels of the ship. I needed to find Holly.

CHAPTER 35

The orlop deck is below the water level. Eric had explained to me that it's the deepest part of the ship with the engine room and, in some cases, the crew's quarters. It was also where I suspected Holly would be. But with Diamond's request for all hands on deck, I figured the engineer would be alone and too busy to notice me. At least for the moment I wasn't worried about running into anyone, and with the belief that our rescue was somehow in the works, I proceeded down the stairs and towards the back of the ship.

Taking my heels off, I slipped by the engine room. The engineer was preoccupied, exactly as I suspected, checking instruments, adjusting valves for impending departure. Ahead of me was a heavy, grey metal, watertight door, behind it the hold. Holly's hold, where Diamond had demanded she be taken and where the ship's cables and cargo are stored. A dark, dank prison. The lock on the door was different than any other lock on the ship. This was an old, round metal wheel shaped contraption with a long lever, like a baseball bat. I leaned against the door. I could feel the cold like a block of ice through my thin t-shirt. I shivered as I pushed the lever down hoping the sound of the ship's engines would mask that of my unlocking it. I felt the heavy hinges engage. I paused, waiting to see if the engineer had heard me, then shoved the door open.

It took a moment for my eyes to adjust to the lack of light. I stepped inside over a watertight lip that secured the door's mounting, and left the door open behind me.

"Holly?"

"Over here." From within the hold I could barely make out her small frame. She was sitting on the top of an old steamer trunk with her arms tied securely behind her to a support beam near the stern of the ship.

"Are you okay?" Silly question. Of course she wasn't okay. I rushed to her side and started to untie her. It was cold and dark and my fingers were stiff from the chill. I worked the knot as fast as I could.

"I'm fine. But Gabi's not. She's over there."

Oh my God! Holly nodded to an area behind her, a crumpled figure that, in the dark, looked more like a sack of potatoes than a human being. She was heaped up against the ship's wall, her hands and feet bound behind her.

"I thought I was alone until I heard her moaning. I tried to get her to speak, but she's not making any sense."

I finished untying Holly, fast as my fingers would allow, then turned around to help Gabi.

"Gabi? It's me, Carol Childs. How are you?" I helped her to sit up. She felt weak and cold in my arms.

"Tell him I'm sorry. He has to know." Her voice was thin and breathy. I could barely hear her. She turned her head in my direction. Her eyes looked glassy, like they might roll back into her head at any moment.

I patted her on the side of her face. "Come on, Gabi, stay with me. We're going to get you out of here. Can you stand?"

She nodded, but as she stood her legs gave out beneath her and she slipped through my hands to her knees. I wondered how long she'd been here. It was freezing, and I regretted leaving the nurse's cape in Diamond's room.

"Holly, help me. We need to get Gabi upstairs."

Holly looked at me like she was afraid to move.

"No way. Diamond's up there. He catches us, he'll throw us overboard. I can't swim, and he'll never let me go alive."

"Holly, look at me." With one arm around Gabi, I grabbed Holly's face with the other and forced her to look in my eyes. "All you need to do is get Gabi upstairs to the poop deck. You know where that is?"

She nodded.

"She needs fresh air and water. I'll go up with you to the mid-deck, but you've got to take her from there. The police, the FBI, they're on the way. Diamond's on the top deck, and once he knows what's about to go down he's going try to get out of here, and I can't let him do that."

Holly took one of Gabi's arms and put it over her shoulder. I took the other. Slowly, we were making our way toward the door, when suddenly the engineer appeared in front of us.

"You," he said. He glared at us, then quickly he turned his attention to a red emergency alarm button mounted on the wall, next to the door. If he pushed it, we'd all be done. It wouldn't matter if Eric, the police, or the entire U.S. Navy were coming. If Diamond heard that alarm he'd come running down those steps and we'd be history.

"I wouldn't do that if I were you." I stepped forward.

"Oh yeah?"

I didn't answer. Without thinking, I charged him. I'm not much of physical contact person; I don't know where this sudden strength, or courage, came from. I only know that I charged him. Like I'd seen my son do during football practice, I lowered my body, tucked my head and, with my hands and arms around me, like I had a football beneath my ribs, I rammed into his lower quarters with all my might. He went flying over my shoulders, headfirst onto the floor behind me.

I heard his head hit first. Hard. Like a melon falling off a fruit truck, splat onto the street. I ran over to his body, splayed on the floor like a green Gumby and checked his pulse. He wasn't dead. I propped him up against the steamer trunk; he moaned and looked as though he might be about to come to. I put his head between his legs, something my limited nursing skills told me might be a good idea and then tied his hands and feet together with a constrictor knot. A knot I knew he'd not be able to untie.

"You do that often?" Holly looked at me like I was some superhero.

"No," I said. I double-checked the knot, and giving it one final tug, stood up. "In fact, I prefer to limit my confrontations to something a little more philosophical, but since he didn't give me a choice, I just went with the flow. Must have been adrenaline."

I took Gabi's free arm and put it over my shoulder. Together with Holly we made it to the top of the stairs at mid-deck. I was about to leave them when four of Diamond's men came running down the stairs and pushed past us like rats off a sinking ship. From the looks on their faces, they had no interest in stopping us. They were racing towards the poop deck to the lifeboat.

I knew instantly they were illegals. One of them was a cook. He still had on his apron, the other two yelling in Spanish behind him, "Esperame! Esperame!" *Wait for me!* I figured they must have seen the flashing light from the *Sea Mistress*, Eric's Morse code response to my SOS, and worried the advancing ship was INS.

I took the steps two at a time up to the top deck. I had to get to Diamond.

I arrived, out of breath, and saw him, his back to me. He was standing at the bow of the ship, beneath the party flags, leaning against the railing, staring out at the *Sea Mistress* and the setting sun. Behind me were the stairs leading up to the bridge and to the helipad. With one quick move, if he turned and rushed me, he could knock me over, and if he made it up the stairs to his helicopter, he'd be gone. I'd lose him for good. I had to stop him.

I looked around for something. Some weapon. Something to protect myself. Something to stop him should he charge me.

There was an ax.

A fireman's ax was attached to the wall of the wheelhouse behind me. I grabbed it, and as I did, Diamond turned around. I felt as though I was looking into the eyes of a cobra, slowly weaving in front me, about to strike.

"So," he said, "this is the part then...where we learn just how good Nurse Carol is with the sight of blood."

His body started to sway, slowly side to side. I didn't know which way he was going to move, but I knew he'd strike.

"Don't move. I will use this." I held the ax above my head, like a bat, my arms shaking. My thin t-shirt was no protection against the cool ocean breeze.

"Come on, Carol, you don't have what it takes to swing that ax at me. It'd be awfully bloody if you hit me. What are you gonna do? Have you thought about it? Swing for my leg, my head? I don't think you can do it."

"You don't know what I can do."

"Don't I?" He took a quick step forward then stopped. He smiled again. Then took another step, this time slightly to the side.

I stepped toward him, the ax still above my head. The weight of it, heavy in my arms. I was shaking. "Don't try it."

"Or what?" He threw his hands above his head, a short sudden move. He was trying to frighten me.

I swung wildly and missed.

"Very good." He jumped backed, his hands out to his sides. "Shall we try again? Perhaps this time I'll grab the ax from you. And we both know I'm not afraid to use it."

I stepped back, just far enough so that he couldn't grab it from me. "Just try. I promise you I won't miss. Not this time." I raised the ax a little higher.

Then suddenly from behind me I heard voices.

"Stop! Don't anybody move."

Diamond froze. I froze.

From behind me, I could hear Eric's voice. "Put the ax down, Carol. He's not going anywhere."

Two red laser dots, the size of a penlight, from a semi-automatic danced on Diamond's chest, directly over his heart.

I lowered the ax and turned slowly to see Eric with another agent, both in their blue FBI windbreakers, approaching, their guns drawn.

CHAPTER 36

I had no idea how Eric and another FBI agent had gotten onboard, but within minutes, the sky and sea around us was full of law enforcement. Like some military exercise, LAPD and FBI helicopters were hovering overhead. Even KCHC traffic helicopter had joined in the action. While in the water, approaching at a high rate of speed was a Coast Guard cutter. Between the wind buffeting the party flags above my head, the chopping sound from the blades of the helicopters, the warning horns of the advancing Coast Guard, and a police bullhorn telling everybody *to freeze*, I felt as though I was in the middle of military assault.

I held my hands up and looked at Eric. *What do I do?*

"Just stay put."

While the second agent held his gun on Diamond, Eric grabbed the rope of party flags above my head, and taking a knife from his belt, cut it down. He stripped it of its flags, then grabbing Diamond by the shoulders, turned him around and tied his hands with the rope behind his back.

"Where'd you come from?" I asked.

Diamond winced as Eric pulled the rope tight around his wrists.

"The poop deck." He looked at me from over Diamond's shoulder, winked, and finished tying the rope handcuffs around Diamond's wrists. "Would have been here sooner, but we ran into a group of illegals trying to jump ship."

I looked behind me. Coming up the stairs were several more blue-jacketed FBI agents. I wasn't surprised. Eric never sailed alone, and crewing the *Sea Mistress* with him were five other agents. They were all on leave together and, like Eric, never traveled anywhere without their GO bag, loaded with the type of stuff any agent in the field might need: meds, guns and ammo. Just in case. I had heard enough stories to know that something like this was just the type of homecoming party a group of well-rested agents relished. The type of thing they'd be talking about years from now, a chance to jump in on a rescue operation after a little R&R in the gulf.

"You okay?" he asked.

"Yeah. And you?"

Eric pushed Diamond in the direction of the approaching agents, who grabbed him and moved him out from between us. Then, tucking his gun behind his back, he took a step towards me, grabbed me in his arms, and kissed me hard on the lips, like I hadn't been kissed in a long time. "Better now that I know you're okay."

The surprise of his move, the warmth of his body, the setting sun, the cool air, there were a thousand reasons why I could have lost myself right there. I felt almost dizzy.

Then above us, from within one of the helicopters, the sound of a bullhorn.

"Agent! I hope that's the reporter."

Eric waved a hand above his head. I laughed nervously and stepped back. "I think I better go downstairs and check on the girls."

Below I found Holly and Gabi on the poop deck sitting together on a chaise lounge, their arms about one another, cold and shaking. I grabbed a blanket and put it around their shoulders. Across from them, the four illegals sat cross-legged on the deck. They refused to make any kind of eye contact. Guarding them was a third agent. He introduced himself, said his name was Agent Dallas, and that he'd been aboard the *Sea Mistress* with Eric when they received a call from Agent Delfino.

"You okay, ma'am?"

I nodded and turned my attention back to Holly.

She explained she had run into the four men who had rushed past us on the poop deck as we struggled to get Gabi up the stairs. They had been trying to lower the lifeboat for their escape when three FBI agents appeared from beneath the deck and boarded the boat.

"They were like pirates," she said. "They were awesome. Then one of them, a tall guy, he took off, up the stairs—two at a time— like he knew something terrible was about to happen."

That had to have been Eric. I glanced over the side of the boat and saw the *Sea Mistress'* small motorized dinghy bobbing in the water. I told her everything would be okay, and for the first time, I really believed it. Agent Dallas interrupted me and told me two other agents were searching the ship for any other conspirators.

"You might want to wait here until I get the all-clear."

I told him the engineer was in the hold below. "I suspect he's got a headache. He took a nasty fall. Fell headfirst over something. I don't know what, but you might want to have someone look in on him."

Moments later, Agent Dallas' cell rang with an all-clear from one of the agents below. Whoever it was asked if I might come down and help them with the girls. I arrived on the mid-deck to find the agents knocking on doors, but to no avail. The hallway remained as it had been before. Strangely silent, the doors all locked.

"You think they're okay?"

"I think they're just scared," I said. "Afraid you'll arrest them."

I knew behind each door there would be a girl, frightened and unsure about what was about to happen.

"You don't think they'd do anything stupid, do you?" The agent in front of Leticia's door shook the handle and looked for a moment as though he was thinking about kicking the door in.

"I have a passkey. Perhaps you might want to try that first." I handed him the key.

He looked relieved and opened the door. Inside, Leticia was

standing at the far side of the bed, holding the earphones to her head. She looked like she was looking for somewhere to hide until she saw me.

"It's okay, Leticia. Diamond's not going to hurt you anymore. The police and the FBI have him now."

I walked with her to the doorway and asked her if she'd help me open the doors and introduce me to each of the girls. The second door we opened was Brandy's room. Every time, behind each door, the situation played out exactly the same. I found a frightened girl—fifteen in all—including Jessie Martin, Marilyn Ann Billings, April Hansen, and several girls from other parts of the country whose names I didn't know. But I did know they were each someone's daughter, sister, cousin or friend, and somewhere there had been a missing persons report filed and a cold case left standing open.

What surprised me most as I gathered with the missing girls on the top deck was the reaction I saw in the faces of some of the girls. There was sadness in a few, tears in others and even cries of "No, don't!" as Diamond was taken away.

I remembered that Detective Browne had said to me, that some girls, no matter how horrid their captors, would bond with them. It was a strange reaction, a kind of Stockholm syndrome, but until I saw it, I couldn't believe it. For some of these girls, Diamond was the only stability they'd ever known in their lives. They had trusted him, and although it was hard to believe, he was a father to some and a savior to others. He'd taken care of them. He dressed them, introduced them to powerful men, took them places they'd never go, and made certain they were housed and fed. Dr. Diamond had provided for some of them what they'd never had: a home and a life. What they didn't know was just how long that life might be. That he'd dispense of them when they were no longer useful to him. That he'd found a secondary source of income, even more lucrative to him than their trade, and that their lives, their bodies, their minds, they were his.

CHAPTER 37

The best thing about radio is that it's live. I didn't have to wait until the press could run my story in the morning paper, or to wonder how it was being received. Our listeners could pick up the phone and ask questions, vent their feelings, and most importantly feel like they were part of the process. I loved that. It made me feel really connected both to the story and to my listeners. But even more, I loved that I was able to describe Diamond's arrest, his last moments on the ship, and the rescue of Hollywood's Missing Girls, as it was happening, live from the top deck of the *Sweet Dreams*.

Holly was at my side on the bridge as I delivered my report. I described Diamond, bound with his hands behind him, his shoulders hunched like a defeated man, as he was escorted off the ship with two armed FBI agents, one on of either side of him. She said it looked like Diamond was about to walk the plank. That got a laugh from Cupid and cheers from a few of the girls who witnessed his departure. A very befitting exit, I thought.

In reality, I told our listeners it wasn't a plank, but a wooden bridge that had been fashioned between *Sweet Dreams* and a Coast Guard cutter that was prepared to take him ashore, and from there, I didn't know. Not yet.

But there was a poignant moment, when Diamond looked back at the boat, this floating brothel he'd created. I wondered what he must be thinking. Did he really think he'd never be caught? Was he such an egomaniac that he didn't care? Or was he crazy? I remembered the pills I found in his medicine cabinet in the bathroom onboard. Maybe he was really was mad...the Mad Dr.

Diamond. He certainly had enough pills in that cabin. It might explain his strange actions, his manic energy, his dark side.

I didn't have the answers. I only had questions, and as I looked down at the girls huddled together on the top deck, I had lots of them. How did they get here? Where had they come from? How many other arrests would there be? Certainly Diamond hadn't put this operation together alone.

Holly leaned up next to me and covered her eyes. We were off the air for the moment. From below deck, the ship's captain and members of the crew were being brought topside. They were all bound, their hands behind their backs, agents surrounding them. The reality of what was happening on the deck below her was maybe too much.

"They're going to arrest me too. Aren't they?"

"I don't know, Holly. I know they're going to want to talk to you. But I don't think they'll arrest you. I think if you tell them what you know, they're going to realize you're as much of a victim as any of the other girls."

She looked at me, her eyes searching mine. *Could she trust me?*

"Tell them what you know, Holly. Tell them everything. How Diamond tricked you, how he threatened you. That he told you he'd kidnap your little sister if you didn't go along. I'll vouch for you. I'll tell them you helped bring Diamond down."

I said goodnight to her, and as I did, one of the FBI agents approached. She needed to come with him. He didn't cuff her, merely asked if she'd follow. I watched as she was escorted down the steps to where the captain and the crew were huddled together. She turned and waved at me, then slowly crossed the gangplank from *Sweet Dreams* onto the Coast Guard cutter. I waved goodbye.

Tyler cued me. He needed me back on the air to wrap-up my report. We were running short of time.

I thanked Cupid and Tyler and even Sheri, who was patched into the show via a phone line, and reminded those listening that I'd be back on the air with them tomorrow afternoon. I'd have more details concerning Hollywood's Missing Girls and the arrest of Dr. Malcolm Diamond then. "Until tomorrow, this is Carol Childs, live from the deck of *Sweet Dreams*, inviting you to stay tuned."

CHAPTER 38

I drove to work the next morning on autopilot. My radio was tuned to the station, my mind full of images from last night's arrest. In the background, the station plugged away with a promotion for this afternoon's show, praising my efforts and referring to me as the station's ace investigative reporter. "KCHC investigative Reporter Carol Childs exposes Hollywood sex trafficking ring. Carol Childs uncovers the truth behind Hollywood's Missing Girls." They were making me out to be a modern day Nellie Bly, America's first investigative female journalist, while in my mind, the events, the boat, the girls, Eric, the arrests, were all blurred together. In hindsight, it was like a dream, or maybe more of a nightmare, that I couldn't quite believe I'd been a part of.

I checked my voicemails as I drove. I had twenty-three messages. Many of them were call-ins from listeners congratulating me. Nice comments after the *LA Times* article concerning my arrest had left some station fans doubting my credibility as a reporter. I skipped through most. I didn't have time to listen to them all. I was searching for something from Eric. His call had come in at four a.m. He said he was leaving a message on my office line because he didn't want to wake me, that hopefully I was sleeping.

"But I thought you'd want to know, Diamond won't be making bail. He's considered a flight risk and the charges against him, in addition to the kidnapping and murder of Monica Channing, could fill a small phonebook. As for Holly Wood, I know you didn't want to see her go with us last night, but she's giving us exactly what we need to make the charges against Diamond stick. Sleep tight, babe. See you tomorrow."

I had mixed feelings about Holly. I had watched as she walked the plank in the company of FBI agents and wondered what would become of her. She wasn't without fault. She had helped to trap other girls into Diamond's sex trafficking ring. She'd told me so. But still, I felt as though she were more of a victim than a conspirator, a young girl in trouble, caught up in a cruel world of human trafficking, and with no idea how get out of it. Diamond had not only threatened her, but also the life of her little sister. What was she to do?

The next voicemail began with a brief recording of *My Way* and I nearly dropped the phone. Tony's voice unmistakably smooth said, "Carol, sorry, I won't be running those ads on the radio. Seems I'm on the move again. But then I'm sure you already know that. Ciao."

I was about to pick up the phone and call Eric's cell, when it buzzed through. It was Tyler.

"I hope you're on the way in, 'cause I need to see you—"

"ASAP," I said. "I know. I'm almost there."

Tyler met me in the lobby. "I think there's something you need to know." He paused. "About corporate and their take on this story."

"Okay," I said, skeptically. "What is it?"

"You know they were never keen on our covering the topic of sex trafficking. That they wanted us to keep with a lighter, more—"

"Yeah, yeah, I know. Lighter, more friendly chick news."

"Exactly. And you know that I did what I could to support you while you continued to investigate."

"Yes." I could tell Tyler wasn't comfortable with what he was about to say. "Go on."

"Well, turns out they're thrilled with the results. That's the good news. However, they'd like to tread lightly on the circumstances concerning sex trafficking and focus on the rescue."

"Okay." I still wasn't getting it, but I wasn't surprised.

"The rescue," Tyler said, "that your *boyfriend*, the FBI agent, did on the high seas. Saving you from certain death."

"The rescue my *boyfriend* did?" I paused. My stomach was suddenly in knots. Not that I didn't agree. I had been rescued, and without Eric's sudden appearance on the deck behind me, Diamond might have taken the ax from my hand and the end result would have been very different. But— "Just how did anyone know it was my *boyfriend* who came to my rescue?"

Tyler explained that while I was busy aboard Diamond's floating brothel taking down the ship's captain while evading capture, and then facing off with Diamond, Sheri was on the air—with Cupid. She described, as best she could, what she knew of my investigation: the pub crawl, my arrest for the break-in of Diamond's apartment, and Tony's disappearance. And, in the course of trying to sound informed, she just happened to mention that I was involved with a handsome FBI agent. Whom she had managed to get in touch with, and whom at that very moment was en route to the *Sweet Dreams* to rescue me.

"She might as well have described him as a white knight coming to your rescue. And I'm afraid, despite all your hard work, that's the story corporate would like us to focus on."

"The rescue," I said. "Nothing leading up to it? Nothing about the girls? How they were targeted and kidnapped? Or Diamond selling organs on the black market? *Just* the rescue?"

"It's a delicate situation, Carol. They're happy for you, delighted you did what you did to bring the girls home. And between your broadcast and what our air traffic reporter in the helicopter above the boat described, we got a real play-by-play of the girls' rescue and exit. But, as I've been told, corporate's put a lot of money behind positioning the station as the feel-good format for women, and they think too much detail concerning exactly what it is these girls have been through might prove upsetting for our listeners. They'd like you to keep it light. However, on the bright side, corporate loves you. Right now you're their new golden girl. So I leave the decision to you." Tyler smiled, disingenuously, I thought.

"Message delivered," I said.

He turned and walked away. The decision was mine. I wasn't going to shortchange this story. I could keep the more morbid details about sex slavery to a minimum, but I wasn't going to omit anything about the pain and fear these girls had gone through. The public needed to know. Sex slavery and trafficking didn't just happen somewhere else; it was happening here, right here in the homeland.

As for Sheri and my boyfriend coming to my rescue, I shook my head. I couldn't fault Sheri for exposing my relationship with Eric, and making a big deal about him coming to my rescue. As a reporter, I know how difficult it is to fill airtime in the middle of a tense situation. When the facts are slow coming in, reporters improvise. We reach for anything, chat about past experiences as we wait for the story to unfold. No doubt Sheri was feeling the same pressure. Trying to explain where I was. Why. And who it was she had called to help. Without even hearing the broadcast I could imagine just how nervous she was, and how she might have gone on about my personal life.

I knew in my mind how it would have gone down. Sheri would have picked up the boys and come by my place for dinner. Exactly as planned. When I wasn't there she would have known something was wrong. It wouldn't have taken her but seconds to check her iPhone for a readout from her fitness watch, and when she got a report showing my elevated blood pressure, and noticed my location, somewhere in the middle of the Santa Monica Bay, she knew I was in trouble. That's when she would have sprung into action, rounding up the troops for my rescue. She would have called everybody, including Cate, exactly like I had told her to. She called Agent Delfino, LAPD, and Tyler, who put her on the air with Cupid.

I had called Cate on the way home. Eric had arranged for a car to take me home and I needed to tell her it was over. But she already knew. She had been following the story on the radio and had talked with Sheri. She asked about the girls. What would happen to them? I told her I didn't know for sure, but that by tomorrow, I'd have some answers. I said she might have to listen to the station because much of what I'd be learning would come from interviews I'd yet to set up for tomorrow's show. Stay tuned, I joked.

When I arrived home, there was a note from Sheri waiting for me on the kitchen counter. *Charlie's with me. Call when you get a chance. Congratulations.* In the refrigerator was leftover lasagna with instructions to reheat it in the microwave.

No, I couldn't fault Sheri. Sheri was family. We may not have been related, but we supported one another. She was there for me and the kids. As for what I did for Sheri? I wasn't so sure. She once said she lived vicariously through me. If so, I figured, at least for the moment, I better come up with something better—I'd had enough close calls to last for quite a while.

Cupid was blasting *I Will Survive* when I walked in the studio. He stood up and greeted me with a big bear hug.

"That's twice now you've saved my life," I said. "Or at least the song did." I explained when I found Leticia last night, she had a small radio with her and that we'd tuned to the station and heard it. "You've no idea just how strong it made me feel."

"Speaking of which." Cupid nodded to the studio window. "Did you know they'd be here?"

Outside the studio Detective Browne, Bessie Bixby and Leticia stood with Brandy. I motioned for them to come in. I had asked several people if they'd come by the studio for Cupid's show. I had no idea how many would show up. I left messages everywhere, hoping I'd get either calls-ins or that those I'd called would show up. In the aftermath of last night's rescue I wasn't certain where anyone would be, and I wanted to get as many people as possible to share their story.

Cupid and I opened the show with Bessie who announced that she was happy to have her granddaughter home and was planning on adopting Brandy.

Tanya Day was our next guest. She was a call-in and said she had been listening to the radio last night when she heard Cupid and

Sheri going on about the rescue. She wasted no time in getting herself down to the marina, where she met up with members of the LAPD rescue operation and insisted she take the girls home. With her, on the air, was Holly.

"I wasn't going to let them keep any of those girls, much less Holly," Tanya said. "After spending several long hours with the FBI and LAPD, they released her to me. She has a long road ahead of her, but she's not going to be spending it in jail. Not if I can help it."

I was glad to hear that.

Earlier that afternoon I had called Mr. King, KCHC's legal guru and Dr. Diamond's attorney. I was hoping to get a statement from him regarding Diamond's arrest. What I got instead was a flat answer. He would no longer be representing Dr. Diamond, but that he'd received a call from Tanya Day, asking if he might be interested in doing some pro bono work for Holly Wood.

I asked Holly how she was doing. She sounded relieved that she had finally slipped beyond Diamond's tyrannical grip and had found someone who could help her find her way out of the nightmare she'd been living. I hoped she was right.

My next guest was Dr. Miles Ericson. He explained he was calling from the hospital where his fiancée, Gabi Garrison, was recovering. He put her on the phone for a moment and she sounded weak but happy to be safe. She said was sporting a nice sparkler on her left ring finger and looking forward to getting back to work. Miles said that on the advice of legal counsel he couldn't comment on the case, only that he was glad to that Tony and Dr. Diamond were out of their lives.

"So," Cupid said, "Carol, you must be feeling pretty good. You've found Hollywood's Missing Girls and, as you suspected all along, Dr. Diamond was connected, but that still leaves—"

"My client, Tony Domingo. You're right. He wasn't aboard the ship last night and I—"

As I was about to explain I'd received a voicemail on my office phone early this morning, Eric walked into the studio. He looked whipped, like he hadn't slept, his hair finger-combed into place.

"Actually, if I might interrupt." Eric reached for a headset and took a seat at the console next to me. "We picked Tony Domingo up at the Burbank Airport less than an hour ago." Eric winked at me and explained that thanks to Holly Wood, they'd been able to track Tony down and make an arrest.

"And one last question," Cupid asked. "What happens to *Sweet Dreams* now that Diamond's been arrested? What becomes of a boat like that?"

Eric looked over at me. The *Sea Mistress* had formerly been a drug smuggling vessel he had bought at auction. I hoped he had no intention of buying this one. He smiled like he'd read my mind.

"That, Cupid, depends upon the outcome of the charges against Dr. Diamond. If he's found guilty, we have forfeiture laws in this country that allow the government to seize property used with trafficking and organized crime, and it's likely somewhere down the road she'll be sold at auction."

After the broadcast, I walked Eric back to his car. It had been a long night and he leaned back up against the black SUV and rested his hands on my shoulders.

"So, ace reporter, is it?"

"That's what they're calling me. Today anyway," I said.

"I have to say, there's just one thing about all this that bothers me." He paused and looked up at the sky, then back at me, a faint twinkle in his eye. "And I'm afraid it's a deal breaker, Carol."

"What?" I couldn't imagine what was bothering him.

"You weren't seasick. I've seen you seasick and you weren't. Not for a moment. I came up behind you on the boat and you were cold, and you were shaking, but you weren't seasick. Diamond would've gotten away if you were, but you were totally in control."

I laughed. Eric was right. Once I had gotten on board and realized Diamond was there and I was going to have to deal with him, that my life depended on it, and so did the girls' lives, I couldn't allow my stomach to rule my defenses.

"I suppose it was mind over matter. Who knows, maybe I'm cured," I said.

"So then, Catalina? You, me, and the *Sea Mistress*, this Saturday?"

NANCY COLE SILVERMAN

Nancy Cole Silverman credits her twenty-five years in news and talk radio for helping her to develop an ear for storytelling. But it wasn't until 2001 after she retired from news and copywriting that she was able to sit down and write fiction fulltime. Much of what Silverman writes about today she admits is pulled from events that were reported on from inside some of Los Angeles' busiest newsrooms where she spent the bulk of her career. In the last ten years she has written numerous short stories and novelettes. Today Silverman lives in Los Angeles with her husband, Bruce and two standard poodles.

In Case You Missed the 1st Book in the Series

SHADOW OF DOUBT

Nancy Cole Silverman

A Carol Childs Mystery (#1)

When a top Hollywood Agent is found poisoned in the bathtub of her home suspicion quickly turns to one of her two nieces. But Carol Childs, a reporter for a local talk radio station doesn't believe it. The suspect is her neighbor and friend, and also her primary source for insider industry news. When a media frenzy pits one niece against the other—and the body count starts to rise—Carol knows she must save her friend from being tried in courts of public opinion.

But even the most seasoned reporter can be surprised, and when a Hollywood psychic shows up in Carol's studio one night and warns her there will be more deaths, things take an unexpected turn. Suddenly nobody is above suspicion. Carol must challenge both her friendship and the facts, and the only thing she knows for certain is the killer is still out there and the closer she gets to the truth, the more danger she's in.

Available at booksellers nationwide and online

Visit www.henerypress.com for details

Henery Press Mystery Books

And finally, before you go...
Here are a few other mysteries
you might enjoy:

KILLER IMAGE

Wendy Tyson

An Allison Campbell Mystery (#1)

As Philadelphia's premier image consultant, Allison Campbell helps others reinvent themselves, but her most successful transformation was her own after a scandal nearly ruined her. Now she moves in a world of powerful executives, wealthy, eccentric ex-wives and twisted ethics.

When Allison's latest Main Line client, the fifteen-year-old Goth daughter of a White House hopeful, is accused of the ritualistic murder of a local divorce attorney, Allison fights to prove her client's innocence when no one else will. But unraveling the truth brings specters from her own past. And in a place where image is everything, the ability to distinguish what's real from the facade may be the only thing that keeps Allison alive.

Available at booksellers nationwide and online

Visit www.henerypress.com for details

FATAL BRUSHSTROKE

Sybil Johnson

An Aurora Anderson Mystery (#1)

A dead body in her garden and a homicide detective on her doorstep...

Computer programmer and tole-painting enthusiast Aurora (Rory) Anderson doesn't envision finding either when she steps outside to investigate the frenzied yipping coming from her own back yard. After all, she lives in Vista Beach, a quiet California beach community where violent crime is rare and murder even rarer.

Suspicion falls on Rory when the body buried in her flowerbed turns out to be someone she knows—her tole-painting teacher, Hester Bouquet. Just two weeks before, Rory attended one of Hester's weekend seminars, an unpleasant experience she vowed never to repeat. As evidence piles up against Rory, she embarks on a quest to identify the killer and clear her name. Can Rory unearth the truth before she encounters her own brush with death?

Available at booksellers nationwide and online

Visit www.henerypress.com for details

CIRCLE OF INFLUENCE

Annette Dashofy

A Zoe Chambers Mystery (#1)

Zoe Chambers, paramedic and deputy coroner in rural Pennsylvania's tight-knit Vance Township, has been privy to a number of local secrets over the years, some of them her own. But secrets become explosive when a dead body is found in the Township Board President's abandoned car.

As a January blizzard rages, Zoe and Police Chief Pete Adams launch a desperate search for the killer, even if it means uncovering secrets that could not only destroy Zoe and Pete, but also those closest to them.

Available at booksellers nationwide and online

Visit www.henerypress.com for details

THE RED QUEEN'S RUN

Bourne Morris

A Meredith Solaris Mystery (#1)

A famous journalism dean is found dead at the bottom of a stairwell. Accident or murder? The police suspect members of the faculty who had engaged in fierce quarrels with the dean— distinguished scholars who were known to attack the dean like brutal schoolyard bullies. When Meredith "Red" Solaris is appointed interim dean, the faculty suspects are furious.

Will the beautiful red-haired professor be next? The case detective tries to protect her as he heads the investigation, but incoming threats lead him to believe Red's the next target for death.

Available at booksellers nationwide and online

Visit www.henerypress.com for details

ON THE ROAD WITH DEL & LOUISE

Art Taylor

A Novel in Short Stories

Del's a small time crook with a moral conscience—robbing convenience stores only for tuition and academic expenses. Brash and sassy Louise goes from being a holdup victim to Del's lover and accomplice. All they want is a fresh start, an honest life, and a chance to build a family together, but fate conspires to put ever-steeper challenges in their path—and escalating temptations, too.

A real estate scam in recession-blighted Southern California. A wine heist in Napa Valley. A Vegas wedding chapel holdup. A kidnapping in an oil-rich North Dakota boomtown. Can Del and Louise stay on the right side of the law? On one another's good side? And when they head back to Louise's hometown in North Carolina, what new trouble will prove the biggest: Louise's nagging mama or a hidden adversary seemingly intent on tearing the couple apart? Or could those be one and the same?

From screwball comedy to domestic drama, and from caper tale to traditional whodunit, these six stories offer suspense with a side of romance—and a little something for all tastes.

Available at booksellers nationwide and online

Visit www.henerypress.com for details

21456548R00142

Made in the USA
Middletown, DE
30 June 2015